"The stories in *Jacked* cover a whole spectrum of crime writing from the grisly to the cozy and everywhere in between, dipping their toes into the murky waters on both sides of the law. It's an impressive debut from Run Amok's brand new crime imprint."
- Joey R. Poole, author of *I Have Always Been Here Before*

"These stories are gritty, bleak, often times funny and brutally honest. Noir bleeds from these pages with deception and a heavy dose of hard-boiled desperation."
- Mark Pelletier, *BookTalk*

" . . . 21 stories of murder, mayhem, and wry mystery that rise way above expectations."
- Beth Kanell, *Kingdom Books, Mystery Reviews*

" . . . every single one was a well-written short story . . . *Jacked* is one of those collections that I'm going to remember for a while."
- H.C. Netwon, *The Irresponsible Reader*

". . . an anthology packed to the gills with good stuff. Vern Smith harvested a handy crop of writers in this one."
- Rusty Barnes, *Tough* magazine

JACKED

A CRIME FICTION ANTHOLOGY

EDITED BY

VERN SMITH

Assistant Editor: Krysta Winsheimer of Muse Retrospect
Book Design: Gary Anderson
Cover Design: Gretchen Jankowski
Cover Photograph: Garth Jackson

ISBN: 978-1-7333526-9-7
Run Amok Books, 2022
First Edition

RunAmok

Printed in the U.S.A.

For Brad and Lyle, who put the good platters on the player as they were being pressed.

CONTENTS

As soon as the word *Jacked* was uttered, I consulted Merriam-Webster, where I found definitions revolving around excitement, custom cars, muscles, injury, and the state of being high. Once we got into colloquialisms, regional idioms, and what some still consider profane (write your own joke here because we have an answer for that, too), the possibilities seemed endless. I remember pausing to think before saying, yes, absolutely. Any good crime story should be able to answer to the concept. That was the truth, the full truth, and nothing but the truth. So, about that time, we ditched our high-minded themes and went off in search of the best fresh crime fiction we could get our hands on, without a single worry of what any of it could be about.

Genre, non-genre—we didn't care. Our only concern was that somewhere a law had to be fractured. Little did any of us know that these authors would have to survive a grueling selection process that saw some four hundred stories auditioned, meaning each had to be very, very good, yes, but also singular in such a way as to give this book another gear.

No pressure.

Although we didn't ask for ID at the door, I can comfortably say that *Jacked* spans five decades of crime writers from five countries, whose stories and novelettes range in style, voice, politics, sexuality, experience, era, and perspective.

Riding with everyone from Emmy nominees to a real-life cop, we find unusual suspects struggling to get by at the end of the biker wars; lavender cowboys robbing a stagecoach in the old west; and a burlesque performer holding up an Italian jeweler at gunpoint. In 1940s Montreal, a budding lawyer is dabbling in tainted love with an injured pin-up model. The art of the Samurai is being corrupted by a rogue ex-detective, circa 1981 L.A., and the ethics of accounting are being violated by a modern pulp-and-paper town bean-counter who can no longer hide from the people she's been cheating. In contemporary Ireland, verbal barbs inside a theater are escalating to actual violence. While somewhere in

England, a man of few means is delivering what might be a head in a bag, or maybe it's just a MacGuffin.

Abuse is clearly a crime on the minds of writers, and the fate of one perpetrator is revealed during a tire-change in Oklahoma as sure as that of another is foretold in Wisconsin, highlighting issues of gender, family, race, and class. Likewise, when gold is struck in the bellies of mountain critters, it's a matter of day-to-day survival, just as it is when your slacker roommate uses your vehicle as a getaway car for hire. If that's not enough, we have patricide, a TikTok murder, a spy in a spot without ID, a murder suspect who's unsure of his innocence, and more than one double cross.

In each case, we find characters lurking in the gray areas, blurring the lines between good and bad, which is where I believe every great crime story starts.

You won't find David Caruso chasing around bad dudes selling good kids bad drugs in these pages. No. As a matter of fact, in one case, the detective is the junkie.

Such characters are three-dimensional people compromised by their lives, loves, lusts, demons, obsessions, affiliations, jobs, and situations. Time and again, the literary trick will be getting inside their heads once the stimuli—crime, in this case—is introduced. That's the human mystery driving every one of these pieces. It's about what real people do when they find someone in the trunk of an alpha car they just stole, as much as what they say upon discovering that said person is a dedicated Nazi.

Talk about blurring the lines.

And look, dear reader, no reprints. All first-run crime fiction here. Not only is the book you're holding a first edition, but every story contained within is a proper first as well—my gift to the experts at the bar.

Anyway, I could go on about these writers and the great stories that they tell, and I will in other settings. But my only real role here was to curate a table of contents—a diabolical mixed tape, if you will—collecting twenty-one authors at the top of their powers, who, together, form a literary murderers' row that's about to challenge your favorite anthology. Otherwise, they need no introduction. So please, let me just get out of the way and hand the mic over to Paul Alexander, wherever he is, to describe what happens when one struggling comedian convinces another to bring a loaded gun onstage.

Vern Smith, July 2022

Paul Alexander is a comedian and author who has appeared on MTV's *Half Hour Comedy Hour*, A & E's *Evening At The Improv*, and Comedy Central's *Comedy Product*. His debut parenting memoir, *Our Baby was Born Premature: the same way he was conceived*, can be found at all the usual places where books are sold even though Paul is currently in the witness protection program in Canada.

SHORTY COCKED HIS GUN

It was a moon cops hate. Full. The sky was the color bats fly in.

And it was the second time I saw Shorty or Short for short. He was driving his '76 white Toyota pickup truck. Russet patches on the hood and doors, dents and troughs in the body, bald tires, and a slipping transmission—perfect for the hills in San Francisco.

It banshee-screeched to a stop in the midst of shiny traffic in front of the Golden Eagle hotel where I was waiting. The *G* in the Golden neon sign was burned out. Guess I'm staying at the olden Eagle hotel.

I opened the squeaky door as a red light changed to a green at Montgomery and Broadway.

Inside—a ripped-up turquoise blue seat that fit two in a squeeze—Shorty got visibly annoyed if his hand touched your leg, even for a microsecond, while he shifted gears.

Short's nature was sore. An unfinished jigsaw puzzle with a few pieces jammed into the wrong places. He wore a distinctive snapping turtle mouth and he loved to snap.

Shorty had come to San Francisco in that truck all the way from Pensacola, Florida, loaded with an acting resume which included a high school play where he played Lenny from *Of Mice and Men.* He had a unicycle. He also had a lawn mower—in case he had to get a day job while trying to make it as an actor.

All this he pledged inside a minute.

We were flying south to Emerson's Bar and Grill in Palo Alto because they were doing a "Comedy Night."

There was a .38 caliber handgun stashed behind the seat, a portable Lloyd's cassette player held together by electrical tape under the dash, and a rancid towel on the floor.

Short lit up a Camel and blew out the smoke as he voiced his ideas on a set at the upcoming bar and grill which was forty minutes away—maybe thirty at this speed.

"I wanna try a character," he said.

I told him, "You should open by taking that .38 out on stage."

He laughed and then got a gleam of excitement in his sockets.

"I'll do it," he slurred, as if daring the world to stop him.

He was all over himself with glee. By the time the Palo Alto city limits were on us he had it figured that he would go out on stage in the guise of a "mental guy" and tell a joke whereupon he would pull out his .38 caliber handgun and point it at someone in the front, and say, "*Get it?*"

I said, "Isn't that a felony?"

Short's confederate jalopy rattled into the parking lot at Emerson's Bar and Grill.

The room was the same as every bar and grill. A bar. A bartender. A waitress. A big screen TV with a football game on and another TV that had Keno on it. And scattered around the room at various tables, a few patrons. The comics were in the corner of the room by a makeshift riser that had a microphone stand on it.

The show started.

Shorty went on early, like second or third. Since the first few acts didn't get anyone's attention it was up to Short to set the pace. After the MC introduced him, my new friend slowly wandered up to the stage in character; making baby steps to the microphone with his shiny six shot held out to one side. He was doing his best impression of a mentally-challenged individual—staring at the lights with an innocent sort of stare—and then he spoke with a vibrato, "Hi. My name's Shorty." At this, he waved his weapon around.

"This is my gun. This one's for killing . . . " And with his free hand he pointed towards his crotch. ". . . and this one's for *fun*."

A man at the table closest to the stage didn't want to be there, but it was too late as Short aimed his gun right at him. "Get it?"

The man was a figurine of panic. His wan smile was frozen in prayer.

And Shorty couldn't see for looking—his preconceived notions of bravado were dying. Disaster had been created. The climb out of trouble was unnatural and time stood still in a place where nobody wanted to be. It didn't matter that nothing followed his opening remarks except an old joke that had nothing to do with anything that came before or after: "What's the first thing Adam said to Eve? Stand back, I don't know how big this thing gets."

Abandoned is the comic who isn't funny; especially one with a gun.

Shorty, bathed in silence, left the stage less gingerly than when he entered.

The guy that ran the comedy night told Short, "I can't have you back, man. I mean—I could have called the cops."

Short shrugged. "You'll hear about me." And walked out, shocked, into the brisk explosive night.

I forfeited my set that was coming up and escaped with Shorty to the pickup truck. Our common ground being no money and no funny. Short vented and put the hammer down until we got back home, wherever that was.

"I forgot to check the chamber before I went on stage. It had a round in it, man," he confessed.

"Now that's funny," I lied, and quickly left the truck.

Eric Beetner is that writer you've heard about but never read. When you finally do you wonder why you waited so long. There are more than 25 books like *Rumrunners*, *All The Way Down* and *The Devil Does't Want Me* so you'd better get started. He's been described as "The 21st Century's answer to Jim Thompson" (LitReactor), been nominated for three Anthony's, an ITW award, Shamus, Derringer and six Emmys.

FIRST TIMERS

We dumped our bikes behind some bushes about two streets away after we'd circled the block twice to see if anyone was looking. We'd found the perfect car.

Ashton and I knew it had to be older. No key fob and fancy starter stuff. I had a screwdriver in my back pocket and Ashton had a rubber mallet, both swiped from our respective Dad's toolboxes. That's how we'd get it going. At least, that's what the YouTube video said to do. We'd never done this before.

"Shit, man, it's beautiful." Ashton's voice was a whisper as we crept up behind the shiny black car. It was some kind of old muscle car, the kind somebody had obviously spent many weekends bent over, torso under the hood or on their backs laying on a roller to get the view from underneath. It looked big and mean and had a chrome number 440 on the side. Beyond that, all I knew about the car was that we were going to take it. At least I was kinda sure.

"You really wanna do this?" I asked.

Ashton looked at me like I'd just asked him if I should screw my sister. "Yeah, dude. This one's perfect."

"I mean, should we do this at all?"

"We'll bring it back. Not like we're gonna strip it for parts or nothing. Just a little joyride. It's not even stealing, just borrowing."

He had a point. And besides, what the hell else were we gonna do on a Friday night in this shit town?

Ashton pulled the Slim Jim from his pant leg. His uncle had given him a lesson and I'll be damned if it didn't work on the first try. The door popped open and he gave me a smile there in the dark of the empty street, like he'd just unzipped the skirt of the hottest girl in school.

One more look around to make sure nobody was spying on us and I slid in behind the wheel. Ashton circled the car and I opened the passenger door for him. I put the screwdriver up against the keyhole and Ashton hammered it home. I let out a quick exhale and turned the handle. The car came to life.

Damn, it was loud. Our laughter was louder. I reached up to the steering column and dropped her in gear and we sped away for the night of our lives.

The engine sounded so sweet. Like a tiger, but one you'd want to have as a pet. We blew through stop signs, took corners too fast, the whole time my brain kept repeating, *You just stole a car. You just stole a car.* It came out my mouth as laughter. We kept the engine revving and the sound ear-splitting until I had to slow down to keep from running off the road. It wasn't exactly a life of crime but it kept the boredom at bay for at least one night. We weren't big drinkers, Ashton and me. And we stayed away from drugs since we'd seen too many people get seriously fucked-up and it's not a good look. You want to never do drugs in your life? Stay sober around stoned people. You see them and think, *hell no, man.*

"Damn, dude," Ashton said. "I wish we knew some girls to go pick up and take for a ride."

We both sat quietly trying to think of someone who would be properly impressed by this vehicle, and someone who also might let us take her in the back seat for a while. At seventeen, girls and the possibility of scoring with girls was always working somewhere in the back of our minds.

In the quiet, and with the engine finally calmed down, I heard a knocking sound. I worried that I'd broken some part of the vintage car, but then I heard a voice. A muffled, very desperate voice.

"You hear that?" I asked.

"Yeah." Ashton and I both craned our necks around to look at the back seat, and we knew the sound was coming from the other side, in the trunk. Whoever it was pounded again and we both jumped.

"Shit, what do we do?"

"Someone's in there, man."

"I know that."

Ashton punched the dashboard. "Shit, man. We gotta help them." Ashton had trained as a lifeguard, kept talking about wanting to be an EMT when he graduated. He had a natural instinct to help people, I guess. I'd have been fine to park the car where we were and walk back to our bikes.

I steered the car to the curb and we got out. We walked around to the back and could hear him clearly now. He pounded on the lid of the trunk, shouting behind that layer of steel to be let out.

Ashton and I looked at each other but had no idea what to do. We could ditch the car, with him in it, but we'd driven miles from where our bikes were and from home. And I had no idea if the guy would run out of air before someone else found him or what. My earlier instinct to run had faded. I knew we needed to help him, too.

"What do we do?" I asked.

Ashton leaned closer to the trunk. "H . . . hey man. You okay in there?"

The car rocked on its shocks as he hammered on the trunk lid. We could hear his shouting more clearly now.

"Hey! You gotta get me out of here. They locked me in here. They have my brother in the house. They're gonna kill us both."

What the hell had we gotten into?

"We gotta get him out," Ashton said.

"We don't have keys." This car was from before remote trunk opening buttons.

"Use the screwdriver." Ashton leaned forward and tapped twice on the trunk. "Hey, buddy. We're gonna get you out. Hold on a sec."

I positioned the screwdriver into the keyhole and Ashton hit it three times with the mallet. It took more twisting and hammering than the ignition had, but we got it open.

The dude was drenched in sweat. His hands were tied, and his feet. He was a white guy, probably mid-twenties. Longish hair, jeans. Just a regular looking guy, I guess, aside from being stuffed in the trunk of a car and left for dead.

"Holy shit, thank you. Thank you." He tried climbing out, which wasn't easy without the use of his hands. "Where are we? We gotta get back to the house."

"What house?" Ashton asked.

I smacked him on the shoulder. "The house where we stole the car, dumbass."

"They got my brother."

"Why?"

"They're fucking psychopaths."

Great. The first car I steal belongs to a psycho. Just great.

"They stuck me in there and said they were coming back for me, after they killed my brother. We gotta go. We don't have much time." He was already moving toward the door. Ashton and I followed him. I tried closing the trunk lid but now it wouldn't close with the lock broken.

I got behind the wheel again and wondered if I'd be able to find my way back. Ashton leaned over the seat and started to untie his hands.

"So who are these guys?"

The dude in the back finally realized he didn't know us. He scrunched up his face. "Wait, who the hell are you?"

Ashton tried stalling him while I put it in drive. "It's . . . we're not . . . it doesn't matter."

"Yeah, whatever man. You saved my life."

I gotta say, that felt good. As thrilling as it was to steal the car, it was a bigger rush to rescue someone. I retraced my route back toward the house, keeping it slower this time. Ashton got him untied and the guy looked out the window, rubbing his wrists. "I hope we're not too late."

"What's your name, man?" Ashton asked.

"Gene."

"Ashton." He pointed to me. "Clark."

"Thanks, guys."

We passed by the bushes with our bikes and I pulled the car

to a stop in the same spot where we'd taken it from. I figured that would be it. Gene would go rescue his brother and we'd get back on our bikes and ride away, forgetting this ever happened. But no.

"Okay, listen, these are bad motherfuckers. We need to go in hard and take no shit, okay?"

Ashton and I looked at each other. We weren't "go in hard" kind of guys. We were in marching band.

"Oh," I said. "I didn't know we were . . . "

"You gotta help me, dude. That's my brother in there. He might already be dead."

Then what help would we be? I wanted to know. Ashton and I tried to communicate with just our eyes, but we came to no decision that way. Gene made up our minds for us.

"Come on, man." He opened the door and got out with a sharp slap to the back of the seat. Ashton and I got out too. We huddled quick by the front bumper.

"I mean, the guy needs help," I said.

"And we already saved his life."

"It's the right thing to do."

"It would be shitty to leave him here alone."

Reluctantly, we walked over to where Gene stood by the passenger door. I'd kept the screwdriver in my hand and I held on to it like it was a rope keeping me from falling off a cliff.

"I'm fuckin' psyched you guys are with me, man. So good to have soldiers who understand the cause." *Cause? What cause?* "Now let's go get my brother." He leaned in the passenger window and opened the glove box, then came back out with a gun. Ashton and I looked at it like he'd pulled a rabbit out of a hat. Or maybe a spitting cobra. He walked toward the door. We followed several paces behind.

Gene raised his leg and kicked in the front door with a practiced swing. We barreled inside and found ourselves in a room with three of the biggest black dudes I'd ever seen in my life.

"Damn right, it's me," Gene said, sounding like a pro wrestler entering the ring. He held the gun out before him. "Y'all motherfuckers didn't think you'd see me again, did you? Now listen up, I want all you dirty fuckin'—"

Gene proceeded to drop the N-word several times in succession. He pointed the gun like an angry finger at the three men in the room and when he jabbed it forward I could see a swastika tattoo peeking out from his T-shirt. We had gotten ourselves on the wrong side of this thing. Ashton and I both knew it. The ignorant shit spewing from this redneck was not a "cause" we were sympathetic to.

"Gene?" A voice from a room down the hall sounded scared.

"Randy?" Gene said.

At least he wasn't dead. I mean, I guess so.

"I got some friends and we're here to rescue you," he said.

I looked at the biggest of the three men and held out pleading hands. "We're not his friends. We just met. He was in the trunk of the car and—"

"We're here for you, brother!" He let another N-word fly and I could see the three men tensing. They all looked at the gun in Gene's hand and stayed put, waiting, I could see in the way their muscles moved like coiled ropes.

"Hey, hey now," I said. Needless to say, nothing changed in the room.

Gene had a whole speech prepared, and it sounded rehearsed. I kept trying to interrupt, but he went on like a preacher speaking tongues.

"Gene, would you shut the hell up." But he did not. I looked to Ashton who flicked his eyes down. I followed his look to my own hand where the screwdriver was gripped in my hand like an orphan chopstick. When I looked back to Ashton he widened his eyes. I didn't want to do it, but I wanted to be in that room even less, so if it got me out, then I would go for it.

I asked Gene one more time to shut up with his racist bullshit, but he ignored me. I took one short step forward and stabbed him in the side with the tip of the screwdriver. It didn't go deep, but it stopped his rant. The men whose house we were in all moved in unison.

A gunshot cut through the room. Gene yelped and went down clutching his leg. I looked around the room and saw a smoking gun in the hands of one of the men. Ashton and I froze. I dropped the blood-stained screwdriver. Two men rushed Gene, disarmed him, and put their feet down on his back, pinning him in place.

"Who the fuck are you two?" the gunman asked.

"Nobody. Just kids. Like I said, we found him in the trunk."

"The trunk of *my* car?"

This might not have been helping. "Yes, but, you see . . . " I froze. Ashton chimed in.

"We didn't steal it. We only borrowed it."

This argument proved unconvincing to them. Before we knew it, we were seated on the couch with guns in our faces while Gene was carried away screaming about white power and taken into the back room with his brother. I figured once the room became available, it would be our turn next.

Ashton said, "Okay, so what happened is this—"

"Man, shut the fuck up."

A conference took place in the corner of the room. Three large men with guns whispered about our fate while looking over at us now and then like we were a stain on the carpet.

The gunman came back over to us.

"So let me get this straight, you stole our car and then when you heard him in the trunk, you turned around and brought it back?"

"Yes, sir," I said.

"So you could raid the place and get his brother back?"

"Yes, but to be fair, at the time we didn't know what this was all about. We don't . . . uh . . . subscribe to the same viewpoint as Gene."

"Or his brother," said Ashton.

"You mean you're not some Proud Boy Klansman and shit."

"Yes, that's correct, sir."

He used the barrel of the gun to scratch his forehead. "Well, I don't know about that. You showed up with this clown."

"He did stab his ass with that screwdriver," the big man said.

"You came kicking in my door."

"Yeah, but they did bring the car back."

There was another conference. While they talked another man who was apparently not important enough to be in the meeting spoke to us.

"We're sitting here calm as you please and these two redneck motherfuckers come knocking on our door screaming white power bullshit and telling us we got to move out of the neighborhood." He shook his head, recalling the story and barely believing the audacity of it himself. "They got complaints like nice white folks used to live here. We're selling drugs. This isn't our America. Really fucked-up shit."

"Yeah, that's not cool at all," I said. He wasn't impressed with my attempt to be an ally.

"Yeah, well . . . it was cool that you stabbed him."

The gunman came and stood in front of us.

"So here's what's gonna happen."

A loud bang from the other room. Gene.

"You two get a pass this time. For bringing the car back and for distracting that asshole."

Another bang. His brother. I wanted to breathe a sigh of relief, but I couldn't find any relief in the situation yet.

"Well, there will be some payback for this bullshit tonight."

Oh, shit. Would it be a finger? Or many fingers? Or would they do worse? We had no money. Damn, it had to be cutting off a finger, didn't it? I thought I heard Ashton crying.

"So y'all jack cars?"

Ashton and I looked at each other. I spoke, "Oh, not really. This was our first, actually."

That got smiles all around. "You picked the wrong damn car for your first."

"Yes, I see that now."

"We want y'all to get some cars for us. Let's say three to call it even and then after that we can talk about future employment."

Ashton and I had to do a double take. "What's that now?"

"You get three cars and bring them here. You seen the kind of car I like. Then after that, we talk about the future. Give you two days."

"We have to steal three cars in two days?"

"You get caught, we don't know each other."

The door to the back room opened and four men came out, each pair carrying the limp corpses of Gene and his brother between them. Ashton and I watched them pass through the room and walk out the back door. We got the message.

"Okay. I guess we can do that."

One of the men tossed me the screwdriver. I caught it, bloody side first. "Go get 'em, tiger."

So we had started out to steal a car, thought we'd saved a man's life, then almost lost ours, and then ended up with a job. Not a bad way to spend a Friday night.

Michelle Ann King is a writer of speculative, crime, and horror fiction. Based in England, her work has appeared in over a hundred different venues, including *Strange Horizons*, *Interzone*, *Black Static*, and *Orson Scott Card's Intergalactic Medicine Show*. Her short story collections are available in ebook and paperback format. "Apples and Trees" came from a love of exploring family dynamics, especially the kind that are usually called dysfunctional. Although, while some people might struggle in the shadow of notorious parents, the ones in this story seem to be doing just fine.

Apples and Trees

Pop stopped short in the doorway and pulled a face. "Jeez, Nika. We pay for this? It's a shit-hole."

He stepped forward gingerly, as if worried about what he might tread in. Not without justification, to be fair—I'll admit Marly's clinic isn't what you'd call a five-star establishment—but people come here for broken bones and bullet wounds, not hair transplants or butt lifts. We pay for our guys to be patched up and put back on the street with no questions asked, and that's what we get. It's not the kind of service that comes with fresh flowers and hot tubs.

But that's my father for you. Nothing and nobody ever quite measures up.

He was no more impressed with Marly herself; just looked her up and down with that pinched, smelled-something-bad look still on his face, and didn't offer his hand. "I don't trust doctors. Or women."

When I made a noise of protest, he gave me a sharp grin and jabbed a finger into my shoulder. "Not you, kid. You don't count."

Was that a compliment or an insult? I was still trying to work it out when he turned back to Marly. "Hey. I know you?"

She shook her head. "No. We've never met."

"You sure? You look familiar."

Now it was her turn to give a little grin. "Yeah. I get that a lot."

She does, too. That famous picture of her mom, the one that

was on all the news reports and book covers? Apart from the out-of-date hairstyle, Marly could use it as her passport photo. You can see it, when people meet her for the first time: the narrowing of the eyes, the tightening of the lips, as they try to remember who she reminds them of. Then, when they do, it happens in reverse: the eyes go wide again and the mouth falls open. The *oh, shit, yeah*, moment. *Her*.

Yeah. Her: Dr. Tamara Fletcher, AKA the Arizona Angel of Death. Marly's mom and the USA's most prolific serial killer. Although, since Tamara was born in England, there's some dispute online as to who claims the crown. A lot of people reckon she moved over here for her killing because she didn't want to lose out to Harold Shipman, who logged a good two-hundred-plus in his day. Others reckon if we knew Tamara's true score, it would leave Shipman in the dust anyway. The numbers are almost as contentious an issue as the mercy killer/serial killer designation: there've been more than a few podcast wars about it.

The next thing people do, once they've twigged it, is start on a whole new set of deliberations—ones that involve apples and trees, and the amount of distance there might be between them. It's the reason she can't get a job in a proper hospital. Well, one of them, anyway. But the truth is, Marly's not like her mom. Not at all.

I started to make that point, but Pop shushed me. "Hey," he said, peering into the gloom at the back of the clinic. "Isn't that Zack Cade?"

I glanced at the man in the furthest bed and shrugged. It wasn't easy to tell, under all the swelling.

Pop turned a suspicious eye on Marly. "Cade's one of Elyse Whitlock's boys. You working for Elyse, too?"

She shook her head. "No, it's a . . . private arrangement. The only deal I have is with Nika."

Pop's face darkened further. "You mean me. Your deal's with *me*, girlie."

I rolled my eyes. "Yeah, yeah, Pop. That's what she means."

It earned me another finger jab, but without the accompanying grin. "I'm the one who gives the orders around here, understand?

She works for me. You work for me. *All* you fuckers work for me, and you'd better not forget it."

As if we'd get the chance. The barest hint of a suggestion that he might want to consider, at some point, starting to think about the possibility of maybe loosening his grip on the reins, and all hell breaks loose.

I understand it, sure. Of course I do. Pop put our whole operation together—built it from the ground up, out of nothing, and made it what it is. It's always been his show.

Thing is, the world's moving on. He'll tell you all about how he grew up on the streets and mastered all the tricks before he was old enough to drink, and that's true. But my generation grew up on the dark web, and we have a whole new bag of tricks to dip into. I don't think Pop, bless his heart, even knows what crypto is, let alone how to execute a DeFi rug pull. It's a whole new Wild West out there, and we need to take advantage of it.

Which means some changes need to be made. Adapt or die, you know? It's just the way shit goes. Transition of power's part of that: it's the natural order of things. The King is dead, long live the King.

Or the Queen.

His hand moved from my shoulder to my cheek and delivered two light, quick slaps. "You listening to me, girl?"

I kept my gaze steady this time. "Yeah, Pop. I'm listening."

He turned that fish-eye stare on me, hard, but eventually seemed to decide he was okay with what he saw. "Good. As long as we're all on the same page."

I nodded, because we were. Change might be natural, but it's also hard. People need time to get used to it. Sudden death might be what you'd call an occupational hazard in this line of work, but it's bad for business.

If Pop checked out now, it'd cause all manner of problems. An outside hit says incompetence. Weakness. An inside one says chaos and disloyalty. Either way, we come out of it looking like turkeys—ripe for plucking—and that's not good. The transition of power is a proper and necessary thing but it needs to be done right. It needs to be *managed*. So yeah, Pop has to stay at the top while that happens.

He wiped a hand over his face, then winced and pressed it to his gut. "Fuck, this place stinks. It's making me feel sick."

"Actually, that's probably the ketamine," Marly said. She glanced at me. "That's what you gave him?"

I nodded. "Pharmaceutical grade, liquid form, fifteen minutes ago. Just like you said."

Pop stared, then made a kind of choking noise and sagged in Marly's arms. I stepped forward to help, but she manhandled him into her chair easy enough. I guess she's had practice at hauling bodies around.

I watched as she strapped him in and ran through a quick set of the tests you see doctors do on TV—heart rate, blood pressure, light shone in the eyes—but I had to look away when she brought out the big needle. I'm not squeamish, but holy fuck. The thing looked like it should be used for inseminating horses.

I swallowed. "That the, er, the whatchamacallit?"

"The neurotoxin. Yes. An experimental compound derived from a new form of MPTP that causes oxidative stress in the nigrostriatal dopaminergic neurons and—"

I held up a hand. "Bottom line, Marl."

She huffed a little. "Bottom line. Okay. Memory loss, cognitive dysfunction, fatigue, muscle weakness, and loss of balance, followed by increasing physical immobility and, eventually, death."

"How eventually?"

She eyed the level of liquid in the syringe. "Eight to ten months?"

I nodded. "I can work with that."

She aimed the needle at the base of Pop's skull, but I stopped her again. "One more thing. Is it going to hurt?"

That's the thing about Marly—it's what I was trying to tell him earlier. People get all worked up about her mom, but while it's true that Tamara killed an absolute fuckton of people, she did it because she thought she was *helping* them. She didn't like to see people suffering, so she wanted to put a stop to it. To put them out of their misery.

Marly, though—like I said—she's nothing like her mom.

"Oh, fuck, yes," she said cheerfully. "It's going to burn through his nerve endings like the fires of hell. But don't worry. Before it went bust, this place used to be a recording studio. It's still fully soundproofed."

"Cool," I said, and lowered my hand. "Carry on."

Pop went rigid as she jammed the needle in. His back arched and his mouth opened wide, but nothing came out. Well, no words, anyway.

I leaned closer and smiled. "I'm still listening, Pop. I'm not hearing any orders, but that's okay. Everyone knows I've heard enough of them over the years to speak for you. It's gonna be fine. Like you said"—I reached out and patted his cheek; two light, quick slaps—"We're all on the same page."

Matt Witten is a TV writer, novelist, playwright and screenwriter who has written for many TV shows including *House*, *Pretty Little Liars*, *Law & Order*, *CSI: Miami*, *Medium*, *JAG*, *The Glades*, *Homicide*, *Judging Amy*, and *Women's Murder Club*. His thriller novel *The Necklace* came out from Oceanview Publishing last year, and has been optioned for film by Leonardo DiCaprio. Matt wrote four mystery novels that were published by Signet, including the Malice Domestic Award winning *Breakfast at Madeline's*, and he has been nominated for two Edgars and an Emmy. His thriller *Killer Story* comes out from Oceanview next year.

THE TIKTOK MURDER

Caroline

Looking in my closet, I'm thinking: I could totally pull off this red blazer for preppie vibes, but my fans would never be into it. How about going luxe punk with this slinky fishnet and the black boots, that could get me another half-million hits . . . But then I see the tie-dye hoodie and think, what if I put that together with the black crop top? Glam plus grit. Oh yeaaah, that is for sure it.

The parents are out of town, so I'm staying out all night long. I figure, first I'll go to Jeremy's birthday party for a minute—he'd kill me if I don't make it. Then I got a sweet gig at this new Hollywood club, the Blind Spot. I get *three thousand bucks* just to show up and dance with the B-listers. I'm not mad about it.

Wasn't always like this. Just six months ago I'm studying for the SATs at Starbucks with my girl Gwen. Total nerd, like me. I don't even drink coffee, not a fan of the taste. But then this V cute guy at the next table, he's like twenty-five—Jeremy, a big TikTok talent manager, only I don't know it right then—and he likes my retro 2000s outfit, so he puts me up on his Insta stories. And suddenly, boom: two hundred thousand new followers! So we start making videos. Last week he shot me finding disco pants at Goodwill and we got twenty million hits. My third time over ten mil. Just turned eighteen and I'm practically in the Hype House!

Think I'll wear these black lace booties. This one A-list director, Randy, is all thirsty for me. I can't be tied down to Jeremy, you know? He's a great manager, yeah, but it was a mistake getting involved with him. I'm not that little girl anymore who thought Jeremy was just the coolest thing ever. Randy's kind of a cokehead, but a fun guy. Says he's gonna put me in his next movie. Maybe I'll get lit with him tonight.

Or else I'll go skydiving—a million more hits!—or skating down the middle of Hollywood Boulevard in my vintage jeans— two million more—or skinny dipping in the ocean—a *lot* more! I check my hoodie in the mirror. Fiiiiire. This is gonna be one of those perfect nights I'll remember forever. Yaas!

Detective Sara Stark

As we walk past the shouting media people to the back of the Blind Spot, then step over the yellow tape, my new partner with the cigar breath says, "I can think of better things for us to do on a Saturday night." I look at the slight leer on his bloated face and think: ignore him. *You twit, go beat off in a corner if you have to. Where's the body?*

Down here. I shine a flashlight at the bottom of the exterior stairs leading to the Blind Spot basement. Blood on the back of her head and the cement next to it. Looks like blunt force trauma.

She must've been standing at the stairway railing here, then she fell backwards, plummeted down to the cement. I stand next to the railing. It comes up above my waist. I'm about the same height as the victim, I think, so the railing went above her waist too. Meaning no matter how drunk she might've been, she didn't fall. She was pushed.

Keep it simple: this girl's standing here, arguing with some-body. Fighting. The guy shoves her. She flails, can't stop her fall, and somersaults to her death.

What about these whitish spots on the pavement, near the rail-ing where she fell? I'll get them tested, but judging by how that black alley cat was lapping it up, I'm guessing it's milk.

But Caroline wasn't drinking milk tonight, not at the Blind

Spot. So what's the deal?

Cigar Breath walks up and eyes the body. "Damn, she was a good-looking girl," he says.

Shut up, scuzzball, and let me think.

Maybe her killer had some milk, set it down on the railing, and then, after they saw Caroline was dead, grabbed the milk and ran, spilling some along the way.

But what kind of killer walks around carrying a carton of milk?

Jeremy

It's two in the morning but I can't sleep. My brain's on fire. Should I tweet about what happened? But if the cops suspect murder, they'll suspect me, and they'll watch every single thing I do on social media. So I'm paralyzed. I do nothing.

Somebody knocks on my front door. I don't answer. But when they start banging, I put on jeans and a T-shirt, go downstairs, and look through the keyhole. A slender woman in her thirties holds up an LAPD badge. Dark eyes, black hair, a mole on her cheek. I open the door—I don't have a choice.

"Jeremy Winston?" she says. "I'm Detective Sara Stark."

"You're here about Caroline, aren't you?" I say.

"How did you hear about her?"

It's beginning. "On Twitter. I was just going to bed when I saw. Come in." I bring her into my living room, still a mess from my birthday party; bottles and stuff everywhere, the brown leather sofa wet with spilled beer. I gesture for her to sit in a dry and relatively clean easy chair. "I can't believe she's dead. People are saying she fell. Is that true?"

The detective stays standing. "When's the last time you saw her?" she says, unblinking.

"When she left the party," I say. "Maybe eleven."

"What was your relationship with Caroline?"

I give her a horrified look. "She was my client. Do you think somebody might've ... pushed her? That's why you're here, right?"

"What do you think?"

"Oh my God." I sink onto the sofa and immediately feel liquid seeping through to my butt. I jump up and sit back down on a dry spot. The detective eyes me like I'm a fish wriggling on a hook. I try to act normal, whatever that would be. "She was such a great person. So alive."

"What do you mean, she was a client?"

"I was her talent manager. We'd brainstorm ideas for her videos, and I'd usually be the one to shoot them."

The detective finally sits on the edge of the easy chair, her posture straight. "Was she having any problems with anyone?"

I think about how to answer that. "Caroline attracted all kinds of people, including some real creeps. I tried to warn her."

"Any creeps in particular?"

"Yeah, Randy Rains." The detective nods: she's heard of him. Who hasn't? How could I ever compete with a movie director whose last two films made five hundred million apiece? "He was trying to put the moves on her."

"What about you?" The detective's eyes knife into me. "Were you sleeping with Caroline?"

I shake my head, giving her my most earnest look. "Me and Caroline were not a thing. We made each other famous. That was way too important to mess up with sex."

"We got into her phone," the detective says. "And we saw her last text to you: *Quit being such a possessive asshole. You're really creeping me out.*"

My head pounds. "I wasn't jealous of Randy, I just thought he was a bad influence." How can I convince this woman? "I found Caroline when she was nobody. I'd never do anything to hurt her. I created her. She was *mine.*"

The detective's eyebrows lift, and I know I screwed up. To escape her stare, I get up and start cleaning the studio. I pick up an empty vodka bottle, a paper plate—

"Where were you three nights ago? Thursday."

Shit, that's the night I parked outside her house for an hour. So stupid. Somebody must have a Ring camera or something.

"Look," I say," you should come by my office sometime. I've got a million gorgeous girls who would do anything if I promised to make them TikTok famous. I'm not obsessed with Caroline, and I'm not some crazy killer."

Those black daggers watch me. I go back to cleaning, picking up an empty Kahlua bottle—

"Kahlua, huh?" she says. "Do you like Kahlua and cream?"

"I'm not saying another damn word," I say.

Gwen

It's ten in the morning. My parents are gone but I'm in my kitchen, because at school I burst out crying every time I thought about Caroline. In kindergarten we pinkie swore we'd be best friends forever. But now forever is gone. I talked the nurse into letting me go home.

The detective is here, and I'm just trying to hold it together. I make coffee for both of us. As I put a hazelnut pod into the Nespresso, I remember all the times Caroline and I were together at Starbucks and the tears start pouring again.

"Caroline always said we were soulmates," I tell the detective. "We stayed like that, even after she got famous and all."

I show the detective a necklace Caroline and I made, that's hanging around my neck. Red garnet, with a silver wolf charm. As I touch the charm, my chest gets so tight I have to gasp for breath. "We used to stay up all night long making jewelry together," I say. "This wolf was her idea. We were planning to start our own line and call it the Gwenoline. Combining Gwen and Caroline. I wrote up a marketing plan and everything."

"It must've been weird for you, though," the detective says. "When her Insta started getting millions of hits, and yours gets what, maybe a couple hundred?"

I'm starting to hate this detective a little. But she's just doing her job. "It was kind of weird, yeah," I say. "But I figured the more hits she got, the more our jewelry would sell."

"What about this text you sent her last Sunday?" I know right away what text the detective means, and I want to crawl inside my coffee cup. She reads, "*I can't believe you would do this to me. How do you think I felt, just trying to be a nice person, bringing you this cute necklace I made for you, and you and your new fake 'friends' just laugh at me?"*

She gives me a hard look, trying to make me nervous, so I look her straight in the eye and get super focused, like my mom when she's on the phone for business. "Detective," I say, "Caroline called me that night and apologized. She said they were all coked up and that's why they were laughing. We were like sisters. Sometimes we'd fight—but we'd do anything for each other."

"From looking at your text exchanges, she didn't always respond to you these last few months."

I shrug. "It's not easy being a TikTok creator. She's busy. Was . . . " I correct myself, and my throat catches. I look down at the bracelet I'm wearing—that I made last week—with rainbow-colored umbrellas for charms. I wish I wasn't wearing it, it feels way extra now.

"Did you go to the Blind Spot last night?" the detective asks.

"No."

"Maybe you were hoping she'd get you inside."

Okay whaaaat is this bish saying? "Do you actually think *I* killed Caroline? I loved her. She's the last person I'd ever kill—and I wouldn't kill *anybody*. I'm seventeen. Come on."

"Accidents happen," the detective says.

Enough. I put my hands on my hips. "I was nowhere near there. I went to Starbucks for takeout coffee, then came home to study for my art history final. You should arrest Randy Rains. The guy who directed *Slow Death* and *Dead Even*. He's the sicko, not me."

Randy

Me and the homicide detective are sitting in my office, with my movie posters behind me. Best pussy lubricant ever. I never had sex with a detective before. Especially not one who was investigating me for murder. What a kick that would be.

"Did you ever think of acting?" I say. A line I must have used on a thousand women, but as long as it works, why change? "You'd make a great detective," I add.

"I understand you were with Caroline at the club last night," she says.

"She was a sweet kid," I say. "Breaks my heart."

"What were you guys doing?"

"Sitting around talking. Or trying to, the music was pretty loud." I imagine I'm in a movie right now. How would I behave? I give the detective an overwhelmed look and put a hand to my chest. "I can't believe, just ten minutes later or whatever, she was dead."

"Did you see her leave the club?"

"No. She must've wanted a break from the noise."

"A witness saw you leaving the club with her."

My heart skips a beat. But maybe the detective is making that up. I wouldn't put it past her. "That's not true."

"Word is, your drug of choice is coke."

I pull myself together and give the detective a sly smile. "What's yours?"

"Providing drugs to a minor is a felony."

"She was eighteen."

"We have witnesses saying that you and Caroline were freebasing cocaine at the club last night."

This woman is starting to be a pain in the ass. I laugh. "Here's the deal," I say. I point up at my movie posters, with their bomb explosions, AK-45s, and corpses. "I make violent movies, but I faint when I see blood. I've never smoked any kind of drug in my life. I smoke sugar and baking powder. I give it to my girls, and if they're in the mood to turn into freaks . . . " I smile. "Then they turn into freaks."

"So what happened last night? Caroline didn't turn into a freak and it pissed you off?"

I lean back in my black Herman Miller Aeron chair. Cost me three thousand bucks. "Sure, I was trying to nail her. So what? I like making movies and I like having sex with young girls. Sue me."

"Your first wife called the cops on you twice."

"Fifteen years ago, for God's sake." Why do people always keep bringing that up? I open my minifridge and reach for a beer—

"You drink a lot of milk?" says the detective.

She must've noticed the gallon on the top shelf. "Yeah, it's wholesome. Just like me."

"When people abuse cocaine, they get a calcium deficiency. Which causes major milk cravings." The detective leans forward. I didn't notice before, but her teeth are kind of pointy, like she's an animal who's been bred to tear into your flesh. "If you were high when you accidentally pushed her off the railing, that's a mitigating factor."

"You are sexy as hell," I say, "and I'm dying to know where you carry your gun. But even so, I'm gonna have to ask you to leave."

Detective Sara Stark

I'm sitting at a Starbucks. The same one where Caroline used to hang out, before she became a TikTok star. I'm sipping coffee and thinking.

Or trying to. I managed to ditch Cigar Breath all day today. He was "doing forensics," which probably meant a two-hour, three-beer lunch and a few long breaks, but now he's back, smellier than ever, sitting at the table across from me. He says, "I still think it was an accident. She was drunk and she fell."

No, not what happened, not with that high railing. Cigar Breath is just trying to avoid work.

Which he proves with his next sentence. "How about we call it a night? Forget this red velvet frappuccino crap, let's head over to Oscar's and have a real drink. We deserve it."

The guy keeps babbling but finally I manage to tune him out. I'm thinking: It's always the boyfriend.

Or ex-boyfriend. Or wannabe boyfriend. I'm not sure which category fits Jeremy and Randy, but they're in there somewhere.

And what about the best friend forever? How dangerous is a BFF scorned?

Cigar Breath is still blathering away. "And another thing I don't get: soy milk. I'd rather put cat piss in my coffee than soy milk."

Milk. If only I understood the damn spilled milk, or cream, I bet I'd understand everything.

Wait a second. I get an idea. I put down my cup so fast I spill coffee on the table, and on Cigar Breath's jacket too, I'm happy to see. As he starts complaining, I go up to the front counter.

Gwen

It's seven o'clock and getting dark. My parents will be at work 'til eight or nine. I haven't eaten anything all day, and I should get up and make myself some dinner, at least yogurt, but it's like I'm stuck to the sofa. I still can't believe what happened last night. I can't make it make sense in my mind. Caroline is dead. She was pushed over a railing—

The doorbell rings. I make it off the sofa, and I see Detective Stark there. Does she know anything more about the murder? I open the door.

"May I come in?" she says.

"Yes. Did you find out anything?"

"I believe so. May I trouble you for another cup of that delicious coffee you make?"

I nod, confused. "Sure." I lead the way into the kitchen and put in a vanilla pod; I need something comforting. The whole time she's talking about the traffic on the 101, and what a nice house my family has, and how real estate prices are starting to go up again. Seriously? Why won't she tell me what she found out?

Finally we both settle down with our coffee. Not that I need any, my heart is racing. "Please. Do you know who killed Caroline?"

She puts down her cup. "First, I just want to say how great it is you stayed such good friends, even after she got famous. Giving her little gifts, like that necklace. Did you give her other gifts too?"

What kind of question is that? "Sure," I say. "We gave each other gifts."

The detective nods and has another sip. "This is such good coffee."

My whole body tightens. I'm dying for her to get on with it. But she just stands up and opens the cabinet where we keep coffee and tea. "Why did you pick up coffee at Starbucks last night, when you have so many different flavored pods right here?"

I blink, taken aback. "Because I wanted an iced latte."

"But you didn't get an iced latte. You got steamed milk."

I feel my jaw dropping open. I manage to pull it back up. "Not last night. I remember."

"So does the server at Starbucks. She also remembers that when you and Caroline used to go there every afternoon, she never got coffee. Her favorite drink was steamed milk."

"So what?" I say. "What difference does it make?"

"The killer spilled milk at the crime scene. As I'm sure you know."

"I told you, I came straight home." My hand is grabbing my coffee cup so tight, my veins pop.

"No. You got her a cup of steamed milk as a gift. Maybe you were hoping she'd get you into the club. But instead she met you out back. She told you to take your gift and go. Get the hell out of her life. Quit embarrassing her."

There's a roaring in my ears. It's so loud I can barely hear her now. Her lips open and close but I can't tell what the sounds coming from them mean. She sits back down at the kitchen table with me. I hear little pieces like "I understand it was an accident" and "You're a nice girl. I can see that."

My mouth begins moving, almost on its own, like it belongs to some other girl. "She wouldn't wear my jewelry," my mouth says.

"That must've upset you."

I manage to shut my mouth again. But then the detective asks, "Did Caroline not like your jewelry?" My lips tremble but stay closed. The roaring gets even louder, but I hear, "She made fun of you, didn't she?"

I have to make the roaring stop. I tear off my bracelet with the rainbow umbrella charms and shake it in the detective's face. "My stuff is legit!" I yell over the deafening noise. "If she wore this in her videos, *everyone* would buy it. Gwenoline would be everywhere! I'd be famous too! But no. No one could be famous but her, and who cares about her BFF forever!"

I throw my coffee cup against the white kitchen wall. It smashes, leaving brown stains and pieces of cup everywhere. I turn back to the detective. "We pinkie swore. That backstabbing bitch. She deserved to die."

I look at the detective's eyes and see a stupid, smug little smile. I should've shut up.

Detective Sara Stark

I book the killer at the station, then step outside into the cold night air. Such a tragedy. One young life gone. Another life ruined. Well, no use crying over spilled milk. I walk on.

Zephaniah Sole's fiction is published in various journals, to include *Epiphany*, *Gargoyle Magazine*, and *Vestal Review*. His first novel, *The Wolves Children Hear* (Black Spring Press), is slated to be published in the Summer of 2022. His work has received support from VONA, the Martha's Vineyard Institute of Creative Writing, and the Tin House Winter Workshop.

Len Bias

Evil. I fight evil. And this morning, evil smells like cat piss and acetone. This Portland-area heroin smells different to me, coming off a dead body, than New York dope. Could be how the best coast Mexican cartels cut it different in transport than the beast coast bad boys using the Caribbean corridor. Or it could just be the cat. It sits, silent, on the dead woman's chest, staring at the foam coming out her nostrils and mouth. I shoo it away before it eats her. I'll never forget the dead body call I responded to back on the beat in Da Boogie Down when I was still NYPD. Me and my partner kicked in the tenement door and the stench of a body that'd been decomposing a week kicked us right back. Elderly man. Kept to himself. Neighbors reported the smell. He died comfortably. On his sofa. But he had three cats and when we got there they were still eating him. I tell all cat lovers, when you wake up in the morning and your darling little pussy's sitting on your chest looking up your nose, it's not showing you love. It's waiting to see if the air is going to stop flowing in and out. In and out. Nicole. Nicole was a cat lover. I fight the sear in my chest from that last thought and ignore the incessant pain returning to my lower back. Fuck cats. Give me a dog any day.

I tiptoe over the urine stains in the carpet, past the dead woman. She's not getting revived. Heart's been stopped over an hour. The boyfriend, crouched deep in the corner of a filthy couch, took too long to call it in. "Can't give her naloxone?" he mutters, running grimy fingers through the hair he has left. I join the officers from PPB Drugs and Vice. Knuckles. Jeff. Donna. Bruce the Sergeant. We stand over the boyfriend. We trade looks. We don't speak. Yet. We know what's what. We got a Lenny. We got work to do. We got to move.

Now. Now it's time to talk. And Knuckles—all red bearded and six two—does most of the talking. I do the listening. That's how these go. Best to use the federal Len Bias Law here. If we get the supplier of the heroin, then the supplier's supplier, the supplier's supplier's supplier, and so on, then we can prosecute every piece of shit in the chain, up to whatever self-fashioned kingpin south of the border or over in América del Sur was responsible for providing the dope that killed this woman—theoretically at least. That's why I'm here. I listen. I take notes. I absorb everything for the federal affidavits I'll need to write. "Let's get 'em my little feebee," Bruce whispers in my ear as he claps my shoulder and walks away. I smirk and nod. I'm the FBI guy embedded in the team.

It doesn't take long to get to the first level SOS. Knuckles, the right combination of intimidation and calm, is best at these interviews. The boyfriend gives up the Source of Supply, quick. A fellow named Geraldo. Knuckles doesn't raise his voice. He doesn't need to. He points to the old-school flip phone on the grungy couch. "Call Geraldo," he says, softly. The boyfriend nods and wipes the snot from his face and grabs the phone.

Now me, Jeff, and Donna, our vehicles positioned outside the boyfriend's house, hide in plain sight amongst the parked cars along the street. Knuckles and Bruce the Sergeant are inside with the boyfriend, monitoring his calls.

Knuckle's static voice comes in over my radio: "Should be twenty minutes."

Donna's voice replies: "Said that two hours ago."

Jeff: "Doper time, baby."

Doper time is right. Another hour goes by, then I'm the first to see it. We had gotten dispatch to check police reports on the identifiers the boyfriend gave us. Dispatch came back with a Geraldo Jimenez and shot his DMV photo to our smartphones. Knuckles had held up his phone to the boyfriend, showing him a rugged face framed by a baby blue background. The boyfriend mumbled, "Yeah, that's him." "That's who?" Knuckles asked. "That's

Geraldo," the boyfriend said. "Good," Knuckles nodded. "What does Geraldo drive?"

Now, here comes the late model Toyota Camry, bluish gray, cruising, intently obeying all stop signs and speed limits. That car is the smart car of the peddlers in the game. It doesn't draw attention to itself, not like the rides ridden by the mopes and the clowns: high-end Sebrings, rimmed-out Mustangs, custom-decaled Hummers.

The Camry pulls up to the house. I get on my radio. "V's arrived." The Camry stops humming. "Engine off." Its door opens. "S getting out."

A pin-up model from 1952 steps out of the car. I make a noise that's something between a chuckle and a groan. A gruckle? A choan? In a way, this is all kind of funny. "S is female," I say. "Bout five eight. Blonde. Approaching."

Donna: "She's got huge tits."

Jeff: "Glad you said it."

Donna: "I can say it. SOS send someone else?"

Knuckles: "CI says no."

I close my eyes. Resigned.

Me: "Just a thought. I say we take her."

Bruce: "Good thought. Do it."

***

Evil. That's what I had told Nicole when she called me after I got home from the homicide scene that night two years ago today. I fight evil. The scene was gang-related which means it was dope-related which means I got called out for the supposed contribution of my expertise—but really it was because they needed the bodies, and the locals don't have to pay me overtime. I fight evil. No, she had responded with the grand authority bestowed by Oregon State University's doctoral program in Psychology. No. You are not fighting evil. You are fighting the wasteland your life has become. I told her, we're all in the wasteland then, and I'm a road warrior baby, holding the line. Keeping the hounds of chaos at bay. She laughed. I could hear her eyes rolling through the high-def reception of my smartphone. It was my birthday, she had said.

You are not a warrior. You are a man with prioritization issues. And this doesn't work for me anymore.

I remember these things as I stare at the blonde's tits. We had cuffed her hands behind her back and sat her on the couch in the boyfriend's house. To get comfortable she has to squeeze her shoulder blades and arch her spine. I stare. I don't care. My back hurts. Worse now. The view's a welcome distraction. Me, Knuckles, and Donna stand over her. Jeff and Bruce search her Camry outside. The blonde's hair is in a mid-length shag that frames her face nice—the same face from the DMV photo, ruggedness replaced with a high-boned smooth.

"Geraldo," Knuckles says gently, and the blonde looks up. "The stuff you gave this woman killed her."

The blonde's voice is hoarse. "That's not my fault."

"I'm not trying to intimidate you. I'm just putting the facts out there. Under the law Geraldo, yes, her death is very much your fault."

The blonde whispers. "My name's Ingrid."

"I apologize. Ingrid. This can end with you and you take all the flak. Or . . ." Knuckles nods to Donna, who holds up the smartphone she seized when she searched Ingrid.

Ingrid looks at me. I toss her a wink. She shuts her eyes and arches further. "Billy," she says. "Billy the Kid. That's my connect. You want, I'll call him up."

"No," Donna says. "Gotta book you in county. You want to cooperate? Give the code."

Ingrid opens her eyes. "Four—seven—nine—one."

Donna unlocks the phone. "What's his contact under? Billy?"

"Kid," says Ingrid. Donna finds the name and catches Knuckles' eye.

"Alrighty," I say and help Ingrid off the couch. "I got transport."

"You don't have to . . ." Donna says, "I can . . ."

"Nah. You guys are better at those UC texts."

"What about the fed affy?" Knuckles asks.

I drone in monotone: "The facts set forth in this affidavit are based on my own personal knowledge as well as knowledge obtained from other individuals during my participation in this investigation including other law enforcement officers and yada blasie blah." I walk Ingrid to the door. "Y'all a be straight without me." I escort her out into the rising sunlight. "Early anyways. Booking won't take long."

***

This doesn't work for me anymore. That's what Nicole had said and I ended the call before I said something back that would taint her memory of me forever. Not that I should have cared, but I did. I cared what her memories of me would be, even knowing I would never see her again. Even knowing her memories of me were not me. I wanted to smash my smartphone. I almost did. But it was the one issued by the bureau and I didn't want to deal with the paperwork; filling out form ten-sixty-this and form thirteen-oh-that, explaining why I now needed a replacement. So, I had taken my anger out on my furniture. In particular, my antique, cherrywood bed frame that weighed a tad more than my lower back expected when I gripped it from the bottom and launched it into the wall. Then, I had pulled my back. Bad. Then, I had to pay someone to repair the cracked and dented drywall. Then, I had to pay someone else to repair the shattered leg and separated headboard of my bed frame. Then, I'd lain on my mattress in pain and tried to sob the poison in my chest out through my face. She was right. Damn it, she was right. I did have prioritization issues. I should have just smashed the smartphone.

I do not remember these things as I stare at Ingrid's tits in my rearview mirror. I remember other things instead. Things that make me pull off 84 East and, instead of heading for Inverness to book her, drive down Sandy then down 105th. Past the chop shops. Past that derelict one-level eight-plex painted that horrendous shade of green. Over the unpaved gravel pinging off the chassis of my Charger. Under the freeway. I pull in behind a group of warehouses. Look around. Make sure we've got no tails. The air gets musky from the marijuana dispensary nearby. I glance at Ingrid in my rearview mirror. She's cuffed in the back seat, passenger side. I shut off the engine, unlock the door, step out. Walk to the rear door, open it. Lean in. Unbuckle her. Uncuff her. She gets out, walks up front. We get back in the car.

Ingrid fluffs her hair and I watch her and I grip the steering wheel tight. She faces me. "How's your back?"

"Hurts," I grimace. Ingrid sucks her teeth, grazes my cheek with the tips of her purple-painted fingernails. "I got you," she says and pushes her hips up off the seat, unbuttoning her jeans, forcing them down over her ass, past her hips.

I gruckle. "They didn't search you so good."

She choans. "Felt down there type quick. Assumed I didn't have a vagina."

"Know what they say about assumptions," I say and stare at an ass that makes me want to destroy the separation of 'you' and 'me.' Especially with those white lace panties on. The panties she reaches into, digging her fingers into herself. I lean forward. Take off my right hiking boot. Take off my sock. Pop open the center console. Pull out a leather carrying case. Unzip it. Graze my finger over the lighter and the needle and the parachute cord and the spoon. Ingrid pulls a small hard sphere wrapped in a black balloon from inside her.

She helps me cook the heroin. She helps me load the syringe. She helps me find the vein I like between my second and third toes. She holds the syringe and she's about to push when I remember. "Call Billy," I say.

"I know baby."

"Use my phone. Don't call the number you gave them."

"I know."

"Tell him don't respond to those UC texts."

"He's not stupid."

"Unlike yours truly."

"You're not stupid."

"Didn't know Geraldo was your proper government."

"You never asked."

"I fucked up."

"Shh," she says and pushes the syringe. My eyes roll to the back of my head. Back, back into the infinite gone. She nuzzles my cheek. She kisses me. She tells me everything is okay.

***

There's a tap, rapping rhythm, and my brain watches a crow pecking at a tree stump. The crow, head cocked to the side, glares at me hard with one eye from a steel-blue-hued land of burned down dreams. Then I come to and the steel blue fades and I see the dancing dark reds I see when my eyes are closed. I still hear the rapping but now it's the unmistakable percussion of little bones on glass, tap, tap, tapping away.

I open my eyes. Ingrid's asleep, her head in my lap. I stroke her hair and look out the window, hoping I'm going to see who I think I'm going to see and to great relief I do. I rock Ingrid's shoulder. She wakes with a sigh. I unlock the door and stumble out of the car. I'm not a big guy, but I tower over the little white boy who made me woke. He looks up at me, bright eyed and head shiningly shaved down to the skin. I like to call him Charlie Brown, but he never gets the joke. Kids his age don't know Charlie Brown.

"Fuck is going on?" he asks. Ingrid steps out of the car to join us. I'm still dizzy. I lean against the hood. "Billy," I say, "you know what's going on." Billy the Kid lets out a breath, clenches his fists, paces a tight circle. "The H you gave Ingrid," I say, "where'd you get it?"

Billy shrugs. "Got two hook ups now."

"And they are?"

Billy holds up his left hand and throws out a name not worth mentioning because it's a chickenshit-little-nobody, upon whom the expenditure of further thought and energy would be an unnecessary waste. But then he holds up his right hand and says, "Brother Stilt."

"Stilt huh?"

"Free Souls got the hook up with this dude from New Generation. Stilt wanna run P-Town and The Couve. Talkin' bout Vagos, Jokers, Brother Speed, push 'em out or get 'em under."

"Everybody wants to get somebody under."

"Might do it."

"If he had the focus. And the will."

"Got hella strength."

"Who's his connect? From *Nueva Generación*?"

"He don't tell me that shit."

"Yeah," I rub my eyes with my forefinger and thumb. "Yeah, I need you to take me to Stilt."

Billy's eyes water. He throws his arms around my waist. "Don't do this."

"Your customer's dead. That's life for both of you."

"Even Billy?" Ingrid asks.

"He's eighteen now, he's Billy the Man."

"Let's just leave," Ingrid says.

"And go where? We're as far west as west gets."

"East then," she says. "Idaho. Montana."

"I stay with you they'll run us down quick."

"North," Billy chimes in. "Canada."

Ingrid clutches at my sleeve. "Let's just leave."

I mull it over. I do. I think about the green of open plain. The orange of clean sunset. I think about the crisp of brook and creek. The rush of river. The trembling of snow. I think about these things. Then I hear a flap and a caw. The crow reminds me these things are not for me.

I rub my eyes and mutter. "Evil. I fight evil." Billy's arms are still around my waist. Ingrid puts her head on my chest. "But we're the evil," she says.

No. I shake my head. No. We are the lost pariahs of a people disconnected. We are the negative space in the portrait. And I want to articulate this, but Billy interrupts my train of thought. "Why you like this?" he says.

"You asked me that when I first met you."

"You ain't ever answered."

I put my hand on his skin bald head. "Got stranded out on the ocean, man. Never made it to shore." Billy lets me go, looks down at his sneakers. "And," I say, "I hurt my fucking back."

I get back in the car, alert now. "My friends move quick," I say. "Don't dance so well, but they can line drive like muthafuckas."

"Stilt's in The Couve," Billy says and gets in the back seat. Ingrid gets in front.

I turn the engine on. "Then let's beat that 205 rush."

***

"If Portland is a poor man's Seattle, and Vancouver is a poor man's Portland, what's the economic metaphor between The Couve and Seattle?" I wonder out loud as Billy directs us through the streets of downtown Vancouver, Washington State.

Billy snaps his fingers. "Vancouver's a nigger's Seattle," he says, with pride. I shake my head. "How can these places be a nigger's anything. Niggers were never allowed here." I pull up to the pawn shop Billy guides me to and we get out of the car. Ingrid follows but I give her the keys and say, "Stay on the wheel. You know . . . " She nods and fights back a tear.

Billy the Kid leads me into the shop. It's surprisingly well-lit. Organized. The six-four, two-twenty-pound skinhead behind the gated counter is also incredibly affable. Or high as shit. I can't tell. Either way, he smiles sweetly at Billy and waves us on. There's an unlabeled door in the rear corner. Billy leads me through it; then up a narrow, musty, two-flight staircase; through another door; and out onto a second-floor loft at least a thousand square feet big.

The loft is bare, save the three Free Souls tying five thirty-gallon trash bags they then sling over their shoulders. Their backs are turned to me and the Kid, showing the blue ankh patches on their biker leather. A jingling comes from inside the bags, like crashing shards of broken glass. They finally look up and approach. They're big, but one in particular, at nearly seven feet, is especially so. This dude, who missed his calling to play center for the Trailblazers, steps to me, his two boyfriends at his side. The seven-footer nods. The boyfriends leave.

I look up at Brother Stilt. "You know me?" Stilt doesn't acknowledge me or the question. He looks down at Billy. "Bad time to bring the piggies around," he says, "'Specially little pork tacos like—"

"Pork mofongo would be a more apt, and funnier, ethnic derision," I cut him off. "But you muthafuckas out here don't even know what a Puerto Rican is. Anywhosie, we can't keep going through Billy. 'Less, you know, you don't want to take full advantage of what I bring."

Stilt glares at me, drops his bags. They clink like fine china. I smell drain cleaner. Stilt says, "Strip."

"Everything?"

"No. Everything except that wire you got on."

"That sarcasm?"

"No," he says sarcastically.

"Cuz my brain don't process sarcasm so well."

"I ain't too sure your brain processes anything so well."

"Not true. Any algebra question. Right now. Ask."

"Everything. Off."

So, I do. My jacket. Shirt. Undershirt. I pull my weapon from my holster and lay the Glock on the ground as Stilt's eyes go wide and he brings his right hand to the small of his back. I unbuckle my belt. Take off my boots. Then my pants.

Stilt's still glaring. "Everything."

I choan. Take off my boxers. Socks. Stilt shakes his head. "What are you selling?"

"I'm a federal agent. Embedded in a local drug task force."

"I know who you are."

"Then you know what I'm selling."

"Keep selling through Billy."

"You ever play the telephone game?"

"What?"

"Exactly," I say. "And my guys are getting a lot more proactive out there. There's too much going on, I can't keep passing the 411 through Charlie Brown."

"He does look like Charlie Brown."

"Right?"

"So what do you want?"

"Direct dealing. No intermediaries."

"I mean how much—"

"I don't have time to launder shit, Stilt. I just want my H steady and costing me free-ninety-free."

Stilt strokes his patchy beard. "You need more don't you?"

I clench my jaw. "Yep."

"How'd you get like this, man?"

"I hurt my back."

"Painkillers?"

"Percocet. Darvocet. Tylenol number three."

"Wasn't enough."

"Was not enough."

Stilt nods. "Common story." I see what looks like empathy in his eyes. "Alright man," he says, "come back tomorrow. Same time."

"Will do. I can put my clothes on?"

"Don't touch that gun yet."

I put my boxers on. "I need a holdover. 'Til tomorrow. Good faith deposit?"

Stilt picks up his trash bags. "Billy'll hook you up."

"Direct dealing," I say again. "No intermediaries."

Stilt grunts, drops the bag he's holding in his left hand. Reaches into his leather. Pulls out a small, resealable plastic packet. Tosses it. It smacks the ground in front of me. I pick it up, note the brownish powder inside. "Thank you, sir," I say.

Free Soul Brother Stilt nods and picks up his bag. Before he exits stage right he turns and says with an offended look in his eyes, "I know what a Puerto Rican is."

***

Now. In an alley a few blocks from the pawn shop, I sit on the pavement flicking the resealable packet. Ingrid's crouched beside me. Billy the Kid stands. "Let's get back over the river at least," Ingrid says. I know why. The hospitals are better in Portland.

I shake my head. "They're on their way. Probably tracking my phone, got no reasonable expectation of privacy on this shit. When they get here, they'll deconflict with Vancouver PD, that buys a little time. A little." I look up at the Kid. "Please leave. They are coming. Please leave."

Ingrid sobs without a sound and the snot from her nose rubs into my cheek. She gives me my works and she kisses me, hard. I don't want to pull away but I do. Me and the Kid trade a glance. He grabs Ingrid by the wrist. He's so tough. They'll be okay. This is a good thing. The right thing. I'm tired anyway. Tired of chasing after her. And by *Her* I mean all of them. And by *Her* I mean none of them. All and none of the ones I won. All of the ones I had and the One I never found. The alpha and the omega. The first and the last. The last. The last who collapsed in on herself, breathing fire when she left. *This doesn't work for me anymore.* That was her refrain. *This doesn't work for me anymore.*

So, I chase a different dragon now.

I mainline the H this time. All of it. Before it kicks in I finger my pocket, make sure my phone's still there. My eyes roll back and I welcome the euphoria, knowing what's coming next. Not sure how much time passes, but it doesn't feel like long before I'm glued to the pavement and I'm having trouble breathing. The world goes splotchy and red and I wish these guys would just find me already.

Another infinity goes by. Then Knuckles' red beard is in my face and he's not talking so gentle this time. "You fucking traitor!" he's screaming and his voice is a continent away. "Where are they?"

I hear Bruce the Sergeant from across an ocean. "Piece of shit," he's saying. How quickly they turn. I was his little feebee just this morning. Knuckles is shaking me. "Who's got the Narcan?" he says, and I hear Donna respond, "Here, here." I tap my pocket, the one holding my phone. Knuckles picks up on this. He pulls the phone out.

"Eight—two—one—zero," I whisper. Knuckles unlocks it. "Stupid ass," I say. "Thought I'd record him with a wire. They got an app for everything now."

Knuckles and his red beard look at me, confused.

"Fuck Billy," I whisper. "Small time. And you weren't getting past him. He had two sources. You wouldna pinned it for sure on the next level up."

"Who's the next level up?" Knuckles asks.

"Brother Stilt. Big pussy. He'll flip on his cartel connect. Fuck Billy and Ingrid. Go get the big dogs."

"Why'd you do this?"

"Cuz my fucking back hurts," I squeak before my neck goes slack and my tongue freezes against my teeth. I tense. I see Her. She's with me now. Her. Now. In my arms. Here. She smells like baby powder. Now. She looks up at me, face damp from drizzling rain. She asks if I have any major character flaws. I tell her about that Snickers bar I stole when I was twelve. She says be serious. I tell her this story. She purses her lips. I tell her I'm sorry. I tried to be good. I really did. She looks out into the rain. Hell, she says, no point in getting all tense over the past. I kiss her head. She cocks an eyebrow. But don't, she says, let me find out you're already married.

"Narcan, come on!" I hear Knuckles shout from a vehicle speeding away from me, got to be doing 85, 90, at least.

"Let the low hangers go," I hear Bruce the Sergeant one last time. "We got a new Lenny. First level, Brother Stilt. We got work to do. We got to—"

Andrew Miller was born in Ohio. He lives in the Silver Lake section of Los Angeles with his girlfriend Genevieve and their two cats, John Wayne and Calamity Jane. He is an author, screenwriter and essayist. His novella *Lady Tomahawk* appears in the anthology *L.A. Stories* (Uncle B. Publications). His short stories have appeared in *Close To The Bone*, *Pulp Modern*, *Switchblade*, *Broadswords and Blasters*, and on Medium.com. His film work includes the music documentary *Soul Of Lincoln Heights*. He is a member of the Independent Fiction Alliance, a network of authors, publishers and editors committed to combating censorship and promoting freedom of expression.

SAMURAI '81

I sat at my desk in the Glass House across from my new partner, Junichiro "June" Genji. We'd closed our first homicide together that afternoon, an open-and-shut, and I was finishing the paperwork when a fresh call for us arrived, hand-delivered by Captain Carnahan.

That winter I was thirty-two, the youngest detective ever promoted to the Robbery Homicide Division. A series of high-profile cases quickly pushed me up the ladder.

"Ford Newcomen, the COO of Goalmart, just got murdered in the parking lot of Yamashiro." Yamashiro was a swank Japanese restaurant in the hills. Captain Carnahan handed a yellow sheet with all the information to June, the senior detective.

"The assistant chief's monitoring this personally," the captain said. "Newcomen had high-up friends and there are irregularities. Witnesses said the killer used a Samurai sword."

A Samurai sword? At first, I thought this might be a joke because June and I are both Japanese, or maybe a hazing ritual because I was new to the division.

An old partner in West Bureau Homicide once told me about how he saw a guy who'd gotten his pinky cut off at a Yakuza bar in Little Tokyo, but even that was years ago. It was 1981 now. People weren't killed with Samurai swords anymore.

***

June drove us down Franklin in a department-issue black Matador. It started to rain. "Have you ever eaten at Yamashiro, Akira?"

I had been there. Yamashiro was a villa built in 1911 to house a millionaire's art. By the time of the camps, it was abandoned and went into disrepair. Today it existed as a discreet restaurant, mainly for rich men to bring their girlfriends. I'd brought girlfriends there, even though I wasn't rich. A few of them were also registered CIs. This was against regulations and I didn't need it getting around.

"I've been to the bar."

"The last time I went, they were playing punk music so loud by our table, Mariko and I could barely hear each other. She asked for a side of rice. The server brought her basmati that had clearly been put in a microwave."

Through the rain, we saw the flashing red lights above us. June carefully climbed the Matador up the winding and narrow road.

The American retail chain Goalmart had over one thousand locations nationwide. Because of Newcomen's high profile in the company, as well as the unusual murder weapon, this case went to RHD instead of the standard divisional homicide detectives.

June parked. At the yellow tape we flashed our shields and were let in. The Hollywood patrolman who took the call was named Martino.

"Follow me," Martino said. "The Yamashiro manager called it in."

We went to the body. It was on the pavement near the front gate, covered by a black tarp and under a tent provided by the restaurant. Blood streamed down toward the entrance below where it emptied into a sewer.

"MEs are running late because of other calls," Martino said.

"Take the tarp off, Akira," June said.

I obeyed and revealed the body of a well-dressed white man in his late sixties wearing a blue, Armani pinstripe suit. Newcomen was on his side. His stiff hands clutched his bloody and bulging entrails.

Martino pointed toward four Japanese men sitting at a table

under an umbrella. "The victim, Newcomen, was having dinner with three visiting reps from Takeshita Electronics in Tokyo. The guy in front's their lawyer."

"Goalmart's been considering Takeshita for a contract," June said. "If the deal is made, Takeshita products will be sold at all Goalmart locations nationwide. It was in the *Wall Street Journal*."

Martino said, "According to the Takeshita lawyer, Newcomen was leaving with his guests when the perp attacked."

June and I took witness statements. Other patrons and staff saw the perp running off with his sword. No one saw the whole kill, just fragments. No one saw the perp's face, except, surely, the Takeshita reps who were hiding behind their lawyer.

The rain let up. I found Tono, a Yamashiro valet I knew. He was close when it happened. "I didn't see, only heard," Tono said. "Some Toyota bigshot was leaving with a young pro when the kill went down. Both of them probably saw everything, I'm almost sure."

"Do I know the pro?"

"It was Yuko. She and the guy skipped fast."

Yuko was one of my CIs as well as an on-and-off girlfriend. She came here with johns all the time. The women in my life were not what I felt like talking about during a case where the assistant chief was watching. I decided to speak with her later.

The medical examiners arrived. While they worked, June pointed: "Despite the brazenness, this cut was precise." A note of familiarity was in his voice.

In '81, my partner June was forty-five years old. He was married and taught yoga classes on his days off, twice a month. His last partner, an old school Irishman named Murray Flannagan, had retired. Despite having put dozens of cases in the red together, Flannagan and June never got along. Flannagan's father was a POW in the Pacific.

June didn't like how Americanized I was. He didn't like my mullet haircut. Still, he wanted to know if he could trust me.

When the ME team finished, Newcomen was carted off in a fire department ambulance.

"I have a fence CI we can track down," June said.

***

He took us to a storefront in Little Tokyo. A yellow-lit sign above the door said *Ashida's Pawn Shop* in English and in Japanese. A Galpin box truck was parked by the entrance. An obvious movie gaffer waited and smoked.

We walked up. "Closed set," the gaffer said.

We flashed our shields. He gave us no trouble.

Inside, it was a regular pawn shop but with a focus on Japanese items. We walked around an opaque divider in the back. Behind it, cables were plugged into a large receptacle outlet. They ran up a stairway.

"Freddy lives up there," June said.

We walked up. A woman moaned sexually. We walked through a doorway. An old Japanese man holding a clapperboard shushed us.

We watched.

Another man was on his knees, pointing a big video recorder down at a naked Japanese woman who laid on the floor on her back. She was being penetrated by the wet tentacle of a live octopus. In the corner, a man stood beside an open portable aquarium on wheels. Beside him the director watched and rubbed a visible hard-on in his jeans and behind him, an older, heavyset Japanese man signaled to June. This had to be Freddy.

The woman's moans built until she came, or at least pretended to. The director called cut and the octopus handler stepped forward to assist the woman in getting the tentacle out of her.

The heavy man rushed over. "Shit," he hissed. "These videos are popular, June. They're a lucrative game for me."

"This visit isn't about your videos, Freddy. Take me to your supply."

He led us back downstairs and across a short hallway in the rear of the building. He removed a rug, stuck a key into a lock in the floor, then pulled open a panel, revealing a wooden staircase leading to a dark basement. We followed him down.

Freddy pulled the chain on a light and illuminated a collection of three dozen heirloom katanas mounted on the walls. All appeared to be in impeccable condition.

"Being an informant isn't a license to do anything you want," June said.

"I have to make money. At least I'm trying to keep a foot in my background."

They spoke Japanese. I understood, but not perfectly and I was terrible at speaking it.

"A man standing on both sides of the fence must split, eventually, down the middle. Did Takezo buy a sword from you?"

Freddy waited. "The buyer sent a man in his place."

"Was the buyer Takezo?"

"It's possible."

I was frustrated on the sidelines. "A man watched his own guts spill out because of that weapon," I said in English. "We need answers."

June gave me a look—*stop talking.*

Freddy said, "Forgive my rudeness, Junichiro-san, but I wouldn't need to deal with anyone like Takezo if I had the business of all the Brotherhood."

June led me back upstairs. We passed the girl, now wrapped in a silk kimono. She bowed delicately. We bowed in return.

Back in the Matador, I said, "Who is Takezo? What is the Brotherhood?"

"I wasn't planning to show you this early."

***

June took me to a big house on Quebec and El Contento, back in the Hills. He used a remote to raise the door and pulled into a four-space garage. There were three other cars already parked here.

Inside, the living room had a wall of windows with a great view of the city below. A bonsai tree was by the window. June led me downstairs.

The rest of the house was built into the side of a steep hill and multiple levels went all the way to the bottom. At the entrance to the second story down, June unlocked a door and held it open. We went in.

It was a windowless dojo. Four men in keikogis and hakamas

practiced kendo with wooden swords and helmets with face grills. They saw us, removed their helmets, and walked over, still sweating. I recognized Eddie Kuwata, the one other Japanese detective currently in RHD. I also knew Homura Yoshimura from my time at West Bureau. Homura was a vice detective. The other two guys I didn't know.

"Welcome to the founding chapter of the Brotherhood," June said.

I waited. *The Brotherhood? Was this why he'd been sizing me up all week?*

"We have a case to work," I said.

"This pertains to our case."

Outside, the wind howled. I looked them over. June introduced the other two as Ken Takakura and Joe Gō, both patrolmen in Northeast Division. "So you brought me to a club where a bunch of Jap cops dress up and play Toshiro Mifune?"

"I told you he wasn't ready," Homura said sharply to June in Japanese.

I sighed. "All right, you meet up, do some kendo and call yourselves Samurai." I used English. "What else?"

"The Jews keep their traditions alive," June said. "The Muslims too. Here, we keep the spirit of our Samurai ancestors alive."

I wondered again if I was being pranked.

"Every Samurai must have a retainer," Eddie said. "The LAPD is ours. Our service to them follows Bushido as best as we can."

"The LAPD would not approve of our Brotherhood, if they knew," Homura said. "No outsider can be told about this."

I nodded. "It's a solid move, keeping this a secret." Either none of them picked up on my sarcasm or they chose to ignore it.

"You're the only LAPD Japanese not currently a member," June said. "We've been considering you, but we heard rumors that you are guilty of discreditable conduct with your female informants."

I swallowed. No one ever brought this up to my face.

June added, "We decided to take a chance, because of Newcomen."

I said, "Takezo."

I waited.

June nodded.

"Who is he?"

"He was one of us, but he was cast out. If you want to know more, we need to know we are speaking to a brother. Are you willing to join?"

Some weird Samurai fetish had driven much of the Japanese element of the LAPD crazy. It was ridiculous, and I wanted no part of it. Just because we shared a heritage, I wouldn't let whatever had infected their brains take root in my own.

"Give me the keys," I told June. "One of them can give you a ride back."

***

I slipped back into the Glass House and I avoided bumping into Captain Carnahan, who was expecting an update on Newcomen.

This late, the file storage room was empty. I flipped through old R&I records of men who'd been assigned to RHD and found a Takezo Murakami. There was a department ID photo. Murakami left the department in '78, a year after making lieutenant. No reason was cited. Before his departure, Takezo had a perfect career. He would now be forty-nine. I pulled his photo from the file and left.

Later, I was standing by my apartment window and looking at Takezo's face when there was a knock at my door.

Yuko stood there in jeans and a tight-fitting Go-Go's T-shirt. Seeing one of L.A.'s hottest working girls standing in my doorway was a relief.

We kissed.

Yuko gave me solid intel and I always made sure she was paid well. Last year, when I was at West Bureau working an armored car heist that left one dead, Yuko ended up on a date with one of the armed robbers and heard him bragging about it at a karaoke bar. My clearance there was a major reason I was pushed up the ladder to RHD so young.

I liked Yuko genuinely. She was sweet and tender. We got along on dates, the first of which was at a Go-Go's show at the Whisky last year. She was one of their biggest fans.

I said, "It's good to see you."

I poured us both a whisky. She took a sip. I handed her sixty dollars. She put it down on my nearby dresser.

"You got the guy at Yamashiro?" she said.

"Were you there?"

Yes, this part of my methods was against regulations, but women saw things. It wasn't my fault they talked the most in bed.

There was another girl I had a son with, but she had moved out of L.A. last year. I'd never met the boy. We agreed I never would.

"I saw the guy's face," Yuko said.

I showed her Takezo.

"That's him," she said. "The most chilling part was how calm he was."

I put down my drink and unbuttoned Yuko's jeans. She turned and bent over as I slowly slid them down to her ankles. She had two tattoos of winding branches of cherry blossoms. They started above her knees, wrapped up around her thighs and bloomed on her ass.

***

I opened my eyes in the dark. Between Yuko's light snores, I sensed someone else in my apartment. A snub nosed .38 was in my bedside-table drawer.

A figure passed across the light from the window.

I shouted, "Hey!"

Yuko sat up fast. I reached for the .38. There was a quick slashing noise. Something wet and warm sprayed my back and legs. Then came a thump.

I aimed and let off four shots in the dark. The figure ran fast out of the bedroom. I chased him. My wet feet were slick and slipped on the linoleum. At my own open doorway, I stopped. I was naked and covered in what I now realized was blood. The intruder escaped.

Back at my bedroom doorway, I flipped the light on.

Yuko's body twitched in the final throes of death. Her head had been chopped off and fell on the floor, her face frozen in surprise. Blood was everywhere.

In shock, I called 911. Then I stepped into the shower. When I turned off the water, sirens blared up the street. I got dressed and put the picture of Takezo in my pocket.

The patrolmen were horrified. I answered their questions but I wasn't really there. I didn't even have a good explanation about my relationship with Yuko.

"She was just some girl," I said.

June arrived. Some of my senses returned. I pulled him into the corner.

"This was him, wasn't it?"

June's expression said *probably*.

My partner and his brotherhood of Samurai cops now felt like my first glimpse at how the world really worked, my first invitation to join a select behind the curtain drama. "Why? If he knew Yuko saw him kill Newcomen, why did he wait until she was with me before making his move?"

"I think he knew you were assigned to Newcomen and he was watching your apartment. He probably saw her presence here as karma. Takezo has a high opinion about what gifts he deserves from the universe."

I scratched my head. None of this sounded like any killer I'd encountered.

"Takezo doesn't want us to come after him like detectives. It will have to be as Samurai."

How did Takezo know I was on Newcomen? Did a cop tell him? Why target me instead of the dojo in the hills? I said, "Do you know how to get him?"

"I know how to try."

In my bedroom, an ME held open a bag. Another gently placed Yuko's head into it.

I said, "I want in."

"The captain and all the higher-ups will have serious questions. Let me handle them. Doing our duty here will require delicacy."

"Fine."

"If you really want in, it must be forever. It can't be only for vengeance."

My career ambitions in the department had dissolved. All I wanted was revenge. "I'll prove how much I mean it."

***

In the dojo, June led a yoga class for the other four. I took off my shoes, sat against the wall, and watched.

I'd spent the last two days answering questions about Yuko from the divisional detectives and investigators from the Internal Affairs Bureau. I kept my answers simple, avoiding any mention of Takezo or the Brotherhood's apparent plans on how to get him. Yuko's decapitation was kept out of the press.

IAB learned I had been in a sexual relationship with my informant. Captain Carnahan told me an unofficial decision was made to ignore this infraction as long as I refrained from doing it with any other still living informants.

I was released, but with many departmental eyes on me.

After their yoga, my induction began. June and the others told me about the principles they stood for—Bushido. I knew about the code of the Samurai, but I was born and raised in America— before now, it meant nothing to me.

"Will you uphold these principles?" June said.

Revenge was still all I cared about and I knew joining the Brotherhood was my path to it. "Yes, I swear I will," I said.

They seemed satisfied.

June said, "Now, we piss on it."

Homura opened a sliding door I hadn't previously noticed. The six of us walked out to a ledge overlooking the yard far below. Each of them reached into their pants and exposed themselves. June looked at me and nodded.

I undid my zipper. Together, each of us pissed off the side.

Later on, I learned this ritual was the Samurai equivalent of becoming blood brothers. They picked it up from Tokugawa Ieyasu, the first Shogun of the Edo period in Japan.

***

We sat on the floor around the table upstairs. Ken poured us tea.

"Takezo was skilled, but undisciplined and addicted to materialism," June said. "He left the Brotherhood and the LAPD to sell himself to the highest bidder. His most recent employer appears to be Watanabe Electronics. Watanabe was on the precipice of sealing a major deal with Goalmart when Takeshita surreptitiously sabotaged the deal and Goalmart began expressing interest in Takeshita."

I almost gasped. "So Watanabe hired Takezo to fucking kill Newcomen in order to scare Goalmart into going back to Watanabe?" They all winced at my cursing. "I apologize, but so much of this is fantastic." I sipped my tea and tried to emulate their composure.

"The US Watanabe corporate offices are in Hawaii," Eddie said. "We've confirmed Takezo took a flight to Oahu yesterday morning."

I looked at June. "Earlier, you said Takezo expected us to come at him as a Samurai. What did you mean?"

"If we confront him as police, we risk having the Brotherhood exposed. Takezo knows we can't have that." June waited. "If we confront him as Samurai, he could lose. If he loses, we can write the ending of the case however we wish."

"I still don't understand Takezo's attack at my home."

June said, "The two of us will follow him to Oahu, where we can ask him face to face."

***

Our flight was a Pan Am red-eye, about a quarter full. We kept an eye out for possible tails at LAX and saw none. June read his tea gardens book. He'd included his katanas with our department issue sidearms in his luggage and experienced no interference from the airline. I tried to read the paper, but I couldn't focus and put it down.

I said, "So the LAPD is our retainer."

The only people within earshot were two businessmen across the aisle in tropical shirts, drinking Mai-Tais with colorful little umbrellas.

June had concocted a cover story for Captain Carnahan about why we needed to go to Hawaii. We would be interviewing Watanabe employees at their corporate offices. He'd successfully argued that Newcomen's high profile and money warranted an in-person visit.

"Since Takezo used to be one of us, solving this officially would bring great shame upon the LAPD," June said. "Our duty is to catch him, but to also protect the department." He waited. "Living this way requires knowing when it's right to bend the rules."

Instead of returning to his book, June began to quietly educate me about elements of Bushido. I was already familiar but he filled in a lot of blanks. He answered every question I could think of.

***

Still wearing my airport lei, I walked out to the balcony of our beachfront room at the Royal Hawaiian. The moon was full. Down the beach I could see the Diamond Head volcano in the moonlit darkness.

Our phone rang. June signaled for me to answer it.

"Hello?"

"Akira," a Japanese accented voice said.

Takezo.

"Are you inducted into the Brotherhood yet?"

I didn't answer.

He gently laughed. "I was just like you. I still believe that the way of the Samurai can be utilized in the modern world, but I had enough of the Brotherhood's hypocrisy."

"So you became a murderer for hire?"

"Business is war. I knew none of the regular cops in L.A. would have had a clue about who I was, but none of them would get the case. I even suspected you might be assigned."

June sat calmly on the bed.

"How did you know Yuko would be with me?"

"The shift manager at Yamashiro told me you were her protector," he waited. "I was watching your apartment, hoping to give you a message when she came to see you. This coincidence felt like a karmic message. I chose then to eliminate a witness against me and to save you from the Brotherhood at the same time."

"I'm still here."

"You are dedicated. I appreciate that. But the Brotherhood's concept of honor is dead. Even they don't follow it. Why not consider joining up with me?"

"Interesting offer. Why don't we meet to discuss it?"

Takezo waited and let out a slight laugh. "A mile down the beach from your hotel, in the direction of the volcano, is a stretch that's closed off. Tell June I'll be there at dawn. No one will bother us."

***

Wearing a gray kimono and sandals, June placed a katana and a short tanto sword into the sash around his waist. I wore khakis, a tropical shirt, and a Members Only jacket covering my department issue .45 in a shoulder rig.

Together we stepped outside and walked down the beach. The rising sun glossed everything pink, a darker shade than the pink of our hotel. June kept ahead of me.

A lone figure waited ahead in the sand. Takezo wore a blue kimono. A katana and tanto were in his sash. The sheath on the long sword matched the patterns on the sheaths hanging on the walls of Freddy Ashida's basement.

June stepped out of his sandals. "Takezo Murakami," he shouted and drew his katana from the scabbard. "I have come here to bring you to justice for the murders of Ford Newcomen, Yuko Kishi, and many others." He used Japanese.

Takezo drew his katana.

Both assumed battle stances.

They rushed forward, kicked up sand, and clashed blades. Takezo was full of rage. June was focused and calm.

The sun was all the way up. People appeared, far up the beach. None of them noticed us yet. The duel went on.

June saw an opening. The tip of his katana went deep into Takezo's bicep. Arterial blood misted the sand.

Takezo wobbled. He went down and dropped his katana. He reached to pick it up. June got close and stepped on Takezo's blade.

Then Takezo jumped up, pulled a hidden blade from inside his kimono and buried it deep into June's throat. June gagged, went to his knees and slumped sideways.

I drew my piece. "Freeze! LAPD!" I shouted, aiming at Takezo. Takezo got up quickly and grabbed his katana.

"Drop it or I'll fire!"

He raised his weapon, once again assuming a battle stance. Blood seeped out of the wound in his arm and dripped from the bottom of his elbow.

June still gargled blood.

He wanted me to pick up June's blade. I wasn't going to let Takezo draw me close. I fired once over his head. He dropped the sword.

The blood loss in his arm accelerated. His skin went pale. Regret settled into his face. The defiant personality I'd spoken to on the phone was fading.

June stopped gargling and went still.

"I formally request your permission to commit seppuku," Takezo said.

Before the Brotherhood, I knew the basics of seppuku. On the plane last night June taught me all the history in detail. Takezo wanted to die honorably.

"I'm an officer, serving the LAPD," I said, surprised at how effortless my Japanese was. "Let's say I was to bend the rules and let you commit seppuku. If you were me, how would you close out Ford Newcomen?"

"The Watanabe men will topple if interrogated by a competent detective. I suspect you are up to the task. They will give you everything you need if you can crack them. You'll be able to deny involvement about what's happened this morning. They'll have suspicions, but the LAPD will accept your story."

I nodded, admitting he was probably right. Then I squeezed the trigger twice, hitting him in the chest. He fell to his knees. He gasped for air.

"You don't deserve an honorable death," I said. "This is for Yuko."

I fired a third shot into his forehead. He fell back dead.

Women began to scream. I hadn't heard them approach. They were Hawaiian girls in grass skirts, probably performers from one of the hotels.

In the distance, over the wind and early waves, police sirens grew louder as they approached.

***

In coordination with Oahu PD, I arrested the execs at Watanabe who hired Takezo to kill Newcomen and extradited them all to L.A.

I was grilled by Oahu IAB about the scene on the beach. My story was this: June and I were there to question Watanabe execs. When I woke up, my partner was gone. I found him on the beach cut dead in the sand with Takezo standing over him with a sword. Takezo charged me. So I opened fire. I could not explain their clothes or their swords. They had history I didn't know about. I didn't deviate from this story, especially not when I ran through it many more times with the IAB guys in L.A.

Neither department believed me. But there was no hard evidence to challenge my narrative. None of the witnesses saw enough. Moreover, I was presenting them with a dead hitman, not just of a high-profile victim like Ford Newcomen, but also of a cop.

After six hours with me in the box, the Watanabe execs started confessing their part in the Newcomen hit, as Takezo said they would. Case closed.

But I knew IAB would be looking into me further. I portrayed myself as a low-key and competent officer and felt I could outlast their suspicions.

Captain Carnahan must have wanted to keep his Japanese guys together, so he made Eddie Kuwata and I partners. Goalmart went forward with the Takeshita deal. The Brotherhood secretly provided security for the contract signing. We wore our kimonos and swords.

Takeshita Electronics became available at every Goalmart location in the country. At the Hollywood Goalmart, I bought a Takeshita Betamax player. I searched for a cassette of my favorite Samurai film, *Yojimbo*. Freddy, now my CI, was able to sell me a copy at his pawn shop.

A shrine for June is in the dojo. I see it every time I'm there. I've met some of the other Brotherhood chapters. They say June died at the "Duel at Waikiki Beach." We were only partners a short while, but I tell them how I was one man when I met June—I had the instincts, but I didn't have any honor—now I am a different man entirely.

I tracked down my son's mother, apologized to her, and began child support payments. I vowed to never behave dishonorably with a woman again.

I paid my respects to Yuko's parents. We had dinner. I emphasized the importance of her bravery. "Her killer won't be hurting anyone else," I assured them both. "You have my word."

Philip Moscovitch writes fiction, non-fiction and poetry. He has an MFA from the University of King's College in Halifax and is the author of the book *Adventures in Bubbles and Brine* (Formac, 2019), which will get you making your own kimchi, among other delicious foods. His short stories have appeared in the anthologies *Soundings* (WindyWood Publishing) and *A Maritime Christmas* (Nimbus). He lives in Nova Scotia. "Carver's Mistake," his first published piece of crime fiction, is in part inspired by the spaghetti westerns he grew up watching (and still loves).

CARVER'S MISTAKE

I was about three days out of Laramie, headed for the Rattlesnake Hills, when Morash finally turned up.

"Where the hell you been?" I asked. He rode at a trot and sidled his horse up beside mine. Jakes didn't lift his jaw from the stream. Just kept lapping up that cool water. Steady horse, Jakes. But fast when you needed him to be.

"It's a big country," Morash said.

I grunted. "Any country's too goddamn big, you ride like a girl in a town parade. Get your horse some water. We gotta be off."

I'd heard good things about Morash. A good shot. Tough, but not so tough he'd bite your face off. Knew how to take orders. Knew how to come up with a plan when you needed one. And he'd worked with Carver, before Carver got caught and took the long drop.

I'd learned most of what I knew from Carver. If he figured I was a good partner, then I figured Morash would probably be all right.

Morash's grey pulled its snout up out of the river, water pouring down off its jaws. I gave Jakes a little dig with the spurs.

Morash didn't say much. He was maybe twenty-five—a good ten years younger than me anyway. Had a couple of inches on me too. Knife scar up high on his left cheek. Showed he was tough. Tough enough to have stayed in the trade after a knife fight— enough to drive a lot of men to dreams of a small farm with a couple of chickens and hogs. He had a long gun on the saddle behind him and more hardware stashed away. Just as long as he knew how to use it. As long as he knew when to use it.

"When'd you last see Carver?" I asked him.

"Last time anybody seen him. He went like a man. Where were you?"

"Working. Up Billings way. Got a job with a gang of rustlers, but I didn't last. Too many people. I've always preferred to work on my own."

We rode. I took my hat off, turned it upside-down and dumped most of the contents of my canteen into it. I flipped it back onto my head and let the cool water drip down the back of my neck and down my shirt. Morash took a little sip of water.

"We going to hit that stage today, you think?" he asked.

"In these flatlands?" I said.

He nodded. "Guess you're right."

I was getting hungry. I'd been getting hungry for the last hour or two, and tobacco had taken the edge off. But now it wasn't working much anymore, and my legs were stiff from the saddle. I looked over at Morash. You could see the green in his eyes, even when he was squinting. That's what he was doing right now, eyes fixed on the horizon, right on the spot where the sun would be setting in a little while. And over to the north were the hills. We'd get to them tomorrow.

Morash looked relaxed. Looked like he was out here on a god-damned holiday and could keep riding all day and all night.

"Better let these horses get some grazing in," I said.

He looked down at me from those extra couple of inches. "You getting scared?" he asked. "Or just tired?"

I patted Jakes's rump. "Horse is my most important partner. And my partner's got to get himself some grazing."

Mars was up in the western sky, just off the side of the moon. I grabbed my saddle bag, swung off of Jakes, and let him loose to graze.

I was sawing a branch for firewood when I heard a single shot. Morash had gone down to the creek. There was some good cover there, bushes on the banks.

I unholstered my pistol and walked towards the creek. No sound. I hunched down, walking slow, making sure I didn't crack any branches or kick any stones.

Morash leaped out of the bushes holding a good-sized hare by the ears. "Too late if you're hunting this fella," he said.

He sat down on the rocks by the small fire and started skinning the hare. I went back to sawing the branch I was working on. I liked a big fire at night. Wasn't anyone around who was going to come after us for it.

Morash looked up from the hare. "Course if you were on your way to rescue me, I guess I would've been shit out of luck."

The hare was good. I had to give Morash that. First fresh meat I'd had in a while. He watched me while I ate it. I watched the fire.

"So how'd you hook up with Carver in the first place?" I asked him.

"Met up back in '88. Didn't like the look of him. I figured him for a cop. We'd just done a good job at the Brady Ranch—3,000 acres, rich family. We got all the money, we grabbed the best horses, and killed old man Brady when he got stupid and tried to pull his old gun out of his holster with his old hands. Against a half dozen of us. Don't know what he was thinking. Well, I didn't mind killing him. He was that stupid, he deserved it."

I took a swig and passed the whiskey bottle back to Morash. He gulped back enough for four or five shots in some of the cheaper saloons.

"Then his boy walked in on us. Good-looking boy. About sixteen. And there's the old man dead at his feet. The stupid old man. The boy looked up at me—he had the prettiest mouth, all soft-looking and red lips. A real girl's mouth.

"Well, he should've been happy. We just speeded up his inheritance. Even if it looked like it was going to be a bit smaller than he'd expected. But the boy was just as stupid as the old man. Same move, only a hair faster. And we shot him too. All six of us at once, I think. We left him there next to the old man."

"Carver in on any of this?"

"No, I told you, I met up with Carver after, in a Laramie tavern.

The Half Acre. God, they got some girls there. Joanie Delaney. Ever had her?"

I shook my head. "Don't think so." Took another swig. Passed the bottle back again.

"Got this little trick she does with her tongue on your cock. Believe me, you'd remember it. Haven't had me a woman in a while."

He carried on. "Well, the next job we did was even better. Half the gang went down, some killed during the job, some arrested and killed later, legal. You probably heard about it. The Ericson bank over in Cheyenne."

"You lost half your gang," I said.

"Whole lotta money though."

He wasn't going to tell me about Carver.

I spat into the fire. My spit sizzled before it even hit the coals.

"You ever knock over a stage before?" I asked him.

"Kid stuff."

"Lot of folks not very good at kid stuff."

"I worked with Carver, remember?" We sat for a while then, swigging from the bottle and looking into the fire.

"They got any good-looking women on those stages?" Morash asked.

"I don't go for that," I told him. "Used to, but no more. All the screaming, the hitting, the biting. I don't need a woman that bad." I tried to look him in the eyes, but his face was in the dark. "And you don't either."

"Been a long time," he said. "Can't let it be too much longer."

"I'll shoot you if you do," I said. I walked over to Jakes, got my bedroll and laid it down a couple of yards from the fire.

Morash took a last swig and went over to his grey. Soon, he was on the ground beside me, wrapped up in his bedroll, pistol by his head.

The clear night air washed over me. Clouds were coming from the west, slowly covering more and more of the sky. I picked up the bottle from the ground beside Morash, took a last pull and closed my eyes.

My eyes shot open. I'd heard a rustling sound. But it was just Morash. I'd spent so much time without a partner, the sound of his rolling around woke me up. The clouds covered all the sky now, except for three stars in a line right over my head. I lay still, made sure there was no one else around, and closed my eyes again.

I was in a warm bed, upstairs from Shelley's Saloon—the Syphilis Saloon, as Carver used to call it. I could feel a woman's lips. They pulled slowly on my lower lip, then moved to the upper. Careful kisses. Good kisses. She was wearing a short black slip that hugged her hips tight and ended just below them.

Her hand moved down to my crotch, as her tongue slipped in past my lips. It had been so long. Too long.

She'd been drinking. There was a sour smell on her mouth, but I didn't care. I reached my hand up to her cheek. It was rough, like she'd been scarred young.

I realized I was dreaming then, but as I realized it, I noticed that the dream carried on. I opened my eyes, grabbed a fistful of Morash's cheek and hair with my right hand and rolled to the left, slamming his right temple down onto the ground between our bedrolls. I grabbed the whiskey bottle, took a pull, swirled the taste around in my mouth and then spat it out onto Morash's face.

He had a stunned look on his face. Maybe he was surprised I didn't go that way, I don't know. I grabbed for the gun by his bedroll before he could get it and waved it in the direction of the night.

Morash hadn't moved. All his talk of being fast, and there he was lying on the ground. His gun was in my hand.

"Go," I said. "Now. Get your bedroll before I put it on the fire. Saddle up your horse and go before I shoot you. I ain't had a partner in nearly a year, and I don't need one now. Carver or no Carver."

He sat up and rubbed his temple.

"Put that thing down," he said.

I did. Morash was no danger to me now.

"It was a little dream, that's all. Must've been that talk round the fire, and the whiskey. I was having a dream about Joanie Delaney.

And it was so sweet."

I ran my hand over my stubble. "Go," I said, but he could probably hear that I didn't mean it quite as much as the first time.

I spat into the fire again. It barely sizzled now. I stood up, walked away from Morash and pissed on the ground about ten feet away. I turned my back on him while I did it, and I left his gun on the ground back there. It was still there when I walked back.

We did have a stage to hit tomorrow. Might be a bad idea to make him ride now. It would be tough to hit it alone, but I'd done it before and I could do it again.

"A dream," I said. "Joanie Delaney."

Morash moved away from me and had a piss too.

He picked his gun up off the ground and tossed it to me. "Hang onto it for the night," he said. "Use it on me if I do it again."

I lay back, his gun by my side, and closed my eyes. Sure would be nice to be in the old Syphilis Saloon right about now. And as I tried to fall asleep, I remembered those kisses, even as I tried to push them away.

***

Next morning the clouds were all gone. I got up just past the dawn and gave Morash a quick kick.

Down at the river, I scooped up some water in my tin cup and had a deep drink. Then I put down my cup, dropped my razor and shaving soap next to it, tossed off my clothes and jumped in.

I cupped the cold river water up with my hands and poured it over my head. Then I sank to my knees and plunged my head underwater.

When I looked up, Morash was standing there by the bank, buck naked. Walked right down to the water's edge without my having heard a thing. His chest had almost no hair on it and his belly was smooth and flat as the prairie.

I stood and let the water drip off me. My balls were huddled together like chickens in a snowstorm. As I climbed up out of the river, Morash was right in front of me.

"Morning," I said, trying to make it sound friendly. Then my eyes traveled down and I saw his meat: hard, thick, and ready.

He took a step towards me.

"What the hell is this?" I asked.

"We're going to have some action later in the day. I need a piece and you won't let me have one of those juicy stagecoach gals. So it's got to be you instead."

He reached down and ran one hand along his shaft, giving it a squeeze at the bottom. I looked behind him. The razor was out of my reach. I should've killed him last night. I'd killed men with my bare hands before, but if I tangled bare with Morash, I suspected I might be the one left dead.

I looked down from his face.

"Like what you see?" Morash said.

I spat. "All that business about the ladies. Joanie Delaney."

"A hole's a hole," he said. "Come on, I need some action."

He grabbed me by the hair and took a couple of steps back. Then he jammed my face downward, into his thick hair.

"Come on," he said. "It's not that bad. Maybe you'll like it. Carver did." A rank smell like sour, wet leather came off his body. We'd been riding all day yesterday, and it was hot.

I closed my eyes, licked my lips and ran them against the bottom of his shaft. The skin was tight there. Tight and hot. I worked my way up to the top and back. It seemed to take hours.

A grin spread over his face. "Suck it now," he said. "Nice and slow. And don't even think about biting." He had one hand on the back of my head. The other clutched the razor.

"All right partner," I said.

"Nice and slow. You might even like it. I promise you won't regret it. You do a good job and we'll get along just fine this afternoon when the stage comes by. We'll get all the money we want 'cause I won't be thinking about getting myself some tail instead. Now get to work."

I could've taken him on. I could've stood up quick, kicked him in the balls and gone for the razor. I could've bitten down hard and rolled over.

But damned if I couldn't feel my one-eyed lizard waking up and groping around down there. He was right. It had been a long time.

I closed my eyes and started bobbing my head up and down, slowly. Each time I pulled up, Morash pushed hard against the back of my head. His grip grew tighter on my hair.

I kept moving, thinking about the job this afternoon, and what I would do about Morash. Maybe nothing. Maybe I'd kill him before the robbery came off and go it alone. You've done fine on your own 'til now, I thought. You can ride away from Morash, leave his body for the coyotes, and hit the stage yourself. Sure, he'd worked with Carver, and Carver was the best. But Carver wasn't around anymore to care about what happened to Morash.

Morash started to breathe deeper, faster, his grunts and sighs more frequent. I reached down and grabbed my cock with my left hand, sliding up and down the shaft, circling the head slowly.

With my eyes still closed, I listened to Morash's breath. It sounded like the breath of the hangman, excited to have my head in his noose at last. I had death in ten states. The hangman had waited a long time. Now that he had me in his hands, he was breathing harder, waiting, ready.

With my eyes closed, I saw the hangman slip the noose around my neck and blow stale breath into my face. He groaned with pleasure as he tightened the noose, yanking it hard so that the rough rope chafed my neck and squeezed it. A cruel moan escaped his thin, cruel mouth. The hangman hit the trap and I fell. As I reached the end of the rope a wet, metallic taste hit my throat.

Morash let out a yell. He had hold of my head with both his hands now, the razor still clutched in one of them. I pulled back hard. He was losing his grip. I fought against him and pulled back so hard I nearly fell over. He released me, sat down, and took a deep breath. I kept my mouth closed and got to my feet. He exhaled slowly and opened his eyes just as I leaned forward and spat his juice out into his face. I grabbed the razor out of his hand when his hands shot to his eyes, then kicked him in the head with my bare foot.

I gargled out of my tin cup, then ripped open a saddlebag and tore off a piece of jerky. I could hear Morash splashing in the water behind me. I whistled low and Jakes ambled towards me, ready to be saddled. Three minutes later, I was on my way.

It didn't take Morash long to catch up. He brought his horse up next to mine. We rode.

***

Morash had his hat tipped back on his head. I had a stage robbery later in the day to think about, but nothing seemed to bother Morash. I was still thinking about killing him before we got to the hills. I'd been sentenced to death more often than most men change jobs, but I'd had my fill of killing. I'd never seen Morash's name on a list of outlaws sentenced to hang. I would've thought that just working with Carver would've been enough to get him hanged some places. But I guess he'd been lucky.

The stage would be headed for Laramie, and then on to Cheyenne, loaded up with men from places like Emblem and Grass Creek. Ranchers making their annual trips to town to deposit money in the Laramie banks and to buy the supplies they could only get in the big city. It probably wouldn't be the biggest or richest stage around, but that would also mean it wouldn't be as heavily guarded.

It would be heavy enough that the horses would have trouble pulling it once they got to the Rattlesnake Hills. The men would pile out and some would have to carry their bags. The women would probably stay inside. The horses would pull the stage uphill while the panting men followed. It would all be easy pickings for us.

I could probably do it alone. Hide about halfway up the hill. By the time the men were up that far they'd be tired and wouldn't want to fight a man waving a couple of guns in their faces. But if any of them got any bright ideas then I might need Morash along.

"We going to talk about how we might pull off this robbery?" I asked him.

He looked straight ahead and didn't say anything.

"I'm the one oughta be mad," I said to him. "Either we're in this together or we get out the guns and finish it now."

A smile played across his lips, barely. "You liked it old man. And you feel better now."

I liked it. Damned if I liked it. "The stage shouldn't be heavily guarded," I told him. "We'll wait 'til they've unloaded for the walk up the hill. We can do it two ways. We can both ambush the stage or I can stop it on my own while you wait up in the hills with the long gun and pick off anybody who looks like he's going to cause trouble."

"I want to be in on the action."

"Good. I don't know how good a shot you are from a distance. Rather have you on the ground beside me."

Morash reached around slowly, pulled the long gun off the back of the saddle and swung it around. The barrel was trained on me for a few seconds on its way past. He let go of the reins, but his horse kept bouncing along at the same speed. Morash pressed the butt of the Winchester into his right shoulder and squeezed the trigger. A red-tailed hawk a couple hundred feet away, towards the hills, fell out of the sky. Morash lowered the gun and stowed it behind him again.

"I don't believe that Carver liked it," I said. "I don't believe that Carver did it."

Morash shrugged.

"Carver wanted that, he would've told me," I said. "I was his partner a damn sight longer than you were. And he survived my partnership."

"The hell's that supposed to mean?"

"He was alive when I went out on my own," I said.

Some men plot and plan. They have every angle down. Study the territory. Know who's going to be riding shotgun on a stage. Know how much money is onboard. Know how many men they're going to run into, how much of a fight they might face.

Outlawing shouldn't be that much work. It's hard enough grabbing what you can get, getting out as fast as you can, and staying ahead of the law. Carver taught me that. Hit 'em fast, hit 'em hard and go. Maybe you could have hit another one and taken more money. Maybe you could hang around and squeeze old Lady Luck for another chance. Maybe you could study your targets and score bigger. None of that mattered to me. I'm not an accountant and I'm not made for studying up too much.

Morash must have felt the same way. He was happy to not plan it out too much. Didn't want to talk it through.

I thought back to the morning. Men turned to each other out on the trail. Happened all the time. Nobody around for days, your balls bursting and a little whiskey in your gut, that guy in the bedroll beside you seemed pretty good—and a hell of a lot closer than the nearest whorehouse. I'd thought about it myself, but never done it. Didn't mean nothing doing it to him. But I ought to have killed him for trying to force me. I probably could have fought him down.

***

The Rattlesnake Hills sloped up ahead of us. I saw a watering hole, pulled on the reins, and hopped off the horse. Jakes could use a rest. Morash got off his grey and walked around back of the horse to tighten one of his saddle straps. Jakes drank enough for both horses. When he was done, the water dripped down from his jaw and he shook his head. I made a fire and boiled up some coffee. We each had a cup, and then we were riding again, my jaw working on some hard biscuits.

We rode into the hills and tried to pick our spot.

The trail cut between two ridges, golden yellow with the color of the long grasses. Not much cover here.

The stage would be by in a few hours. I wanted a good steep rise to make sure all the men were out. And I needed a spot that gave us cover, so that the stage wouldn't turn and bolt.

We climbed, then at the end of a gentle rise, reached a peak. I led, and Morash followed me as we started our way down the other side. We rode a couple of hundred feet down the drop. The trail curved to the left and hung close by a ravine. It wasn't deep, but it was deep enough.

"Here," I said.

Morash grunted.

We led the horses down into the ravine and tied them.

As I climbed back up, I could hear Morash loading the rifle and checking his guns. I pulled myself up to the lip of the ravine. From here, we had a clean line of fire a couple of hundred yards down the trail on the one side, and all the way up to the top of the ridge on the other.

All there was left to do was wait.

Morash climbed up beside me, leaned with his back against the edge of the ravine, and closed his eyes.

I looked down the trail and imagined the stage on its way up. The men would be walking. The horses would pull ahead of them, tired as they got near the top. Morash would stay behind, in the ravine. I'd fire a couple of warning shots. That ought to do it. Most men don't have half the fight in them they think they do. We'd grab what we could, and I'd leave Morash guarding the men while I got the horses. Then we'd race down out of the hills and head for the Colorado line. Simple. I was wanted in Colorado too, but I didn't have death there yet.

I checked my guns. "Your guns ready?" I asked.

"They were last time I checked."

I could hear hooves now, far away but not too far. Rumbling.

"Hear 'em?" I asked.

"I hear 'em."

"Ten minutes. Maybe less."

I looked at Morash. "Ever hit a stage with Carver? Best stage man I even knew. He'd get in, grab the money, and get out. And most of the time, nobody'd get hurt."

"Nobody?"

"Nobody."

"That's 'cause he never hit one with me."

"Listen," I said to Morash, my voice harder. "Nobody gets hurt with me either, understand? I'm not in this for the killing or the women. I'm in it for the money, and that's all." I looked him in the eye. "I'll kill. Kill anyone—if I have to. But I don't want to have to. Used to think Carver was squeamish when he didn't want to kill. I learned he was just smart."

"Carver looked after himself," Morash said.

The rumble grew louder. I looked down the ravine. Jakes was grazing on the needlegrass. Morash's grey stood, staring.

Suddenly, they broke round the bend. But it wasn't the stage. It was two men on horseback. Marshals. I should have known then. I should have known right away. Instead, I thought I'd made a mistake. I hung back in the ravine, let the marshals ride past.

But Morash was ready for action. Too ready. Just as the stage rounded the corner, Morash raised the long gun and hit the right flank of the tallest marshal's stallion. It slammed to the ground. The other one hauled back hard on his reins and turned towards us.

They hadn't spotted us yet. The stage came up behind the marshals and stopped too. The wheels creaked and groaned near my head. I looked up. Marshals. Two more of them. One riding shotgun, and one on the running board. And that was just on my side.

I looked back down towards Jakes. He stopped grazing and looked up at me. Silent. Good horse, Jakes.

Maybe I could get out now. But there was no other way out. The ravine was too choked with bushes and the only other way was past either the stage or the marshals up the hill.

I looked at Morash. "You wanted a fight," I said.

"I'm ready."

There would be killing now. There was no way out of it. Must have been some load on board that stage to warrant all those marshals. Something worth killing for.

The first marshal leaped off the running board. I fired and watched as the bullet from my Colt ripped his lower jaw off his face. His body jerked up into the air and then fell to the ground.

"Take the next one!" I yelled to Morash.

I saw him pulling his revolver out of a holster. Slow. Too slow. The marshals up the hill were running back down towards us now, and I was making my way up the ravine towards them. It took me farther away from the stage, but if nobody saw me, maybe I could cut them off from behind. I heard a loud report. Morash, I figured, hitting the second one. A bullet slammed into the ground five feet in front of me. I rolled. Bullets were thick in the air. I looked up and saw the boots of one of the lawmen up on the trail. He was firing back towards where I'd been a minute ago. What the hell was Morash up to? He ought to have dropped that other marshal by now.

I fired twice, straight up, then rolled hard down the ravine. I stopped up against a bush and saw the body of the man I'd just killed. If I hadn't moved, he would've fallen on top of me. Bullets ripped into the ground near the spot. Some hit the dead man. I saw him jerk and toss.

I could see the stage now. It had barely moved. Instead of breaking for the head of the ridge, it was waiting.

I reloaded and clawed my way back up towards the spot where I'd left Morash. I could hear the horses whinnying and stamping, but they still weren't moving. Too scared.

Morash was on the ground, his head near the stage's running board. One marshal leaned over him while another raced towards them. I snapped off three shots. The running man paused, took a step backwards and fell to the ground. Red burst out over Morash's head. Blood from the marshal who took my bullet while he leaned over him.

The firing had stopped. I could see the men I'd shot lying around like dice in a craps game that broke up fast. I looked for the men Morash had shot, but couldn't see any.

I stepped out onto the trail and turned, slowly, looking around. No fire. Either they were all done, or they were lining me up. I broke for the stage and ripped the closest door open. Nobody. I grabbed blindly for whatever cargo was in here, but my hands just pawed the air. Suddenly, there was light. The opposite door flew open and a bullet tore into my left arm. I raised my pistol and fired. A body lurched forward onto the floor of the stage. It filled with the sticky, hot smell of blood and that raw meat scent of fresh death. I looked down at the body. It was the only thing in the stage.

I held my gun hand up to my wound, and felt my own blood leak out through my fingers. I dropped down to the ground and kicked Morash.

He grunted as I wrestled the body on top of him out of the way. Then I rolled him over onto his back. His pant leg was ripped where he'd torn at it to get to his wound. It didn't look serious. One of his shins was smeared with blood. Morash's eyes rolled back in his head.

"Don't give me that." I slapped him hard on the cheek. His eyes snapped back into place.

"We going?" he said weakly.

"We're going."

I loaded up my pistol.

"It's all right," Morash hissed. "I think we got 'em all."

I nodded. "I got 'em all."

"Tried my best."

"I know. Just didn't work out for you. Thought you'd make yourself some money."

"Thought you'd make money too. We both would. Next time, I guess."

"How'd you know we didn't?" I asked. "You never looked inside. I never heard of anyone got rich robbing empty stages."

"Empty?"

I leaned down close and grabbed him by the hair. He kicked at me. I stepped on his injured leg, then reached down and pulled him up to his knees by the hair. Handfuls of it came off his head.

Morash tried to scream, but instead let out a sound like a dying songbird.

I pulled my good arm back and slammed it across his face. Morash fell. I leaned over and hauled him up by the hair once more.

"I heard you were Carver's last partner. I knew Carver had it coming eventually. Didn't figure it was because he'd trusted you. And here you are dumb enough to try the same play on me."

Morash opened his mouth, and I could see a tooth hanging loose from his upper jaw. I flicked my gun barrel against it and knocked it out. Blood poured down onto his tongue. He gagged on some of it and spat the rest out.

He looked up at me, his eyes clear as the mountain air. My finger on the trigger, the barrel of my gun up against Morash's chin. Blood drying on my arm and the flies growing thicker by the minute.

"Water," Morash managed to say.

I slammed the barrel against another top tooth before he could close his lips, and he fell to the ground with his hands on his face. I walked down to the ravine and let Morash's horse loose.

"Go," I said and gave it a slap on the hindquarters. It went.

Then I got Jakes and led him back up to the trail.

"You've got death now too," I said to Morash. "Death for killing Carver and death for trying the setup on me."

I leaned down and kicked him in the nuts. While Morash puked into the ground, I pulled a few solid lengths of rope out of my saddle bags.

"You're going for a ride, Morash." I unhooked the stage and held on tight to the reins of one of the horses. Then I cut the saddle straps off it and let the saddle fall to the ground. I hoisted Morash up onto the horse's back and hog-tied him there, laying crosswise.

"Word's going out fast. Death, Morash. In every state I know. You might live a week, you might live a year. You might die tonight. I'd stay away from Joanie Delaney. She might know a new trick to work on that stinkin' cock of yours once she hears the news."

I drove a spur viciously into the side of the horse. It broke up the trail, bouncing Morash on its back like a baby in the hands of an angry giant.

I leaned against Jakes, then climbed on. His hooves hit the hard ground, then went through something soft lying on the trail.

We rode away from Morash. Down out of the hills, towards the Colorado line.

Jenna Junior works as a Writing Center Coordinator for Tulsa Community College and lives in an old house with her partner and two orange cats. She has been published in Oklahoma University Press's *Voices of the Heartland Volume 2, The Tulsa Voice*, the Ghost Orchid Press anthology *Dark Hearts*, and placed first prize in prose in the debut issue of *The Tulsa Review*. She is the host and creator of the horror podcast *Scream Service* and co-runs the zine press Pizza Funds Press alongside her partner. She wrote this story while waiting for her tires to be fixed to avoid watching *Judge Judy*.

MITSUBISHI MURDER BALLAD

David was working the counter because Jimmy needed to leave early that day; his son had fallen from a tree, quite a ways down, and had broken his arm in several places. David had eavesdropped on the phone call, hearing Jimmy's wife fight through panic and tears as she asked him to come as quickly as he could. Jimmy tried to apologize, over and over, about how he would make up the hours and how he was sorry to leave David short-staffed. Jimmy was the kind of family man, the kind of good ole boy, that David almost didn't believe in anymore. It sickened him sometimes, how wholesome Jimmy could be.

"Go on, go on!" David had cried, almost begging with the man. Finally, after an obnoxious amount of nervous fumbling to find them, Jimmy had his coat and his keys and left. His truck could be heard squealing out of the lot onto the highway and David released the sigh he was holding in since Jimmy's ringer went off.

David found small pleasures in mundane aspects of working the front. He was able to make himself a cup of coffee from the bulky plastic machine wedged between used car batteries. It tasted like motor oil, but, then again, so did everything in here. He was able to watch TV if he craned his neck just right to stare at the mounted screen. *Judge Judy* was on. He wouldn't admit this to the guys, but he liked that lady. She knew how to handle people in a way that David found sensible. She was quick-witted and logical and, even better, funny as hell. He found himself smirking when she hit someone with a one liner: "Beauty fades—dumb is forever!" If one of the mechanics walked in and asked David why he was watching that shit, he would lie and say something like he couldn't find the remote, which he had earlier tucked behind the safe in the corner for just such an alibi.

David had just fired up the popcorn machine when he heard the electronic bell chime from behind. The air now smelled like gas leaks and fake butter, which somehow comforted him and made him feel more at ease than he had before. He turned around, a genuine smile on his face to greet the customer, and stopped, his foot still hovering over the floor. It was her. She was here. Older, much older than the last time he had seen her, but it was still her nonetheless. Samantha Adams. The first girl he had ever loved. It was a statement that would make him grimace with embarrass-ment—how corny could he get? But there, as he was frozen in the middle of a hot afternoon, his heart couldn't figure out a way to be sarcastic about it. It was just the truth, powerful enough to glue him to the spot where he stood.

She looked rough, he thought with a touch of guilt. This caused his shoe to lower, hesitant in its footing. He had always imagined her to be forever young, her eyes still twinkling with mischief and a smile that had a wattage to it. This woman's eyes were worn down, the blue irises muddled and flat, and though she smiled at him softly, it felt like he was approaching a wounded animal. Sure, he had to be realistic about the situation. People got older. Himself included, a beer gut to prove the passing of time. Yet she was be-yond just *older*; she looked like she had gotten the life sucked out of her. When they were young, he had always been envious of how free she felt; how relaxed she could be in any situation. The energy that filled the lobby was taut, nervous, and approaching a breaking point. Maybe it was because of all the nights he had spent in her arms or maybe it was just plain enough for anyone to see: Samantha was in danger.

"Sam," he found himself sputtering after much too long a pause. It was then that he clocked the tiny figure hiding behind her legs. A girl. Same blue eyes as her mother, with a pouty lip that he didn't recognize. She was dressed in a pink ballerina costume that had stains dotted along the spandex. Her tutu hung limply at her waist, which David could not help but notice was incredibly small.

"And who's this?" he asked. Samantha tousled the girl's high pony in a shabby attempt to be lighthearted.

"Introduce yourself, honey," she said in a voice that pained David to hear. So small and quiet. Was this truly the girl who would laugh so loud she'd get dirty looks from strangers? This could not be the same girl who would pick the worst songs at karaoke bars they were too young to be in, wildly singing They Might Be Giants for a crowd of chain-smoking bikers. This could not be the girl who would go to animal shelters just to read library books to the ugliest cats and dogs she could find. This could not be the girl, or the woman, who made David wake up in a cold sweat for years, disappointed to find his bed without her. But it was, and now a smaller, different version of her stood staring at him, probably weirded out by his long silences and questioning stares. He kept trying to remind himself to smile. Keeping his lips tight enough so that his jaw would refrain from falling open.

"I'm Abigail," the girl said, her voice also barely above a whisper. David could feel his stomach twisting. He had always imagined seeing Samantha one day, maybe even with the hopes of reconnecting romantically. It was a scenario he would run through his mind as he worked on the underbelly of Chryslers, Jeeps, Dodges. He always imagined himself skinnier in those scenarios and he could admit that was a naive hope. However, he always imagined Sam vibrant in his daydreams, and he never once stopped to think that maybe she wasn't someone who could shine anymore. He had never imagined feeling nervous for her, and worse, afraid of her.

"You look like you've seen a ghost," she said. She gave him a pathetic half smile, one that didn't touch her eyes. She knew what she looked like, David realized. She knew what he was thinking and it made him feel ashamed, dirty. He tried to respond with genuine humor.

"Something close! What has it been, twelve years?" Each of those years lived clearly in the wrinkles carved into Samantha's face. It reminded David of counting the rings on a tree, marking all the time since the girl he had loved had been rubbed away into someone else.

"Sounds about right. Abigail here is turning seven in March," Sam said. The child smiled slightly at that, revealing her missing teeth.

"Well, happy early birthday to you, Abigail," David said sincerely. She seemed in dire need of a happy day.

"You ladies didn't just come in here to catch me up on the birthday news, did you?"

Samantha shook her head and pointed behind her.

"Got a flat while on the road. Was wondering if someone could patch it up; we're in a bit of a hurry."

"Dance recital, perhaps?" David asked with a wink to Abigail. She blushed and retreated back behind her mother's legs. Samantha herself looked a little nervous at the question.

"That's right," she agreed. She pointed again. "Shouldn't be a big fix; just need a patch and we'll be on our way."

The car outside surprised David. By the way the women were dressed, he expected a jalopy rusting on the pavement. Instead, a brand-new Mitsubishi was parked right in the sun, sparkles highlighting its pristine condition. Looking at it made David uneasy. Why would this car be so immaculate when its passengers looked so worn down? He found himself feeling like a court procedural, examining evidence to something he didn't fully understand. He was on edge, something he rarely felt anymore, and it hurt his heart to think that the reason behind it was Samantha, someone he had always remembered with a lustful, hazy admiration.

He remembered when he got his own first vehicle, a Toyota Tacoma his dad had pulled from a salvage yard. He and the old man had coaxed it back to life and David drove it with pride, not caring that it wasn't vintage or hell, even relatively in fashion. It was sturdy and it purred as he led it through winding country roads and empty highways. When Samantha started to come around, he would take her along for those trips, where music filled the silence like a soundtrack or her laugh was the only song he needed that night. When things progressed, he would make good use of the bed of the truck, parking it in boggy creeks long forgotten and lover's lanes unknown. It wasn't all the hot and heavy stuff, either. David remembered the sex clearly and with a fond excitement, but he was also a secret romantic. He could remember the way Samantha's eyes looked when she stargazed next to him, buried under the crook of his arm. She would tell him about her dreams, the same dreams every country girl had: to get out of this town, to find herself in a city where no one knew her and she could find herself in the chaos. With other girls, ones he had never gotten this far with, he smirked at how ridiculous those ambitions sounded. With Samantha, he started to believe that maybe one day, he too could find himself in a city that didn't know his past. Maybe together, they could whittle out a life in such a place.

The Mitsubishi in front of him was a grim reality check that those starry nights were just fancy notions after all. Samantha did not escape. She didn't make her way to crowded streets and cluttered traffic. She wasn't writing poetry next to coffee shop windows. She wasn't taking day trips to the beach to get away from all the noise. She wasn't living in a high rise, the kind that had a man downstairs who opened her doors and knew her name. She'd stayed where she was and it had eaten her alive.

It wasn't just her physical appearance that sickened David. It was the lack of energy in her; someone dead already with years left to go. A walking corpse carrying a smaller version of her misery beside her. Then again, what the hell did David know? He was still in this same goddamn town as she was. His friends were the same dumb fucks he met in high school. He drank the same cheap beer from the same gas station down the way, watching the same shows on TV every night. He never learned to play guitar or write a song. He never made it past high school graduation. Tinkering with cars, cars that he didn't even own, was his fate. Maybe they both were miserable and David just knew how to bury it deep.

He walked back into the lobby. Samantha was watching *Judge Judy*, her eyes hard. The case was the typical run-of-the-mill boyfriend says this, girlfriend says that. They were fighting over who owed what to each other, disputing over which one of them gets the cell phone, the dog, the Playstation. Samantha's lips were pressed so tightly together that they were white, almost invisible among her sallow skin. Her hands clenched her handbag like claws. Her eyes flicked to David and she popped her lips back into a quick, embarrassed smile.

"I hate these things," she said, gesturing to the television. "Always brings out the worst in people."

"That's true," David said as he walked slowly to the computer. He typed in the car information for their records. "Judy's pretty fucking funny, though."

He froze as he realized Abigail was still there, pulling a hole in her tutu even wider. Samantha waved away his worry.

"She hears far worse, believe me," she told him. David didn't know what to make of that, but returned to the keyboard. Samantha frowned, realizing what he was doing.

"You don't have to do all that," she said.

"Yes, unfortunately I do. Store policy."

"Oh, I . . . " Samantha paused and calculated something in her mind. "Don't go through the trouble. It's just me and my stupid tire."

"No trouble, only takes a few clicks."

"Seriously. Don't."

The anxious tension was back. The thing that was scaring David was rising from its hiding place. He had never seen Samantha look so fierce. It reminded him of a feral animal.

"It's really not a problem," he assured her. Samantha shook her head, furious. As her hair swayed, David caught sight of a bruise along the side of her neck. Fingerprints, impressed in purple.

"Please. I don't . . . " Samantha looked at Abigail, still working away at her tulle. "I don't want anyone to know I came in. Okay? Please. For me."

"Are you in trouble, Sam?" David asked, his voice low. She

smiled, slightly, and for a moment, the ghost of the girl she once was appeared on her face.

"No, of course not," she put her hand, skeletal with skin like paper, over his and squeezed. "Still . . . maybe skip the paperwork."

How could she say she wasn't in trouble, he thought, when trouble was spelled out in black and blue ink along her throat? Her nervousness made perfect sense to him now. That caged animal energy was crystal clear.

"You got a husband?" he asked. He usually would never be so blunt, and in past reveries he imagined asking her this question only to receive a flirtatious denial. He could remember the face from guilty drunken nights stalking her on social media. A big man, probably even bigger than David, with a cocky smile punctuated by a single, shining gold tooth. Now, though, he wanted to hear a yes and he wanted to hear a name to put to that smug grin. It would make looking for the bastard easier if he could look him up before kicking his ass.

"Recently separated," is all she offered.

Well that was something, he supposed.

"How recent?"

Her eyes narrowed, and he knew that look well. It was her "don't fuck with me" glare, something she spared only for the deserving.

"Recent enough for it to be a sore subject," she said, her voice low enough to be heard as a threat. She could hear the coldness in her own voice and tried to smile, like what she said was a joke, but she only could manage a grimace. David nodded and looked back at the car. He hoped it was his. He hoped that she won it, a sorry prize for leaving a shit bag like that. Maybe the prize was her life, though, he thought with a sinking feeling. Maybe the prize was the ability to live long enough to go to another dance recital. He didn't want to get deeper in this. He didn't want to uncover the whole truth, raping the image of his innocent first love with something dark, sinister, and close-by. He wanted to retain what scraps of sweetness he had left with Samantha. He nodded again, more a confirmation to himself than to her, and jerked his thumb at the car.

"Gimme the keys and I'll roll her in and fix the patch myself," he told her. Usually there would be one other person here besides David and Jimmy. They had a rotating list of tough guy wannabe teens who got to roll up their sleeves and show the tattoos they got in a friend's garage. But today it was just David, and he was relieved that Jimmy's kid shattered his tiny arm today; and he was relieved that Wayne, the guy he would've called, was too hungover to come in. He was thankful for their miseries. When God breaks a bone, he opens a window.

He drove the Mitsubishi into the garage, feeling strange being in her car without her beside him. He expected it to smell like smoke, or even vomit, based on the haggard way she and Abigail looked right now, but it smelled only like the pine tree hanging sharply on the rearview mirror. He was impressed. Samantha was quite the slob when they were kids. Her car usually was littered with burger wrappers and coffee cups, maybe the occasional parking ticket thrown into the mix. Her bedroom had so many newspaper clippings and band posters tacked up that you suspected these were the walls, that no wood and plaster laid beneath the thumbtacks and glossy images. It was a secret worry of his as a teenager, that maybe when they moved to that big city apartment together, he would have to go over what qualifies as cleanliness. They broke up long before that conversation could happen, for reasons that he couldn't even recall anymore.

He pulled off the tire and examined the hole. A shard of glass was wedged in, a jagged edge surfaced above the rubber. He yanked it out and let the tire hiss in anger as he looked around the shop for his tools. He found the plugger and got to work, knowing that in a few minutes he would be done and Samantha would leave his life again. He hoped that she left happier. He imagined her smile returning, maybe in the audience of that recital as Abigail twirled her now-ruined tulle around the stage. He looked up to look at them through the glass pane that separated the lobby from the garage.

Samantha had her hand balled into a fist, pressed tight against her mouth. She was looking up at *Judge Judy* again, but David had a feeling she wasn't really watching. Tears slid down her face. Her chest hiccupped with a silent sob. Abigail was further off, practicing a pirouette in the corner. Her little face was so concentrated on her feet that she looked angry. He could see Samantha in that determined face, the way her mouth screwed up slightly and her cheeks reddened from the fire within her. David looked back at Samantha, wishing she could see this moment, her daughter unconsciously impersonating the girl she once was. He noticed something, though, that made him pause. He had first thought Samantha's chest was moving with a cry she didn't want Abigail to hear. Now, he saw her mouth. She was laughing. He didn't think she was doing it audibly, because her laugh usually could be heard from rooms away. Still, it was a laugh, one that had her belly bouncing. The tears continued to fall down her face, but they accompanied an unbridled joy he had worried left Samantha years before. He felt warm knowing that the girl he loved was still there, behind the dimmed eyes and worry wrinkles. Samantha was still alive.

He turned back to the car in case she caught him smiling at her. He wanted her to have her private moment of laughter without him being a creep staring at her. The tire was done, a quicker fix than he wanted. He didn't want her to leave, not yet. That nagging feeling, that touch of dread he had felt before, was still moving around slowly in his guts. He had hoped it would dissipate when he saw her laughing, but it stayed put. Was it the bruises on her neck that made his insides churn? No, he realized. This felt more primal. This had the hair standing up on the back of his neck. Something was wrong, more wrong than seeing Samantha like that, which was enough to make him sick as it was.

There had been a predecessor to this feeling, a trigger he had buried deep years before. The ghost of it rose from his guts, unwound itself as he opened the car door, thinking again about when he had looked up Samantha on Facebook. Sure, he had done it many times before—only briefly with embarrassment— but on this night, he was feeling particularly sorry for himself. He was drunk, he knew he shouldn't be doing it, and he buried down his feelings until they hazed into nothing. Now, they came back. He saw that she had gotten married. He saw a stranger's hand wrapped around Samantha's waist, a protective circle around her tiny frame. He saw her smiling, and at the time, he felt like she was faking it and scolded himself for having such an ego. He was just jealous, that's all. He was jealous that someone was tied to her so strongly and that it wasn't him. Now, he knew he was right. This was beyond a high school sweetheart's jealousy or a former lover's nosy curiosity. No amount of Bud Light could erase how well David knew Sam, not really. She was not really smiling but posing as someone happy. The man next to her was smiling, too, like he had won the best prize in the world. David knew that was true, and didn't blame the guy for that. The smile, though, was more than smug. David saw, on his right canine, that gold, blazing tooth and it had sickened him then. Now, the image was holding him as tight as a knife against his throat: that gilded, false brilliance covering something rotten beneath.

He felt himself outside of his body, looking down on his body in the garage. A knowledge was given to him, one that he never owned before, that seemed to know the pinpoint for his discomfort. There was something wrong with the car. He didn't know how he knew, and if he believed in God, that would be his best bet at why he was so aware that it was the truth. But he didn't believe in God. He didn't believe in the supernatural. All he knew to believe were his instincts, now pulled taut with anxiety. He knew something was very wrong with the car.

He fired up the vacuum and decided this would be his alibi. If Samantha, already tense enough, came asking what he was doing, he could just blame his serviceable nature. He knew that the car was spotless, but maybe he could blame it on old habits and even tease her about how sloppy she once was. He glanced at the glass to check that she was not looking his way. She was still watching *Judge Judy*, a lingering smile on her lips. He climbed into the car, holding the vacuum hose at his hip like a holstered gun.

The floor wasn't as immaculate as he imagined and he was slightly comforted at the sight of it. Potato chip shards and loose hair ties were hidden beneath the floor mats. He was relieved to see parts of humanity in this car that felt more like a mausoleum on wheels. He vacuumed up the food scraps, deciding he could be a Good Samaritan and a snoop at the same time. The backseat was done and he hunched over the arm rests to get to the front. The passenger side had nothing to clean up; he could even see the lines of a previous vacuum job. So, Abigail's territory is where Sam was still allowed to be her old, messy self. Things changed when you got to the front. He pulled the driver's side floor mat up and instinctively dropped it back into place when he saw it. Here it was. Here was the apex of the dread; the proof of the sinking feeling that something was absolutely not okay. It lived here, hiding beneath the mat, in a car that David wouldn't even look twice at. The home of horror was a small focal point, laying in the carpet, waiting for David to finally see it and finally understand. The vacuum screamed in his hand but it was just white noise as he stared down at the thing on the floor.

A tooth. A gold tooth. Surrounded by a crimson red halo of blood.

He knew Samantha before, and now, with a sharp twist in his guts, he could see her in the stark present tense. She was once a girl, but now she was a woman who had a child to protect. The same fiery teenager he knew, who could memorize Sylvia Plath poems and change a tire herself without his eager help, had now grown into someone who had seen a lot. She had felt a lot. Things added up for her. Every beating was a tally mark, building up to something. He didn't know what the last straw was. Maybe an argument about the dance recital. Maybe someone stared at her too long in the grocery store. Maybe nothing happened at all. David realized that he had never known Samantha to be a weak girl, and he was ashamed to have considered her a weak woman now. She never changed, not really. She had only waited until the timing was right. Today, it seemed, the timing was perfect.

He glanced up, wanting to look at anything else besides the tooth, and this time, Samantha was staring back at him. She didn't seem embarrassed. She knew what he had seen and she knew he was smart enough to put it all together. Maybe that was her plan, all along, to let him know. It wasn't for some romantic reason, either. She didn't want him to view the tooth as a glimpse into the future they could have together. Maybe she was saying goodbye this way. Maybe this was her letting him know she was still the same and that she was okay. Now, she was watching him knowing that he had a choice to make.

There was a phone in the garage, only a few steps away, and three digits could get the police here in less than ten minutes. She couldn't leave; he had her keys in his pocket. She could get caught by him, or by someone later down the road, David thought. Or, she may never get caught at all. Abigail could grow up, get clothes that didn't have holes in them because finally she had a parent who gave a shit. She could keep dancing and maybe one day she'd even get to fall in love with someone who wasn't like her dad. Maybe she would meet someone like David, who knew deep down it would always be Samantha. Maybe Abigail would reverse the bruises and be able to finally leave this fucking town. David hoped that years from now, when he was regretting the decision he had already begun to make, he would see Abigail drinking coffee in some city coffee shop's window and know that he made the right choice. He stood up, flicked off the vacuum, and began walking the keys back to Samantha, the first woman he had ever loved.

Allison Whittenberg is a Philadelphia native who has a global perspective. Her novels are *Sweet Thang*, *Hollywood and Maine*, *Life is Fine*, and *Tutored*. Whittenberg is a three-time Pushcart Prize nominee. If she wasn't an author, she'd be a private detective or a jazz singer. She loves reading about history and true crime. "Killing in Periot" examines the complexities of family relationships and the conditions of class and race.

KILLING IN PERIOT

I wasn't just Solly's brother; I was his protector. Over the years, I had done a pretty good job of it considering what I was up against. Nick was my stepfather. He was Solly's real father. He was our main adversary. Everyone else, I could handle.

It all came to a crossroad late that fall when I was fifteen, nearly sixteen, and Solly was younger than that. We both upped our ages so we could work long hours at shit jobs because that was what Nick told us to do. Nick pimped us out to honest jobs since his own illegal exploits were going slow. Between Solly and me, we pulled an all right grip; the only hitch was Nick took it all.

Now, I was no dummy, so for quite a while I'd been holding back, in one way or another. You know, deep pocketing some of the money. Most of the time I'd leave some pinned to the inside of my shirt, then when I got inside I'd stash it in the fraying fabric of a chair in our room. That evening, I was careless.

"Empty your pockets," Nick demanded. He would not let Solly or me pass him to get inside of the house where it was warm.

"I did," I said.

"You're coming up short," he insisted. I could tell his ire had already formed. Like a bull in a ring preparing to charge, his nostrils flared. "You two worked forty hours between you two. This doesn't add."

I maintained a poker face while I lied, "It's all there."

He looked from me to Solly. "What do you know about this?"

Solly wore a blank look. "I don't know anything."

In disgust, Nick shook his head. "You can say that again."

"Look," I told him. "You got your money."

Nick shot a look over to me that could split rock, but I held myself together. As he advanced toward me, his gaze switched like a light bulb going on. He pushed me down.

"Hey—" Solly began.

"Shut up," Nick said as he raised his hand to him. I hated when he did that. That was worse than the slap itself. I couldn't tell if Solly flinched from my vantage point. I turned over and sought to get back to my feet.

That's when he grabbed me again. He had me by the foot and wrestled my right sneaker off, then my left sneaker. It was there he grabbed the funds. For a moment, his anger turned to laughter. He kicked his head back as if it were all good fun.

He paid me a back-handed compliment. "You know, Boy, you're pretty smart."

He got like that with me. My name was Jonah; how hard could it be for him to call me that? When he referred to me as "boy," I knew he wasn't just highlighting my age, it was his way of never letting me forget that I wasn't all the way white.

After Nick quit laughing, he pocketed the money, leaving out one bill—a twenty—which he tore into pieces.

When I stood up, he spat on me to further his spite.

I felt a shiver go up my spine.

What was I going to do?

I swallowed hard.

What could I do?

Nick was a big man, a least a few inches over six feet. He was muscular and picked Solly and me up like we were babies. He had both of us by the back of the neck, throttling us; then he crammed our faces way down deep into the snow.

Before I knew what was what, Solly's whole head was so deep into the white it was drowning him. Solly was gasping for air and coughed up chunks of the freeze each time his father let him up for air.

I was fainting worse because not only was it impossible for me to breathe, but since I had a slimmer neck, Nick could get a tighter grip on me. Kneeling in the chest high snow, Nick bore down with his might. Nick swept up a hand full of snowy gravel and slammed it down into my face. He braced me still and worked the wet and cold rocks into my eyelids, cheeks, and lips—grinding them against my teeth.

I hollered and spat and squirmed, but I could not escape his clutches. Each new fist full of gravel brought a fresh array of scraping. My flesh tore and seared and stung and all I could do was yelp and buck like a wild horse. I could hear Solly close by still coughing and coughing, it sounded like a lung was coming up.

I wished for a weapon, anything. If only there was a large rock or fallen branch within grabbing distance, I wouldn't have been so helpless. A few minutes passed, I didn't have the strength to struggle free; I was looking for the stamina to just stay conscious. I did stay alert, barely. After my stepfather let me go, I saw that Solly was in the same bad shape I was.

Like me, he couldn't even make a crawl for it.

Nick strutted in front of the moaning lump of torn meat, which was better known as me and said, "Tell me was that worth it?"

I didn't answer. This was already way past being a bad movie. What was the point?

Then he walked over to Solly and gave him a series of kicks right to his ribs. "And you, Oink, I'm your father. You're barely related to him. Don't you ever side with him over me."

"He didn't know," I managed to get out.

"Shut the fuck up, unless you want some more," he told me.

So, I shut the fuck up, and there was an end to it.

He walked away, leaving us to our wounds.

In the past after such attacks, I always thought about Solly first, since I was his protector and all, but I admit right then I wasn't thinking about how Solly was doing and then suddenly didn't even care. I was concerned about me. At the very moment when I regained my bearings, I got myself vertical, and I didn't concern myself with helping Solly up.

I just ran.

I ran and ran.

By this time, barely within earshot, I could hear Solly calling after me, asking me where I was going. But, as I ran, I could only hear this faintly and then more faintly still till my brother's voice all but disappeared.

In Periot, Wisconsin, the houses are spread out like sailboats along a shoreline. I went heading for the Lelands'. I wanted to talk to the man of the house; I needed to borrow something.

Knocking on the door, I nearly collided with Mr. Leland's granddaughter, Lori. Our eyes hooked. She had extraordinary irises of emerald green, intense and searching. She had some books in her mittened hands, and she was all suited up in a coat and scarf as if she was just about to run an errand. She asked me what happened.

"Nothing happened. I'm alright. I'm just here to see your grandpa."

Lori said my face looked like a used razor blade.

"I'm fine," I repeated.

"Sure, you are," she frowned. "Come on, I'll get you something for your cuts," she said, taking my arm.

I pushed her away. "No, I want to see your grandpa."

She knitted her brows together and told me Mr. Leland was around the back in the shed.

I walked around to the back, slowly, with measured steps. It was hitting me now. I felt so queasy in the core of my stomach. My fear bubbled. I kept waiting for a pop. *How in the hell was I going to ask for this?*

I approached Mr. Leland's bent figure. Over a sanding board, he was just filing away. He didn't notice me till I was right up on him. He was a funny looking old man. Stocky as a bulldog, he wore his graying blond hair in a ponytail. He straightened up when he saw me and put his hand to his lower back. He shook his head in a pitying manner.

"Why don't you just stay out of his way?" he asked me.

"It's not so easy, Mr. Leland."

He tilted his head to the side and told me, "You don't have to make it this hard."

"You think I asked for this?"

"All I'm saying is you gotta do what he says. Everything he says. Maybe you've heard that old saying: the life you save may be your own."

"I've heard it," I said.

Pause. Then more silence as he peered into me more deeply.

"Where's your other half? Where's Solly?"

"I left him," I said, taking a visual sweep of the room. "It's all right though. The storm is over."

He nodded and frowned. "Why don't you go inside? My wife will clean you up. She's in there making a pie. You can stay—"

"I didn't come all the way over here for pie, Mr. Leland. Or to get cleaned up."

He nodded again, this time more slowly. "Well, then, what did you come here for?"

"I came here for a loan."

"Sure, sure. Take what you want. You know, I promised you many years ago I'd always be here for you and your brother. What do you want?"

I didn't hesitate for an instant.

"That," I said and pointed to his gun rack.

He turned and looked behind him. "That?"

"Yep."

"Well, this is a fine time to think about that. You want to hunt, now? When I took you boys out last month—"

"I ain't hunting."

"Say what? Are you crazy? You want a rifle, but you don't want to hunt with it? What are you talking about? That man must have hit you too hard in the head."

I smirked. It was funny because, if anything, the sense had finally gotten knocked into me, not the other way around. At last, after many episodes, I was going to move from a defensive posture to an offensive one.

That is why I had picked Mr. Leland. He was an old soldier, Vietnam and all that, so he knew all about shooting and shot positions. Since Lori had little interest and he didn't have a grandson, he had shown Solly and me everything about how to wield a rifle, even how to fire from a prone position. I guess it was only natural of me to turn to him at a time like this.

"I'm thinking clearly, Mr. Leland, I need a gun for protection. I'm not going to get beat like this ever again."

More silence followed. I shattered it by telling him that I'd been thinking of this for a good long time.

Mr. Leland's color rose but his smallish, green eyes didn't tell me anything. He shook his head. "You don't want what you're asking for. You're fixing on doing something you're going to be sorry for."

I nodded. "I'm just going to have to be sorry then."

"Wait a minute. Have you thought this through? I mean really thought this through. This ain't the way. This ain't you, Jonah. You don't go around doing rash things."

"Mr. Leland, I have thought this through—"

He talked over me, speaking quickly using wild hand gestures. "Jonah, I've been mad. I've been crazy mad, but you have to believe me that sometimes the smartest thing to do is to hold your fire."

"Mr. Leland, I don't have any fire. That's what I'm here about."

"Look, you and Solly, I know you have had it rough, but this ain't no way. You're about to blow this thing sky high . . . You two made it this far. Just keep doing what you're doing. Don't do this, I'm begging you."

I shook my head. "Don't beg, Mr. Leland."

"I will beg you. I will. I am begging you."

"You're begging me and my brother to wait—"

"Yes, wait."

"With all due respect," I said as I eyed the rack of weapons, again. "But it's gotten past waiting. Who knows what's going to happen next? I don't want to get hurt or worse, and I don't want to see my brother hurt or worse and that's it. End of story."

"But it's not the end. You do this, and it's only the beginning."

"My mind is made up. It's set. If you don't want to help me, don't. I'll get it from someplace else. This is Periot. Everyone has a gun, except for the people who need one."

I was prepared to leave right then when he again said, "Don't do it."

My brown eyes met his green ones, which were just like Lori's— emerald, searching. I wished he'd cut it with all the grave concern. All it did was add another layer to things that were already deep enough.

"All right, I won't take it," I said to him but that was a lie. A big one. As soon as Mr. Leland turned his back to go inside, I knew I had only a short period of time to get what I'd come for.

In every bad situation, there's always time to act but only a second or two before the cliché comes true, bad goes to worse.

I walked toward a side cupboard. The floorboards creaked beneath my footsteps. I opened a drawer and pulled out a short, heavy revolver. They call this type of weapon a snub nose. It's also called a belly gun because it's just right to shove against someone's stomach. And sure, there was nothing brave or noble about anything I was doing: stealing, plotting a murder, etc. But I wasn't aiming for those descriptions. What's the use of honor? I'd rather be safe.

Maybe this would work out for the best because a small weapon is more portable and I figured Mr. Leland wouldn't notice it missing for a while since as far as he knew my interest was in his rifle. I took the gun and slipped out with it.

It felt good to be out in the air. Out of the corner of my eye, I saw the large white clouds floating across the sky. I caught my breath. Though I had secured what I'd come for, I knew this was just the start of things. Mr. Leland sure got that part right.

I came in like a cat burglar. I clawed at the pane until I was able to squeeze through. Solly walked by, just as I fell to the floor. In surprise, he nearly dropped the large can of ravioli he was finishing.

Solly and I had the exact opposite way of diffusing stress. He ate, and I didn't. At least so far, he hadn't turned into a blimp, and I hadn't gone full manorexic.

"What's wrong with the front door?" he asked.

"I saw his pickup. I thought he'd come back."

"Naw, he ain't here," Solly told me in between shoveling down spoonfuls. You'd think he'd grown up in a great big family where you have to stake your claim early. His habit of eating fast was so that barely even pausing to breathe was his way of keeping the food warm. "Where did you go?" he asked.

"I went over to Mr. Leland's."

"Did you see Lori?"

"Yeah."

Solly smirked.

"What are you smirking about?"

"Nothing . . . She likes you."

I didn't answer his lead. I went into the bathroom and got my first look at the damage. My lip busted, pink and purple. My whole pan was bloody with lacerations.

"Did you hear what I said?" Solly called after me.

"Yes, I did." I wet a small towel so I could use it as a warm compress.

From the other room, I could hear Solly still on the same topic. "Lori's not bad looking. She talks too much, but she has pretty eyes."

"I don't have time for girls; I've got too many problems," I told him flatly, but in a muffled voice on the count of I was holding the cloth to my mouth. "Besides she'd be better paired with you," I said, thinking of her wide mouth and dizzily curling blond hair.

"Don't push her off on me. I got just as many problems as you have."

And we were silent again.

I came back to the room and sat on the bed. I felt a little more composed. I was at least breathing steady. "Let me see your ribs," I said to him. That was the last thing I recalled from the attack, his father kicking him there.

Solly came closer to me and lifted his T-shirt. What I saw was definite, half-moon-shaped bruises made from his father's boots—tip and the heel.

"How does it feel? Sore?"

Solly nodded. "How does it look? Do you see any swelling?"

Solly was a husky kid, so the words: "No more than usual,"

slipped out of my mouth though I didn't mean it the flip way it sounded. If his ribs felt anything like my face, it didn't matter how meaty he was built, he must be in real pain. I laid my hand against the skin there to see if I could feel any heat. Pain draws heat, and there was radiating heat coming off his skin. I began to worry.

"Maybe we should swing by the hospital?"

"That's too much waiting. We'd be there half the night."

"But, I can't tell. I ain't a doctor. Maybe there is really something wrong. Remember before—"

"Of course, I remember before. How could I forget when I had to wear that thing for two months?"

"Solly, maybe you have some broken ribs or something."

"They can't put a cast on my ribs, can they?"

"No."

"Then how do they fix it?"

"I think they tape it."

Solly put his hand up as if to say he didn't want to hear it. "Skip it. I don't want to be taped."

He pulled his shirt down and ate the last of the ravioli.

"Solly . . . " I began to whine. I hated to whine, but I was so tired and achy and cold and pissed off. I just wanted some cooperation from him. I only wanted to help. I laid back on the bed totally forgetting about the gun. It was between my waistband and the back of my jeans.

I quickly sat bolt upright. I removed the weapon I had secured to my lower back.

Still not noticing, Solly chucked the empty can in the trash. Its clank made a violent sound.

I held up the weapon for him to plainly see it. "I got this."

"That's a gun," he said after a double take.

I nodded.

"Is it loaded?"

"Not yet."

He motioned to me to let him hold it.

I did without reminding him to treat it like it was armed even though it wasn't because I knew he already knew that.

Solly held it for a while, examining it. He checked the chamber and said to me, "It's cute."

"Cute?" I asked. Of all the adjectives in the world, how did that one pop into his mind to describe a weapon? I gave it a deeper look.

"Yeah, who'd think that something so small could actually hurt someone. But it'll get the job done," I said before taking it from his hands.

"What job?"

I got up, placing the gun on the desk. I began to pace.

"I didn't even know Mr. Leland had this type," Solly said. "I thought he just had hunting stuff."

"He's pretty well armed."

"Why?" Solly laughed and winced. "He ain't in Alpha company anymore."

"I suppose, he's got to protect his wife and Lori."

Solly frowned, now holding his side. "He must have like twenty or thirty guns. That's real stupid."

"What's stupid about it?"

"He only has two hands."

I stopped pacing. "I guess it helps him to sleep nights."

"Is that what you got the gun for, Jonah," Solly asked, "Sleeping?"

That made me think. I mean really think and think and think and think. I thought until I was trembling all over and my head felt dizzy.

"Jonah? Jonah? Earth to Jonah? Come in Jonah?" Solly kept asking. He clapped his hands in front of me.

I snapped back into the present.

For a second or two, I took stock of his face noticing how clear and boyish it looked for a change. There wasn't any of the acne that so often polluted his complexion since his father had been back. Usually after a beating, Solly was so bruised up that his face was distorted and outsized. This time he looked like himself, with his delicate features. How his father called him an Oink was beyond me. His nose especially was too finely cut to even be mistaken for a snout. It looked like something a plastic surgeon would construct, a showpiece even.

"What's the job?" he asked me.

"Huh?" was my reply.

"You planning to stick-up a bank?"

I gave a nervous laugh, took a deep breath, then spoke in a blue streak. "I've had it with your father, Solly. Ever since he came back he's been flying into his rages on us. I'm sick of being boot kicked and bitch slapped and thrown across the room. This shit has been going on for too long. Today just capped it off," I told him. "Why can't we keep our own money? We earned it. That man wants everything. Everything. And I'm sick of it."

Solly's mouth was open. Then, he closed it. Then he gestured to the gun, "So what does the gun have to do with that?"

"I just told you, Solly, we're getting out."

"Out? Where out?" he asked.

"He'll cripple us if we don't."

"We can't leave. We can't leave Ma. What about her?"

I went back to pacing. I thought long before I spoke, considering heavily if I really wanted to say this next part. "What about her?" I asked finally.

Solly looked at me incredulously. "Well, we just can't leave her behind."

"She's the reason we're in this mess."

"How do you figure that?"

"She hasn't done one goddamn thing—"

"She's doing the best she can do—"

"This is the best that she can?" I said lifting up his shirt.

He jerked my hands away. "That's not her fault."

"Yeah, right. She doesn't have to keep taking him back. She could stop this if she wanted to."

"What do you want her to do?" Solly asked.

"You're not listening to me," I shouted at him.

"I *am* listening," he shouted back.

"Then why are you talking?!"

Solly gave me a piercing look and went quiet.

I began, "Last week, I promised myself the next time he puts his hands on us, he's dead—"

"Don't you have that kind of bass ackwards? The next time—"

I spoke over him. "What did I say about talking?"

He went quiet again.

"I got a gun, and I plan to use it."

This time he waited a good few seconds before he asked, "On my father?"

"Yes, Solly, yes," I said. "On your father."

At that instant, Solly's skin turned sweaty and clammy. "You decided this all last week, and you didn't clue me in before now?"

I nodded. "I know it is a lot to get down all at once."

"You only had a week to think of it . . . Jonah, you're really going to kill him? Like shoot him in the head or something?"

I shrugged. Those were some blunt questions he was asking me. "I'll do what I need to do."

Solly didn't have much of a reaction after that. He just glanced away for a moment. He looked toward the window.

Outside, the dull yellow sun had set and pitch had settled in for the night. Solly's eyes came back to mine. He said, "Good."

Shane Leavy is a writer and researcher based in the rainy north-west of Ireland, with work accepted by publications including *Popshot: The Illustrated Magazine of New Writing, The Ekphrastic Review, Loughshore Lines,* and *Poems from the Lockdown.* After a cinema trip was ruined by four chaotic teenage boys—boys who responded to calls for quiet with astonished anger—he wondered how they perceived the disagreement. He wondered, too, what would happen if both sides chose to escalate.

FIGHTING THE LAST WAR

Myself and Mulligan and Gaffney and Robber are at *James Bond,* all sprawled out at the back with a few sweets and big cups of coke. A shitty day: that prick Moloney had called me up in maths for not doing my homework and then it was lashing rain for PE and I cut me knee doing a sliding tackle. Mr. O'Donnell said we had to wash the cut 'cause of the muck and he splashed some fuckin' Dettol on it—Christ that hurt! Then I went home and the house was freezing with no food, and me mam was out. She'd gone and left the front door open again, 'n all.

Anyway, Robber's brother works in the cinema and he got us a few tickets so we're having a good laugh. Myself and Robber are right up at the back and Gaffney and Mulligan sitting in front of us, which was good craic, obviously, for taking the piss! This bird comes on one of the ads and she looks a bit like Gaffney's mam, so I lean forward.

"Is that your mam, Gaffney?"

"Fuck off," says he.

"Jaysus, I didn't know your mother was an actor," says Robber, kinda getting into it.

"She's a porn star," I say, and Gaffney tells me to fuck off and we all have a good laugh.

The lights go down. James Bond is with this blonde bird and Robber gives me the nudge.

I'm like: "Would yeh ride her?"

"I would," he says.

"Would you ride Gaffney's mam?" I say, and I say it a bit loud so the lads can hear.

"That's a fine question, sir," says Robber, putting on an oul voice, "I believe I'd ride her from behind and shtick an oul bag over her head."

We have a good laugh at that and then Mulligan says Robber'd give Gaffney's mother some fucking disease after the shtate of his girlfriend, and we're laughing our heads off.

And it's a lovely feeling, being in the dark with the lads, drinking ice-cold coke and stuffing me gob with sweets, and I feel sort of free, for a minute, and I don't have to think about school or home or me Mam.

Then this voice comes across in the darkness from the seat next to Mulligan and whispers up to us: "Fellahs, keep it down."

And there it was again, that rush of fuckin' dread, that empty feeling in me belly, like I'm a little kid again with that prick of a man my mam was seeing shouting at me, telling me I'm shit, saying my mam should have had an abortion. I'm sitting on these lovely comfy seats in the cinema, in the dark and warm, but in me head I'm back home on the fucking tiles being screamed at by this massive fucking man with his shirt off.

And at the same time, I'm in school with a smarmy fucker like Moloney or Mrs. McGoldrick making me stand up and read in front of the class like a retard, all: "M-m-my s-s-school is S-S-Saint Columcille's," and all these other shits sniggering at me. Like I'm a retard.

And at the same time, I'm coming home from a game and getting in at eleven and the front door's open, the lights are all off and my mam is sitting there with a burnt-out cigarette in the dark and I'm fucking terrified, terrified, but I can't show it, can I?

All these thoughts—thoughts that're more like feelings—flash through me, and I can feel my skin crawl with it. I'm sure I stink of fear for a second, I'd say a dog'd know anyway. Sour, that's what fear smells like, like rotten milk.

Robber says: "What?"

And I can get a better look at him, this man in a nice jacket and a fancy fucking jumper, a specky fucker with a bird beside him. He says: "Keep it down."

Fuck me, I am filled at once with hatred for this evil little shit for making me feel like this, like I'm a little kid getting screamed at, or a retard in school. I want to break his fuckin' face. I want to stab the bastard with fuckin' scissors. But I keep thinking, calm down mate, calm down, you can't get into trouble because you have to look after Mam.

The lads all settle down a bit and we're watching the film but I can feel Robber getting restless beside me, he can't sit still. Sure, he's after eating a full bag of pick 'n mix and never had dinner, so I know the feeling. He keeps twisting and turning in his seat, and I start to snigger. Then Gaffney turns around and says, very loud: "SHHHHH!"

Well this sets us off and I have this little gush of relief as we laugh, I'm bathing in it like a hot bath. I feck an M&M at Gaffney and it bounces off his head and hits the specky stranger's shoulder. I can tell he felt it, he sort of stiffens for a split second, but he doesn't do anything about it. So I nudge Robber and he rests one of his feet up on the back of Specky's chair, just to see, but he doesn't do anything.

Fuck him—straight away I can see he's all bark, right? He's not going to do shit, so we get back chatting and throwing sweets and having a good laugh. I'm guzzling away on me coke so I have to go take a piss, so off I go, and most of the anger's dropped away now, it's hard to be angry at a total loser, you know what I mean?

I head out to the toilets and I'm standing at the urinal when the door opens and it's Specky. I'm not sure what to think about that, but then he moves right over beside me and doesn't unzip or anything; he's staring at me taking a piss and I'm like: "What are you watching me for, yeh pervert?"

And he says: "You need to keep it down, I'm being polite."

Like a teacher. So I go: "Fuck off."

And he says: "Oh really? You tell your little friends to shut up or I'll have ye thrown out."

I finish my piss and zip up, and that gives me a bit of courage, so I move to go past him and just mutter: "Fuckin' queer."

And I'm not really thinking anything of it, there's gay lads in my football team and I don't have any problem, but I just want to make this prick feel as fuckin' small as he makes me feel. But suddenly I feel my hoodie tighten 'cause he's grabbing me and I'm staggering backwards into the urinal, which hits me at the back of me knees and one of my hands sort of lashes out for support and wipes down on the front of this pissy urinal.

My jaw is on the fuckin' floor and I look up into Specky's face and—fuck me—it's all red blotches and his eyes look really small and I can tell his teeth are ground together like a fucking wolf. But for a second I'm not scared or even angry, for a split second I get this weird flash like: maybe someone called him "queer" before, maybe this Specky cunt in his nice jacket had a shitty time when he was a kid like I did.

I'm completely fuckin' confused, a part of me wants to talk to this poor bastard to see what the fuck happened him, but then I can see him pull his shoulders up and down as he tries to calm down, and he goes: "Prick." And he walks off.

And it's charging back, that evil fucker with his shirt off screaming at me: all the spit flying in my face, me on the tiles, Mam smoking and crying behind him—all in that one word. And for a second I'm going to deck him, but I'm telling myself to calm down, fucking hell, calm down and stay out of trouble. And Christ, I think, he didn't look hard, but he's a tall enough bastard and he sent me flying a minute ago. It feels like someone has poured petrol down my throat, all this poisonous mixture of fear and hatred, I want to poison him and burn his house down, but I'm stuck, terrified.

Then the door opens before Specky gets out and it's Robber and Mulligan. I know if I play this wrong I'll get the piss taken out of me and I'm fuckin' cold in my belly with horror, so quick as a flash I point at Specky and shout: "This fuckin' queer was trying to watch me piss."

Mulligan cracks up but I can see Robber's noticed my face and he's walking in to Specky and Mulligan follows. Mulligan's the tallest of us and he's bigger than Specky, although Robber's got more scrappin' experience and I'm the one who got cautioned by the Guards.

"What are you fuckin' doing you sick fuck?" says Robber.

"Fuckin' pervert," says Mulligan, then he blurts out, "paedo," which seems odd since I'm not a kid but I can see Specky's ears are red and he's clenching his teeth as he goes for the door.

"Excuse me," he says, but the lads are in the way and—fair play—they're standing in close, making him uncomfortable so I rush in close too, right behind him.

"Sick fuck," I say.

"Paedo, they should cut your fuckin' balls off, you're disgusting," says Robber.

Specky tries to go round but the three of us are in his face now and I can feel this delicious hot blood feeling in my face, the feeling you get before a fight when you can nearly smell your own blood. Because I hate this fucker, I hate him and I want to stamp on his stupid glasses with his face beneath them, and now we're calling him pervert and paedo and maybe we'll fight, but—fuck me—I can't be the first one to throw a punch or I'll have trouble and I can't leave my mam alone.

"Fuck off," says Specky in a high pitch, and this sets us off.

"Ooh *fuck off*," says Robber in a girly voice, prancing about with his hands over his mouth. "Or what, you're going to finger us to death?"

"Aw, you sicko!" Mulligan cries. "Arses to the wall, lads."

"Don't tell *us* to fuck off," I say, and I can hear the fuckin' weight in my own voice and it sounds good compared with Specky's pathetic voice. "I'll put your head through that fucking wall."

Specky lurches for the door but Robber gets in front of him, grinning. Specky switches and tries to go the other way, but me and Mulligan close up and all three of us are shouting at him now and laughing, and he is fuckin' losing it, and at last he snaps.

"Fuck *off!*"

And he grabs Mulligan and throws him, hard, staggering back towards the door. Now I said Mulligan's the biggest of us so I'm a bit shocked but at the same time he's reaching out to grab me and his face is this incredible storm of blood-red rage, I can see his cheek bones popping, he's clenching his teeth so hard. He grabs my hoodie and I don't know if he's going to deck me or what so I swing a punch up and clip him on the mouth and Robber tries to put him into a choke from behind, but Specky's too tall and Robber's arm doesn't go around his throat. Specky roars and shakes me back and forth—fuck, he's strong! My head is rattled and then I'm flying back again and crack the back of my head on the wall hard enough to make sparks pop in my eyeballs, and then the door opens.

Fucking hell, it's like slow motion, it's like something out of *James Bond*. There's a middle-aged fellah with a big belly and a soft face and he's carrying his daughter, a tiny little kid, they're probably in *Addams Family* or *Encanto* or something. The girl is gabbling away but the man freezes when he sees the three of us and we all freeze too. Specky lets me go and shoots for the door with his face all red.

"Excuse me," he says, and he disappears.

"Alright here, lads?" says the man.

"We're right as rain," says Robber and the three of us look at each other and have a good laugh.

But I'm not laughing inside. I can't think straight, my guts are all cold jelly and my legs feel weak.

The man takes his daughter into a cubicle and I've no reason to stay, but I hang back, waiting for Robber and Mulligan to piss, then the three of us march back through the cinema, back to *James Bond*. The lads are in good form and I'm trying to keep it up, shouting and laughing and sort of shadow boxing, but I'm seeing this specky cunt's face with his tiny eyes locked on mine and I'm sure there's a lump growing at the back of my skull where I hit the wall. And, Christ, I can feel this horrible heavy wetness behind my eyes like I'm going to cry, so I break into a run and the lads run with me and we pound up the steps to take our seat, while all the time I'm dreading the thought that Specky is up there in the darkness already, sizzling with rage.

Because he's not all bark after all and I don't know what shit he went through before, but when he grabbed me I swear he wasn't just wanting to hurt me, he wanted to kill—not me—kill someone who fucked with him in the past, someone I reminded him of.

We see Gaffney still shoving popcorn down his gob and that nearly does make me laugh after everything.

"Four Eyes has fecked off," says Gaffney and I see that the seats where Specky and his bird had been sitting are empty, thank God.

We sit back down and then Mulligan blurts out: "You knocked me fuckin' popcorn over!"

"I didn't knock it," says Gaffney.

"Must have been that specky prick," says Robber.

Someone further down the audience turns back and says: "Shhh"

"You shush," says Mulligan and Robber says in a high-pitched nerdy voice: "Fuck off, madam!"

We're all laughing away and the lads are swearing at the memory of Specky and telling Gaffney about it, but inside I feel like my guts are full of cat food and my head is properly stinging. There's a big noisy action scene on *James Bond* so I lean right back and pull my hood up, and I'm able to hide my face a bit so the lads don't see my eyes are wet. I just feel fuckin' awful, full of pain and fear and humiliation, and more and more I can't get Specky's face out of my mind and the fact that we outnumbered that prick three-to-one but we let him walk away. In my mind I'm getting his face all mixed up with the face of that prick of a boyfriend of Mam's, standing with his top off, three times the size of me, screaming as I cry and screaming at me to stop crying, and for a second I think I'm even confused and think Specky really *is* my mam's old fellah, but he can't be, he's too young.

So I'm there all hollow as James Bond is murderin' lads on the screen and I grit my teeth and wish I had a fucking machine gun or I could shove a hand grenade into that cunt's mouth and make it go off, but the lads have no idea; they're sitting there laughing and taking the piss and fecking popcorn at each other. The film's getting on so I wipe my eyes and pull myself together.

The credits come up and the lights go on and we all scramble for the steps to get out of there, chatting away and laughing. The whole crowd is trying to get out at the same time so the steps are clogged with people and we're getting impatient, ducking into the little pockets that open up in the crowd. I'm laughing, even though I'm all shit inside, and as we're getting to the door I swipe in between two people but one of them moves at the wrong second and we bump arms for a second. I look up and meet the eyes of the other person, who's a biggish fellah with a big, black beard and I hear him mutter: "Fuck's sake."

I feel like I've been punched in the fucking stomach, but we work our way outside and Gaffney's nicked some cigarettes so we're lighting up as we cut through the carpark.

"O'Donnell'll be telling ye off for smokin'," says Mulligan, 'cause he's not on the football team and the rest of us are.

"Oh yeah, he'll be like: 'That fat lad Mulligan said ye were shmoking tobacco!'" says Robber.

Then Mulligan laughs and goes: "Fuck off Robber, ya bollocks."

Mulligan gives Robber a push and Robber pushes back and Mulligan is a bit off-balance so he steps back and his foot comes down on my toes. Now Mulligan is a big bastard and his full weight comes down with this shock of pain; I can feel my toes sort of crunching together in my runners, so I let out a howl and bounce backwards on the other foot with the lads all laughing, and next thing I'm smashing backwards into someone and I hear this mutter behind me and when I turn I realise it's the beardy guy from before.

"Watch where you're going, will you?" he says.

And I'm just a wound, I'm pain and fear and anger all over. My head is throbbing, my foot's all red-hot with blood, I'm sure I'll be out of football for a week and O'Donnell's going to kill me, but above all I feel like I'm just a frame of fucking bones around this ice-cold, fuckin' salt water belly. I'm afraid I'm going to puke or sob like a baby and now this beardy prick is telling me off like a fucking teacher and I don't know what I'm doing, but I snap out a punch and crack him across the nose.

He cries out in a high voice that surprises me: "Ooah!"

I can hear the lads sort of gasping, they're not expecting it. Gaffney goes: "Easy, easy."

"You hit me!" the man cries with a hand dabbing his nose, which is all bloody. "You little brat. I'll have the law on you, you brat."

And I see Specky, and I see my mam's old boyfriend, and Moloney in school, looking through this man's eyes and I just pummel at him with both hands and one of them seems to click on bone—I can feel a needle of pain run up my hand. Yer man falls, falls like a tree and it's like slow motion, this big, beardy face going backwards and hanging for a split second before he vanishes and I hear this terrible crack—fuck me—it's like the crack of a coconut when me mam opened one up with a hammer at Halloween a few years ago without thinking to get the water out first. Wet, it sounds, and hollow.

But for a minute I'm all rage and I can hear myself saying: "You fuckin' prick, you cunt!"

I'm hearing this, and I know it's my voice, but it seems far away, and the lads' voices are far off too, but I stand there and slowly I can hear them more clearly like I'm turning up the volume. I can see the cigarette in Mulligan's mouth, because his mouth has fallen open and it's sort of stuck with spit to his upper lip, which is hilarious. I'm remembering, as well, another kid in school who used to walk around with his gob open and the lads called him "Fly-catcher." And these strange memories come out of nowhere and make me laugh.

"Fuckin' hell, oh no, oh my God," says Robber, and that wakes me up because I've never heard Robber make that kind of sound.

I hear myself say, "What?" and there's still laughter around my mouth.

"Come on, mister," says Robber and he hunches down where the man has fallen. "Come on, wake up mister."

"Don't touch him," says Gaffney, "fingerprints."

And now I'm beginning to wake up a bit.

"Fingerprints?" I say.

"Fuckin' hell, I don't think he's breathing," says Robber.

I hunch down and the beardy fellah's out flat on the tarmac. His eyes are closed, he actually looks peaceful, as if he's asleep. But there's blood coming out his ear.

"We need to call an ambulance," says Mulligan, but he doesn't sound serious, it's like he wants us to disagree with him.

"Fuck the ambulance," Gaffney says in a hiss, "we need to get the fuck out of here or we're going to fuckin' prison."

Robber drops his fag and goes to step on it but Gaffney says: "Fuckin' hell, Robber, evidence!"

So Robber picks it up and holds it in his fingers, this little ember still hanging on, looking pathetic. All three of the lads stand up and they're looking left and right in the carpark and I know they want to see if anyone saw us or if we were on CCTV that they sometimes have in carparks.

"Lads, we're in the clear," says Robber in this wobbly voice.

I don't move and Mulligan grabs my hoodie and pulls me, so I stagger a few steps with him but shake myself free and stop.

"Fuckin' hell, do you want to get the shit raped out of you in Mountjoy fucking Prison?" Gaffney says, and I just say: "No."

I say: "Lads, go on. I'm going to call an ambulance. I fucked up, fellahs."

They're looking at me and now it's Robber who has tears in his eyes and Mulligan looks terrified. Gaffney just looks amazed.

"Sorry fellahs, ye won't be in any trouble. It's not your fault. Go on home, I'll handle it. Robber, will you pop in to my mam on your way? Just . . . make sure she's alright."

"I will," says Robber and he's crying and sniffing.

The other two lads look like they got the sense punched out of them by Tyson Fury or something. Mulligan just shakes his head and says, "Good luck," and Gaffney says, "Seeya."

Then they're off, sprinting away off down the street like we did a million times together, but instead of shoutin' and hootin' with laughter they're silent. I hunch down beside the beardy lad again and I phone 999 on me mobile. It's a woman's voice and I'm surprised that she starts giving me advice about how to check his breathing and airways and all this stuff, but I'm a wreck and I can't get a pulse and finally I start sobbing; I can feel it tearing up through my chest and my throat, I'm coughing out sobs and my face is all slimed with tears. Eventually they get me to put him in a recovery position, and I take off my hoodie and put it over him, just to keep him warm.

It's fuckin' freezing, in fact, I can see my own breath all twinkling with silver bits in the streetlights and I keep thinking: that's the last time you'll see your breath outside, free, and I want to do a runner but this poor bastard is so calm-looking lying there with a big, black wound on his head, so I'm frozen to the spot.

And I think how I've fucked up and my mam won't have me, but I know she wouldn't want me to run away from something like this, at least when her mind is clear, so I have to be a man for the first time in my fucking life. That thought calms be down a bit and although I'm sad, like really, really sad and ashamed because I know that I'm losing my life to prison, I'm calmer and a bit proud. I'm doing the right thing.

Something moves in the carpark and I hear footsteps running that I presume are the paramedics, but instead my head goes sideways with a burst of yellow stars. It's weird and I don't know what's happening; the world turns red and I hear words that seem to come from somewhere else and smell a gust of beery breath that reminds me, of course, of the shirtless man screaming in my face, and I'm falling.

All slow motion again—fuck me! I'm falling backwards and I see Specky standing over me as I fall and his words come out in slow motion: "Not so hard now, are we?"

He'd hit me! I'm nearly proud of him, he's strong after all, because it feels like I've been punched by a pneumatic drill; my head seems to have broken from my neck and at last I hit the tarmac with a bang. I am looking through this red filter of blood at Specky standing above me, smelling all beery, so now I know where he went after the cinema, and at the same time he's the shirtless man, and Moloney, and somehow he's also sort of my house with the front door open and all the lights off at night in the dead of winter.

His eyes move from me and I guess he's seen the beardy lad and all the rage falls away from his face and he looks fucking terrified as he looks back at me and then runs; I can hear the footsteps pounding away to silence. And like an echo I keep thinking of the noise my head made when it met the concrete.

It's like the crack of a coconut when me mam opened one up with a hammer at Halloween a few years ago without thinking to get the water out. Wet, it sounded, and hollow.

Christine Boyer has been published in *The Little Patuxent Review*, *The Tahoma Literary Review*, and *So It Goes: The Literary Journal of the Kurt Vonnegut Museum and Library*, among others. She is a student with Harvard University Extension School and lives in Massachusetts.

Skeleton Filing

The crowd had already formed around the entrance of the mill when Alma pulled into the parking lot. She was always the first employee in each morning, walking against the tide of departing third-shifters, but today there were already people milling around. A few stood smoking in a loose huddle.

She parked her Volvo. She watched the sky lighten in the east, the cloud cover turning a fleecy grey as the sun rose behind it. There was a promise of rain, judging from the deep ache in her bad knee. She thought of the bottle of codeine on the windowsill in her kitchen and promised herself half a tablet after work.

Alma climbed out of her car. She gripped her briefcase and walked up to the crowd, her low heels thudding on the pavement.

"Hey, Alpo!" someone called. Her stomach sunk at her high school nickname, and she turned to see her cousin waving at her from the crowd of smokers. Bobby said something to the men, then stubbed out his cigarette and trotted over to her.

"You just get here?" he asked. He reached into his pocket and shook out another cigarette. He tapped it against the cardboard before lighting it with a cheap plastic lighter.

Alma glared at him. He worked with the chemicals in the pulping mill, and his face was perpetually ruddy from the exposure to the heat and noxious fumes. He kept his black hair short, the scalp peeking from underneath.

"Don't call me that," she said.

"Alright, alright." He tucked the cigarette into the corner of his mouth and asked again if she had just arrived.

"Yes," Alma said. She gestured to the men standing around. "What's going on?"

Bobby took a deep drag on his cigarette. "Door's chained shut," he wheezed. Blue smoke plumed out of his nostrils.

Alma strode to the double doors that led into the mill. Thick chains were threaded through the handles, and a large padlock secured them. She was staring at them, dumbfounded, when Lou came up behind her. She smelled him before she saw him—that cheap aftershave—and she turned to face him.

"Good morning, Alma," he said, his voice somber. "You've seen the doors, obviously?"

She nodded and he continued, "Insolvency." His voice dropped in volume. "Do you know what that means?"

She did, but Lou never had much faith in his bookkeeper. He had been her boss since she started at the Abenaki Paper Mill decades earlier, and he had a low opinion of women and their capacity for critical thinking and math. She had found, years ago, that it was best to let him assume the worst.

"It means that we are bankrupt." Color rose in his jowls.

"What does that mean for us?" she asked, even though she already knew. Thunder sounded in the distance. A lone droplet of sweat formed between her shoulder blades and began its maddening journey down to the small of her back.

"It means we are out of jobs," he said. "Abenaki can't make payroll, let alone pay the bank."

She shifted the briefcase from one hand to the other. "I didn't see this coming. I knew we were cutting shifts . . . "

Lou smiled sadly. "The paper industry is tanking. It's as simple as that."

Alma looked over at the growing crowd of men in the parking lot. Swallowing hard, she asked, "Do you need me to do anything? Will there be an outside auditor or . . . ?" She trailed off, looked at Lou, and then shifted her eyes to the chained doors again. Her stomach gave a lurch at the thought of some state auditor, rifling through her meticulously kept books.

Lou reached out and patted her arm. He gave her a weak smile. "You go on home now. Once things settle down here, I'll write you a letter of reference."

The crowd in the parking lot began to rumble, the men demanding to know what was going on. "I guess one of us has to be brave around here," he said, squaring his shoulders. He gave her one last appraising look. "Take care of yourself." He turned and walked away.

"You too," Alma said. She walked through the crowd quickly and climbed back into her Volvo. She laid her briefcase onto the passenger seat and took a final look at the mill.

Alma drove away.

***

There was nowhere to go. She could go home, but the thought of her house at nine in the morning was depressing. It would be too quiet, just a ticking clock hanging over the kitchen sink. Alma tried to think of the last time she had a day off.

"It must have been when mom died," she said to the empty car as she drove.

She thought about that year in purgatory, her mother dying from lung cancer but making a brave stand with chemotherapy, experimental lasers, positive thinking. Alma had taken time off to drive her to Bangor for treatments.

Now, she drove for a few hours, circling the town, bisecting it. She drove past the brewery, a Gothic monstrosity in red brick. She drove down the highway, past the fast-food joints and bank branches and car dealerships. She drove past the high school, past the business college where she took accounting classes. She parked for a while at the cemetery where her parents rested companionably under a granite headstone. She thought about checking on their grave, but she continued driving instead.

Alma pulled into the narrow parking lot of the bar without realizing it. The Last Chance Inn was her dad's old haunt, a refuge after regular double-shifts at the plant before heading home. Alma's father had grown up in a family with six brothers, and he had seemed baffled by the quiet and cleanliness of his adult life with just a wife and daughter.

Alma couldn't begrudge him the fraternity he found at the Last Chance Inn, even if it meant that, from time to time, she'd had to fetch him from the bar to bring him home. Like when the Sox played, and the men in the bar had alternately leered at her breasts and retreated from her face.

She climbed out of the Volvo and walked into the bar. Her eyes took a moment to adjust to the gloom, but it smelled exactly the same—like cheap cigars and spilled beer. The walls were paneled in mismatched faux wood. Beer posters with women in bikinis covered the holes in the wall from when patrons got too rowdy and tossed each other around.

"Hey, Alpo!"

"Damn it," Alma muttered. She half-turned towards the door to leave, and then changed her mind and walked towards the bar. Bobby was spun around on his stool to face her, a mostly full glass of beer in his hand.

"Hey, Alpo," he said again, grinning as she walked up to him. He nudged the man sitting beside him. "Tony, this is my cousin Alpo. Alpo, this is Tony, the recently unemployed." Tony glanced at her and grunted.

Alma settled into the stool beside Bobby. "Tony and I have met before," she said.

"Here, I'll buy you a beer. We just got here." He gestured to the bartender, a leathery slip of an old woman who poured a beer into a theoretically clean glass and slid it across the laminate to Alma. "How do you and Tony know each other?"

"From the plant," she said. A few years back, Tony had become divorced, and he needed help sorting out the changes to his paycheck with alimony and child support. Alma had patiently sat with him and sorted through the financial nightmare of a man with several kids scattered across the nearby counties. He had smiled with his cornflower blue eyes and dimples, and he had thanked her, touching her hand.

She'd been charmed and had spent a couple of days thinking about him, sparingly, in the quiet moments between bank runs or balancing the books. She replayed the smile he gave her over and over, how he had thanked her. Her mind sometimes drifted beyond their time together. He worked in the shipping department, and Alma had spent a few weeks walking purchase orders down to the warehouse herself. If she wore her nicest skirts or wore a touch of lipstick when she went there, well—did she really need a reason to look nice?

It was only a month later when she overheard him in the breakroom. Alma had been sitting a few tables over and eating her usual peanut butter sandwich when she heard a peal of men's laughter. It sent an icy chill down her spine, like she was in high school again, but she heard Tony all the same, telling the guys at his table about the beast in accounting who had a crush on him.

"Did you know about the bankruptcy? Before this morning, I mean," Bobby asked.

She shook her head and took a sip of beer. "No, I just found out today . . . " She trailed off, thinking of the balance sheet and bank statements she reconciled every month. She knew firsthand how easy it was to hide problems, to shift balances around under innocuous pretenses. Deceit was easy, as long as you knew the books.

"Lou came over and told us this morning. Said it was the out-of-business kind of bankruptcy, not the restructuring kind. He saw the papers, said they got filed quick overnight."

Alma nodded. "Skeleton filings. It's when the important forms are filed first, and the less important ones are filed later."

Bobby drained his beer and signaled for another. "Doesn't matter what it's called," he said. "All it means it that we're screwed."

Tony slapped his hand on the bar. "I'll drink to that," he said. He called the bartender over and ordered a round of shots. "Just leave the bottle, honey," he said, hooking the whiskey bottle by its neck. The bartender batted her lashes at him and his winning dimples. Tony glanced over at Alma and winked.

***

The three of them drank through the morning, when the place was empty save for a handful of day-drunks drinking away their pensions. They drank through the lunch crowd: white-collar types who used breath mints to hide their problem. They drank through the afternoon lull, and then though the steady stream of regulars that made the Last Chance Inn their first stop after work.

They ordered pizza from across the street, the grease soaking through the flimsy cardboard box, the burnt cheese and yeasty dough sponging up the booze in their stomachs. They bade the night crowd farewell and closed down the bar with a few remaining regulars and the old bartender, who kept their glasses full. When she started to slack in her duties, Tony dialed up the charm.

"Hey, sweetheart," he called when their whiskey bottle was low. The bartender brought them another, and Tony laid a hand over her wrist. "You've got really beautiful eyes. You know that? Real deep and soulful." The bartender smiled and went back to her few other patrons. Alma swallowed a mouthful of beer.

"You told me that, y'know," she said to Tony over Bobby's head. Bobby had laid his head down on the bar earlier, sometime between the regular crowd coming in and then leaving. He snored softly into his folded arms.

"What'd I say?" Tony asked. "What'd I tell you?"

"That I have beautiful eyes." It sounded garbled to her ears when she said it aloud. She took a steadying breath. "When I helped with your paycheck," she said, annunciating clearly. She tried to remember if he had really complimented her eyes or if she had pretended he had when she thought about him late at night alone in her bed.

Tony laughed and poured a shot of whiskey. "Never said that." He threw back the shot and poured another.

She finished her beer. She had tried to pace herself, drinking plenty of water in between the whiskey shots and beer, splashing her face in the bathroom with lukewarm water. She still felt loose, like a marionette doll, her limbs unattached and free. She raised a hand in front of her face and wiped the beads of sweat dotting her upper lip. "It's okay," she said.

Tony turned and looked at her, his blue eyes bloodshot.

Alma put her hand down on the bar and looked over at Tony. "It's okay. I know I'm not pretty." The alcohol roared in her blood, and it made her brave.

"The kids at school called me 'Alpo' because I'm a dog. But you know what? It's okay," she continued.

Tony laughed again. "What's okay about that?" he asked.

She stood up, unsteady in her heels, the room shifting and tilting like the funhouse at the county fair. "I'm ugly, but I'm smart."

"What good is smart? You're up the same shit creek as the rest of us." He turned halfway on his stool to give her an evaluating look.

She crept towards him until she was inches from his face. "Do you know what a smart person can do, at a company like Abenaki with a boss like Lou?" The words rolled out of her in a fog of alcohol.

Tony shrugged and started to turn his stool back to the bar. "I don't care," he said. He picked up the whiskey and lifted it to his mouth.

Alma reached over and plucked the bottle from him. "You aren't listening." She waved the bottle under his nose and then held it away from him. "Do you know how much money a person can take if they are very patient and very smart?"

"Bullshit."

"A lot. They can take a lot." She tilted the bottle to her mouth and took a swig. She laid a shaky hand on his chest, toying with the button near his throat.

He batted her hand away. "How much is a lot?"

"Almost eight hundred."

Tony scoffed. "Big deal. Eight hundred won't even cover my bills for a month."

She reached out to fiddle with his shirt button again, and then she leaned against him. "Eight hundred thousand, dummy," she said. "Little by little, month by month, Lou signed off on the cashier's checks for a dummy account. Eight hundred thousand, cash, sitting in the bottom of my dad's footlocker from Korea." She thought of the trunk in the guest room, holding her father's mementos from the war, and her own secrets as well.

Tony grabbed her, hard enough to dig his fingers into the meat of her upper arms. "Liar."

She struggled against him. The two tussled for a moment, the booze throwing their equilibriums off. Alma tottered as she tried to break away, and Tony fought to keep his seat on the stool.

"Interested now?" Alma asked, out of breath as she pulled against him, her hair hanging in her face. "Funny how that works. The guy who called me a beast is suddenly paying attention. Guess all that child support doesn't leave you with much at the end of the month, does it?"

"Shut up."

"Between my Abenaki account and my parents' life insurance and my house, I'm a goddamned millionaire. What are you, Tony? You a millionaire?"

"I said shut up."

"Nah." The two stopped struggling against each other, and Alma looked into his blue eyes. "Tony's just a broke skirt chaser with a year or two left before his looks are gone." He narrowed his eyes at her and tightened his grip on her. "What'll you be then, Tony?"

He shoved her, hard. She fell to the floor, her teeth clicking down over her tongue with a jolt of pain. Tony slid off his stool and stood over her, his hands closed into fists. Alma tasted blood, and she suddenly felt very tired and very sober. The old bartender came around the bar and stood between them.

"You need to get out," she said. She pointed to the door. "You can't drive, you call a taxi from the pay phone out front."

Tony stepped over Alma and stormed out of the bar, and the door banged behind him.

"You alright?" the bartender asked. She offered Alma a hand, helping her to her unsteady feet.

"I'm okay," Alma answered. She dusted off her skirt and winced. Her tongue was on fire. She walked over to the bar and fumbled in her purse for her wallet. "How much do I owe?"

The bartender waved her off. "That one," she said, jerking her thumb at the door where Tony had stomped out, "has a tab. I'll put it on his. And if not, I'll put it on his." She pointed to Bobby, his head upon his arms, snoring. "You sure you're okay to drive?"

Alma nodded. The buzz of the beer and whiskey has subsided, replaced by her aching tongue and a sick feeling in her stomach.

She thought of the stacks of hundreds safely hidden in her dad's footlocker. Over two decades of patience and planning, and she bragged about it to the first man she flirted with. *Stupid, stupid, stupid*, she thought.

She stepped outside. The night was hot, but the wind was picking up and there was thunder close by. She reached into her purse for her keys when her head exploded into a million stars of pain. She fell to the gravel, her bad knee twisting painfully. Someone reached over her and yanked her purse from her arm.

"What," she said. The word was thick in her mouth, and she thought of what to say next when a heavy steel-toed boot swung into her field of vision and connected with the soft part of her abdomen, low in the belly.

Alma slept.

***

Alma tried to open her eyes. She raised her lids a fraction, allowing the florescent light to flood in—past the cornea, down the optic nerve, and straight into the center of her skull—setting off a Klaxon horn of pain. She raised a shaky hand to the side of her head, probing gently with fingers that felt thick and stupid.

"It'll grow back." The voice was somewhere beside her. Cold fingers took the pulse in her wrist.

"What," Alma said. Her tongue throbbed, and she remembered the click of her jaws as she'd bitten it.

"Your hair," said the voice. "It'll grow back."

Alma turned her head gingerly. The voice belonged to a nurse, blindingly white in her uniform. "The doctor had to shave part of your head so that he could stitch you back up."

"Stitch?"

The nurse smiled. "You've got a nasty goose egg, but that'll go away. The scar is yours for life, but once your hair grows in, no one will be the wiser."

"How . . ." Alma started. She took a deep breath, ignoring the pulse in the side of her shaved head. Her thoughts were like a worn record, skipping from thought to thought just as she started to get her bearings.

The nurse shook her head. "The police will be in shortly to talk with you. I'll let him know you're awake." She gave Alma squeeze on the wrist and left.

Alma raised herself onto her elbows and sat up. Her head throbbed in time to the pain in her belly, a symphony of hurt playing across her body, all discordant minor chords. She touched the side of her head again.

There was a knock in the doorway. She turned to look, wincing at the pain. The cop standing there looked barely old enough to drive, let alone maintain law and order.

"Morning, Alma," he said. "I'm Officer Laurant." He stepped into the room and closed the door behind him.

"Good morning."

He pulled a notepad out of his pocket. "I've been up all night, running down calls. The town's gone to hell quick with the mill closing."

"How so?"

He pursed his lips. "Drunk driving. The tow trucks were as busy as we were, pulling cars out of ditches. There were domestic calls. And then there were bar brawls, simple assaults." He gestured to her, lying in the hospital bed. "As you know."

She shook her head gently. "I don't remember anything."

He flipped open the notepad. "What can you tell me about Tony Bosco?"

Officer Laurant ran her through the missing pieces of that night: the bartender had gone to lock the door and found Alma lying outside in the gravel, bleeding from a flap of scalp. She had made sure Alma was breathing and then called an ambulance and the police. Alma's purse and car were long gone, and the weapon lay nearby in the gravel—a chunk of asphalt that had broken off from the road, Alma's blood crusting on it.

While Alma was being stitched up, the police got a separate call of a car in a ditch out near the county line. It was Alma's Volvo. The driver, presumably Tony, was long gone and had left only a watery puddle of vomit behind in the passenger seat. There was an all-points bulletin out to the staties to look for him: Anthony Bosco, six feet, two inches tall, approximately 220 pounds. Possibly on foot. Wanted for questioning regarding an assault, but they might as well pull him in for the two outstanding warrants in Androscoggin County while they were at it.

"I've seen his type before," Officer Laurant had said. "I bet he's long gone. We won't hear from him again until he gets picked up in another state." He had filled out Alma's statement as she told him what she remembered. She left out some points, such as her embarrassing flirting and the reveal about her embezzlement.

"What do I do now?" Alma asked the policeman as he drove her home in his cruiser. She raised a hand to her bandaged head and probed the lump until it started to throb again, like a rogue heartbeat above her right ear. The sun was setting, and the streetlights had misty halos around them that throbbed in time to her head.

"Nothing," he replied. "Just lock your doors, take some aspirin, and rest. I'll keep you updated on the case."

She looked out the window. The houses on her street were all the same model of split-level ranch, built in the '60s by a local developer who was tired of the same saltbox houses from when it was a company town. Alma's house alone was brick though, and it sat on a double lot, back from the street a bit. She blinked away a tear forming in the eye on her stitched-up side. That eye kept watering, making her vision tremble like a desert mirage.

"Seriously," she continued. "If he's still out there, he has my keys. He has my purse with my driver's license. He knows where I live."

Officer Laurant angled the cruiser into Alma's driveway and parked. "Why would he care where you live? He got drunk, cracked you over the head with a rock, stole your cash and car, and fled. He probably sobered up and thought he killed you, which is why we'll probably find him a couple states away."

He turned the engine off, and he reached into his breast pocket to pull out a business card. "If you need anything, don't hesitate to call. I'll keep you updated on the case." Alma nodded and climbed out, and she gave him a half wave as she watched him pull away.

The house was as still as a graveyard at midnight and as neat as she left it. The clock in the kitchen thundered each second off as Alma plucked her mother's half-empty bottle of expired codeine from the windowsill.

She kicked off her shoes and opened the cabinet above the sink. She pulled expired food out—a bottle of corn syrup, crusted over with crystals; a container of ancient cupcake sprinkles—until she found her mother's dusty bottle of crème de menthe. Alma poured herself a tumbler of the atomic green alcohol. She had promised herself half a tablet a lifetime ago when her knee was aching from the weather, but the agony in her head and belly dwarfed that pain. Fishing three codeine tablets out of the prescription bottle with trembling fingers, she chewed them up and washed down the bitter taste with the crème de menthe.

"I should eat something," she said aloud as she carried her glass and the dusty bottle into the living room. She raised her glass to the picture of her parents over the mantle—from their 25th wedding anniversary, two days before her dad dropped dead from a massive coronary. "Bottom's up." She drained the glass and poured another.

The sharp edge of her pain was dulled enough for her to think. "I know he's going to come here," she told her parents' picture. "He could rob me blind and I couldn't do a thing about it and he damn well knows it." She plopped onto the sofa, beads of sweat forming along her uneven hairline. She knew she should eat, but the thought made her stomach turn in protest.

"What should I do?" she whispered to the picture. "I don't know what to do." She stared at the picture, willing her father to turn from his position in half profile and answer her, willing her mother to climb out of the frame and run her hand through her hair in that comforting way she had. *Just to be touched again*, Alma thought.

Alma's eyelids grew heavy and the bottle of crème de menthe dropped out of her hand. She nestled into the sofa, mouth open, and snored softly.

Alma woke with a start. "He's here!" she hissed to her parents' picture. She crouched low to the shag carpeting and strained to hear. Every nerve in her was alight; her skin prickled with the fear that Tony would appear behind her suddenly. She stayed low, keeping her back to the wall, her eyes darting to every shadow in the room. She tripped over something, and her trembling fingers fumbled until she found the culprit: the bottle of crème de menthe. She grasped it by the neck and held it in front of her like a cudgel. She moved as quietly as possible from the living room into the hallway towards the back of the house.

The Day-Glo alarm clock in her room said that it was a little past three in the morning. She crept past her room and slipped into her parents' room at the back of the house.

Her father's footlocker from Korea sat in the corner. It was covered with a half-finished afghan that her mother had been crocheting before she died. She slid the blanket to the side and undid the clasps of the locker quietly.

Inside was her father's uniform, and the Silver Star and Purple Heart he had won when the PVA attacked his machine gun nest in the battle of Hoengseong. Underneath was the flag that had draped his coffin, a scattering of snapshots from the war, a Nambu pistol that he stole from the dead body of a North Korean soldier. His discharge papers. Underneath, nestled in the bottom and wrapped in black garbage bags was the money. Alma reached in and pulled out the pistol.

Her father, despite the protests of Alma's mother, had taught her how to fire a handgun. When he died, her mother had sold all of the guns to his brothers and nephews, but she had forgotten about the war memento. Her father never used the Nambu. He had only shown it to Alma once, so that she knew where it was and that she wasn't to play around with it, since there were still a couple of eight-millimeter bullets in the magazine.

Alma stood up, her head tilted to listen to the house. It was silent, and she padded down the hallway back towards the kitchen, the pistol a comforting weight in her hand. She sat the gun down long enough to shake a couple of codeine tablets into her palm.

She tossed them into her mouth, chewing them, wincing at the bitterness. The pounding in her head lessened. She ran her tongue over her teeth, sucking out the last grains of the opioid. She picked up the gun.

"I know you're here," she said, her voice loud in the still house. "Come on out, Tony." Her voice sounded brave in her head, despite the blurring shadows in the kitchen. The faint light from the streetlights gave everything the barest, hazy outline, causing her to squint. The eye on her stitched-up side watered.

A shadow in her periphery moved. She took a steadying breath, smooth and even like her father taught her, and she fired at the shadow on her exhale, pulling the trigger once, twice. Three times.

The Nambu—stored for over thirty years in a trunk after a young American sergeant thoroughly dunked it in the Seomgang River after stealing it—misfired. Alma pulled the trigger once. The bullet, without enough grains of functional gunpowder, stalled in the barrel of the pistol, waiting to be cleared. Alma pulled the trigger again, sending the second bullet into the first, blowing out the side of the barrel and throwing a piece of shrapnel through Alma's skull. In a split second, the razor-sharp piece of metal tore through her prefrontal cortex, the seat of decision-making, and Alma squeezed the trigger one last time, the hammer falling on an empty clip.

The shrapnel, slightly diverted, exited through her superior frontal gyrus, where laughter lives. Already falling, Alma saw herself from above in that endless, finite moment—the gun tumbling from her hand, her bad knee hitting the floor, the flickering streetlight and codeine making the shadows move and dance.

Alma laughed.

Gregory Jeffers' stories have appeared in a dozen or so literary journals including *Chantwood, Suisun Valley Review, Typehouse Literary Magazine, Corvus Review,* and *Bards and Sages Quarterly* and several anthologies including *Hard Boiled,* and *If This Goes On* (Parvus Press). His stories took first place honors in the 2019 Writer's Digest Short Short Fiction Contest and in the Sixfold Summer 2019 Fiction Competition. Other stories were short listed for the Himes Prize in 2020 and Fish Publishing's 20/21 Short Story Contest. Montreal is the closest metropolitan area to Mr. Jeffers' home in the Adirondack Mountains and his favorite city in the Americas. His Quebecois grandfather immigrated to New York State in the 1920s.

FROSTBITE

Instincts convinced me my first criminal case would be a piece of cake. It had better be. It was high profile and would make or break the rest of my legal career. It was pretty clearly a case of self-defense. She'd been denied bail the first go round, but my boss got us a second shot at it, citing the incompetence of her first—and court-appointed—lawyer.

Turned out, my only obstacle would be the client.

I bounced my shiny saddle leather briefcase against lampposts and snow-capped trash cans along Boulevard Gouin O, trying to break it in a bit. The one-legged news boy at the intersection of Rue Tanguay was shouting about Hitler declaring himself Fuhrer as I strode past.

Five minutes later, on my way to an interrogation room, the slap of my boots echoed off the tile walls of Montreal's oldest prison.

The sight of her with a prison haircut set me on my heels, what with most of her scalp newly exposed. Only one ear, badly mutilated. The other missing altogether. Frostbite had ravaged both two years earlier. Common knowledge in many circles but being face to face made me wonder how beautiful she must have been before that tragic evening on the train. Because here in the Bordeaux Prison, even disfigured, she was still a stunner.

I'd seen pictures of her, some in the Gazette and some in the files recently sent over by the chief defender's office. But in those photos, she either still had ears, or had long hair covering the mutilation. Still, none of the pictures had prepared me for the doozy she was in person.

"I'm not going to answer any of your questions if you keep staring at me like that." She shifted in the straight-back chair, not out of uneasiness I was certain.

I sat at the pale oak table across from her and pulled a legal pad out of my briefcase. "I'm sorry, Miss Stone. I don't mean to stare." She thought I was gaping at her deformity, but in all honesty, I was enraptured by her beauty. I turned my focus to the pad.

"It's not like I'm one of those legless guys in The Red Light District, pulling himself along the sidewalk with a couple of fisted bricks."

I stammered something both unintelligible and completely forgettable.

She leaned forward in the chair. "How many murder trials have you handled?"

I looked up. "This is my first."

"How old are you, if you don't mind me asking?"

I tugged the Windsor at the top of my tie. "Thirty."

"Never. Twenty-six maybe."

Tough customer. Figured, considering what she'd been through. But she was right. She was ten years my senior.

She pulled a box of matches from her prison uniform pocket, pried one out with a fingernail and struck it, the tip sputtering before flaming yellow. She lifted it to the cigarette resting between her lips, inhaled deeply and shook the match out casually, the grey smoke wafting before being obliterated by the white flume of her exhale. She fell silent, looking at me through the shroud.

I didn't need to ask about her early history. It had been in all the papers. High fashion model—one of the most prominent—in the late '20s. A rising star. Destined for cinema.

The incident happened my senior year of university.

Suzanne Stone and her handlers had boarded the streamliner,

the *Zephyr Bullet,* in Philadelphia. They'd been doing a shoot for some fur company, headed for the Big Apple for a week-long job modeling lingerie. *Modeling lingerie.* Tabloids liked to play that bit up.

The streamliner took a curve too fast, the rails were icy as a cheap cocktail. To boot, the engineer was joed from too many turnarounds. Half a dozen cars left the tracks, including hers, and slid down the embankment, crashing into trees before plunging onto the shore of the Schuylkill.

Two of her party—an agent and Suzanne's hair gal—died. Suzanne lay pinned between a seat back and the crushed roof of the car. It took almost three hours to cut her out. By then the temperature had dropped well below zero.

She'd have lost her nose and perhaps her lips as well if she'd not managed to withdraw her face into the collar of her mink coat.

Though I knew most of this, procedure dictated I go through it with her.

She acted accommodating enough. But then it's not like she had anything else to do. I was happy to have the use of the interrogation room to prepare for the bail hearing. No small comfort, not having to sit for hours on end in her cell.

Finally, she took the last long inhale of her cigarette and stabbed the butt into the jade-colored glass ashtray on the table between us. "What'd you say your name was? Romero? First or last?"

"Beauregard Romero."

She tutted the last trace of smoke from her mouth. "Beau Romero? Get serious."

"Born in New Orleans. My Dad was from Montreal, so I have dual citizenship. Mom thought I'd get a better education at McGill."

"Don't hold back," she said quietly. She moved her stare to the blank wall. "Yeah, well, I don't fancy Beau much, it's a little light, so I'll stick with Romero." She finally stopped grinding the remains of her cigarette and swept the short red bangs off her forehead with a gesture so grand I felt sure it was a remnant of her former life. She stared straight into my eyes.

"How much does a freshman lawyer like you know about the fashion world, Romero? You have one of those calendars with the pin-up girls in your kitchen?" She did not give me time to answer. "If you're one of the lucky girls, that's where it starts. Pin-up shots. That's the bottom of the fashion world. But most girls aren't even that lucky."

She picked the pack of Chesterfields from the table and tapped one out. She placed it in her mouth as if it were a cherry and looked at me for a very long moment.

"Not much of a ladies' man, are you?" Another couple seconds jerked by. "You going to light this snipe or not?" Looked like a wry smile, but it's not always easy to read an expression when a woman's got something in her mouth.

I tilted in my chair and snatched the Zippo from the pocket of my suit jacket, flipping it open halfway to the cigarette. The flint wheel let out a tiny croak as I spun it with my thumb, and the flame lent her cheek a tangerine hue. She held my eyes as she took the first draw.

During our time together, she'd often light up a cigarette, and in those interludes would not speak. She seemed to enjoy the intense comfort it gave her to get away, deeply inhaling, often exhaling through her nose. I was so distracted by her physical appearance I couldn't concentrate during those silent spells. I would leaf through files and occasionally glimpsed the distinct ways she had of holding a cigarette. The first one was thumb on the bottom, two fingers on top, a grip usually reserved for cigars.

Now, I watched her from the corner of my eye, pretending to be rummaging through my briefcase.

It seemed to take forever for her to finish that second cig and start talking again.

"I was one of the lucky ones. A pin-up. Started in short shorts and a polka-dotted blouse knotted just below the sternum. Sometimes a bathing suit. You've seen those shots, right?"

My face burned. Sure, I'd seen them. Not a sin. I couldn't figure out why it should embarrass me. Seemed as though the heat was coming from her.

Then, as if she read my mind, she said, "No big deal. Those calendars are all over the place. After that I started working the advertising circles. Better work. But the crumbs were even worse than the pin-up producers. Big shots. Bums who thought you were desperate to have their meat hooks on you. Pickled after lunch and out of control until they stumbled out of the photo shoot at five-thirty to return to their wives in the suburbs." She rubbed one cheek with her fingertips. "You sure you need to know all of this?"

"The more I know, the better the job I can do."

"Maybe. But I haven't seen you set that pencil onto the pad the whole time we've been here."

I drew a doodle, then stopped, realizing how stupid a gesture it was.

She tutted again.

***

The second way she often gripped a cig was between the first two fingers, with the pad of the thumb resting on the nails of the curled tips of the ring finger and the pinky, a grip I would later learn was called Gentry.

She finished and looked at me with a furrowed brow.

"Romero, you ever been cold? I'm not talking about shivering. I'm not talking about numbness or cold bones or a chill you can't shake. What I'm talking about occurs an hour or two after the type of cold that drives you nuts. I'm talking about having a gasoline-fueled fire on both sides of your head. A fire you can't reach because your head is trapped somewhere you'll never be able to reach with your hands. All you can do is hope it hits your brain soon and ends the agony."

I felt my face skew into an expression of discomforted concern and compassion.

"Don't get all sappy on me." She crossed her legs. "Just saying it was damn uncomfortable. And I've never been able to shake it since. Even after they took the one ear off, the fire still raged. And what's left of the other one burned just as hot."

"Do they still . . . burn?"

"Nah. Now I'm hot all over."

***

I had never seen anyone hold a cigarette the way she did on our first meeting the second week. Thumb on the bottom and only the middle finger on top. She pointed her index finger at her nose in a relaxed arc when she inhaled, the ring and pinky fisted. The whole posture had a toughness to it. A dare and a challenge to engage, it seemed, although I had no idea exactly what she was challenging me to engage in.

I adopted this method of smoking briefly in the privacy of my boarding room, often in front of the mirror during the infancy of my adulation. I didn't smoke that way in her presence. At least not then. But I did flaunt it at the local bars after work. It seemed to improve my stature among the other young associates at the office.

But that day—the Monday of the second week—we reached the part of her story I knew the least about. Her denouement. The fall took a couple of years, but the rags had summarized the inglorious descent into the few juicy bits they used to sell papers. Her downward spiral into accessory modeling: purses, shoes, wrist and finger candy. Then personal escorting; and finally, high class prostitution. Even the office files had little info on this time in her life.

"Listen, Lucky." By then she'd taken to calling me Lucky as often as Romero. "I honestly had little interest in sporting jewelry for Spiegel or shoes for Macy's. The catalogues pay tin and the hours are long and tedious. But worst of all, no glamour, you know what I mean? No juice.

"No one wanted me for head shots anymore, even though my hair could cover . . . this." She lifted both hands, the fingertips touching where her ear lobes had been. "I tried going back to the full body shot, but even the big lines weren't interested. Everyone in the industry and most glamour magazine customers knew the score. I was worse than washed up. Worse than damaged goods. I was mutilated."

"That's a bit of a stretch, isn't it? You're still very attractive."

She threw me a hard stare. "Did you just cross some sort of professional boundary here?"

"I guess I did." I stroked my necktie. "Sorry."

"I don't care. But I can tell you that being told you're still attractive is more than a letdown after having men call you gorgeous."

She rotated the Chesterfield package a couple of times on the table.

"Then there was the escort work. It paid really well, although the jobs were spotty. And the butter and egg guys thought they owned you. At one dinner party, a louse brushed my hair with some fond pretense only to discover my ear was missing. The shock spread across and down the table like the smell of bad beef.

"There were even worse times. One Saturday, dancing cheek to cheek in some juke joint, the John dives in for a nibble. He shrieks and spills out the door."

***

Just before the bail hearing, we were into her year of high-end prostitution.

"The other girls were too pushy about their wares. What worked best with the crumbs was to gaze over the tops of their heads when they showed up in the parlor. Like I didn't give a shit. Because I didn't. But no way I was going cheap. Twice the going rate and they paid it. Then I discovered if I pulled my hair back on one or both sides to reveal my ... *uniqueness*, I could charge three times the cabbage. Weird, but joes would go limp as dynamited fish if they came unexpectedly upon a mutilated ear, but if they spotted a mutant, they were suddenly juiced.

"I latched onto a really rich guy—well you know the guy, that's why we're here—about four months ago. He got dizzy on me and insisted on buying all my time. He didn't use anywhere near all of it, but he didn't want anyone else to have it either. So, he paid my all-night rate every night. Rented me an apartment in a nice part of town."

I scratched the side of my head with my pencil. Sure, I knew of the guy. Racketeer by the name of Bruno Zelski. Babe Zelski in the social circles. Ran whiskey into the States.

"I'd been on his motor yacht twice before. But it had only been the two of us, and the crew, of course. But when he'd phoned before this trip he said it was going to be a party and I should be sure to be looking sexy when his driver picked me up. *Sexy.* That was his word. God, we had hit all-new lows on the vocabulary side of things. But I was so far beyond caring what people thought about me I played along. Besides, I was lonely if you can believe it, so I was looking forward to a party.

"The clambake turned out to be mostly men—his torpedoes and some others I didn't recognize—and some very hard-looking women. You know. Nazis. Professional lady wrestlers is what they looked like, but with hawk-like attractive faces. Attractive in a dangerous way. I'm sure some of the zoots were Nazis too. And Babe's connection at Seagram's, Harry Gromfield was there.

"After an hour of bumping gums and the third round of giggle juice, Babe led me below deck and introduced me to my new handler, although he called her my 'assistant'. She took me to Babe's cave—the forward stateroom. Alone inside, she explained that some wealthy business associates wanted to do some private blue filming. This wasn't new to me, but frankly I wasn't into the idea. I was ready to tell Babe the bank was closed and demand a launch back to shore. But she sensed this I think, because as I was looking at her with the most disdain I could muster, she handed me an envelope.

"Open it," she said.

"I did. It was twenty-five large, U.S., all in McKinley's.

"I stuck around and let them film some opiated stud doing me in a couple different positions. But things went circussy fast and I sensed there was not only kinky but dangerous intent aboard. I blew my wig. I threw such a fit about reporting him and his merry little band of perverts, that Babe told everyone to leave. They did, shouting drunken and cocaine-induced olés and adióses from the launch as it churned toward shore.

"Babe was sore and things got rough. I'd never been punched in the face as a model but had as a whore, so I knew how to shake it off. And I knew the vulnerable spot on a man and I wasn't afraid to plant a foot or knee there. I did that with him, twice. Once with the foot, once with the knee.

"On all fours, he pulled a .38 from the sideboard. I gave him a heel to the chin, then we wrestled for the bean shooter. It went off in his gut, and I crawled away across the floor to watch him bleed out. He called me a lot of rotten names, but nothing I hadn't heard before. He wasn't such a bad person. Just demented and sadistic. My standards had dropped pretty low by then."

"Self-defense," I said. "Pretty clear. He was going to shoot you."

"Good luck with the witnesses on that theory."

"You don't have any names of the people on board?"

"What do you think, Lucky? Think I have some names? Other than Gromfield? And no way he's admitting being there."

The bail hearing was the following Thursday. I felt pretty strong about the self-defense approach but knew it would take some doing during the actual trial to overcome the tarnish of the tabloids. But it was just the judge for the bail hearing and I did pretty well, all things considered. Bail was set at ten grand.

"Where in hell do you think that's coming from?" she asked that afternoon.

"You must have something left, you know from . . . "

"From what? The heydays? There's nothing. I'm beat."

One of the partners at the office knew a bond guy and I managed to come up with the money. The judge let her out on my reconnaissance.

I felt pretty large as we exited into the hall.

She shrugged her coat further up her shoulders. "Now what, Lucky? Buy me a house?"

"What?"

"Where to?"

It dawned on me I had no idea where she would go. I hadn't thought of it. "Maybe I can rent you a room somewhere." I shifted my briefcase to the other hand.

"Going to bring my meals over? And aren't you supposed to be keeping an eye on me? Make sure I don't jump bail?"

"Why would you do that?"

"So I don't end up with a slug between the eyes. I have the goods on Gromfield. And you can bet he's not happy I killed his most profitable bootlegger."

There was no chance of having her at Mrs. Barrington's boarding house, so after half a dozen phone calls, I rented a furnished flat over on St. Laurent and we moved in that afternoon.

On the first night, I bought a bottle of Five Star, thinking we might celebrate with a low ball. But one turned into three, and she towed me into the bedroom.

Twenty minutes later she took a breather, laying back into the pillow. "You've never done this before, have you?"

"Well of course. I've been with women before." How could she tell?

"That's not what I'm saying, Lucky. I'm saying you've never done *what we just did* before."

She was right. What she'd been doing was something I had never experienced. Five minutes later she was doing something I had never even imagined experiencing. And after that, something I'd never imagined as even remotely possible.

And she was right about being hot. I mean she was physically much warmer than a person ought to be. From that next morning on, she would be uncovered next to me when I awoke, regardless how cold it was in the room.

On that first morning, I rolled her gently toward me and started up again, but she pushed me off. "Lighten up, Lucky. I'm hungry." She let out what passed for a laugh, got out of bed graceful as a ballerina, and stood full on in front of me. In that moment, I knew I was a goner for her.

"This can work," she said, "but only if you promise not to fall in love with me."

"It may be too late."

She bent and placed two fingers on my lips. "Shh. Listen. You have to at least promise you won't fill me in if you fall in love. Deal?"

"What if I can't make that deal." What an idiot I was. I needed to shut up.

"Then no deal. Deal?"

"Deal."

***

133

The next two months were—and still are—a dream. Even now the details are sharp and clear, but they swim about in an ether more overwhelming than the actual memories.

We spent weekends at museums, matinees and cafes. Weekdays I'd check in at the office, maybe do a little research, then head out to "interview the client" and "prepare for trial" and we'd lie around on the couch reading André Gide or necking.

My salary was spent, what with the new apartment and all, and an extra mouth to feed, but I was enchanted with this new life. I blew the last of the week's wages on a hand-knit wool scarf for Suzanne for Christmas.

It was the only thing under the meager little plastic tree. Christmas morning, she opened it. Her eyes glossed over. She wrapped it around her neck, leaned into me and kissed me deeply, tugging at my hair like a child pulling on her parent's sleeve.

"I won't live without it."

As happy as she made me, I could never seem to jar her out of her essential melancholy. Perhaps I projected much of that onto her. Maybe she had simply lost interest in life. Because the few times she chose to respond to my optimism about the prospects of the trial, it was with comments like: "No worries, Lucky, they'll give me the chair, then you can move onto a real girlfriend", or "Don't think this is pro bono work you're doing here, kiddo. I'm leaving my entire estate to you." She'd say it with absolutely no affect, while peeling an orange or steeping tea.

Her hair had grown out a bit since the day two months earlier when we'd first met. It was no longer the flaming red of her youth when the style magazines all sported her as "This Year's Stunner." But, still, the red overwhelmed the silver and the overall effect was the berries.

New Year's Eve, I splurged and took her to dinner and dancing. Swell night, but cold. Nonetheless, we decided to walk home. She insisted we stop for a smoke at the center of the Jacques Cartier Bridge. As usual she enjoyed her cigarette in silence. I often wondered where she went in those moments.

She flicked the butt into the dark water thirty feet below, its ember trailing a small comet tail. "Perfect spot," she said, with a trace of a smile. She moved her stare to me. "On the canals in Ottawa you can skate all night and never return to where you started."

"Sounds nice."

She nodded to the black water below. "My Dad used to say if this river ever froze, you could skate all the way to the moon."

I felt a smile spread my cheeks. "What would you do there?"

"Fall in love, maybe."

I wanted so badly to confess I was already there but had not forgotten my end of the deal. "Perfect night." I pulled at the other side of her chin, gently forcing her to face me and moved a strand of hair off her cheek. "Perfect girl."

"Perfect sap. No need to get so far off the cob." She squeezed my cheek. "Come on, Wordsworth, it's getting cold. Let's get under some covers."

Her lovemaking that night seemed more about maintaining contact for every instant, as opposed to the famished sex of the previous two months. Not a moment crept by in which we were not caressing, or simply holding. I fell asleep thinking my life could end right then and there.

Perhaps I told her I loved her as I fell asleep. In some recollections of the evening I told her. In some, I told her more than once. In other recollections, I simply fell asleep.

I awoke around five, shocked by her absence, as if her body had been replaced with a bag of ice. I bolted out of bed, the knowledge of the situation slamming me in the forehead.

I pulled on my boots and snatched my gab off the rack, spilling into the hall. Minutes later I was sprinting down Boulevard Dorchester. Too late, I realized the temperature had fallen dangerously below zero and I had left my gloves and hat at the flat. My lungs were burning, but my hands, face, and head were so cold they were numb. Even at this pace, I was ten minutes from the bridge, but I was out of time and kept running, alternating jamming my hands into my jacket pockets and clamping them over my ears, or my nose and lips.

By the time I reached the center of the bridge, my entire head was in flames.

The scarf. It was knotted loosely over the rail. Hot tears stung my already blistered cheeks.

I untied it and wrapped it around my head and face.

A paper drifted out of the scarf and fell to my feet. I jammed it into my pocket and stared into the black water until convulsive shivering jolted me back to the moment.

***

Her body was never found. Everyone at the office thought she'd played me for a sap, even if they didn't say so. I'd let her jump bail, and I was liable to the bond broker. I lost my job and never practiced law another day since. But she didn't chisel me. It wasn't like there was another guy. Or even some loot at the end of it all. Just peace, I guess. And I can't fault her for that.

Unlike Suzanne, I kept both my ears. Like Suzanne, I now burn all the time. I long for a cool breeze, a chilly dip in the ocean, a lover who can lower my body temperature. A skate to the moon.

The note? The paper that drifted off the scarf that night? I read it every week or so.

Hey, Lucky. Slip on your skates and I'll see you on the moon.

P.S. I forgive you for breaking our deal. Please forgive me for keeping my end of it.

Meredith Craig's fiction has appeared in *Variety Pack* and in a forthcoming issue of *Rock Salt Journal*. Additionally, she writes about travel and culture for magazines including *Lonely Planet*, *Delta Sky*, *Times Union*, and *Vice*, among others, and has written and produced for television. She lives in Brooklyn with her husband and son.

LIVING THE *DolceVita*

Ginger Price's white-gloved hand twirled the diamond tennis bracelet around her wrist. "I'll take them all," she said to the shop assistant, who didn't speak English. With the other hand, Ginger pulled a Tiffany-blue Glock out of her Ferragamo tote and pointed it at the shopgirl, who understood perfectly now. She swiped the diamond necklaces, opal stone brooches, sapphire rings, and jewel-encrusted tiaras into a velvet bag. "Don't forget the Viva Diamond." Ginger motioned with the gun for her to bring the clearest red diamond ever excavated around to the other side of the counter, away from the cameras and the emergency bell. "*Grazie*," Ginger said, smiling through her mask. "I thought it'd be bigger, but you know what they say: with diamonds, size isn't everything."

Ginger hopped on the waiting Vespa and told the driver to step on it. "Get me to the ferry station. I've got a cruise to catch," she said. The driver took off like a rocket down the winding Positano streets, pressing his foot on the accelerator even as the tires screeched. The grape arbors were no match for the construction of the motorbike which cracked through them as easily as a curtain. "I'll give you a tip if you get me there in one piece," she said, as they blew past a church, barely missing tourists slouching across the street. Pedestrians screamed, pointing. "It's like they've never seen the Queen of England on a Vespa before!" Behind her, tire marks charred the street where they had taken a sharp left, plowing past an outdoor café, almost knocking over a basket of lemons, and coming to a full stop in front of the *DolceVita* cruise ship.

In the roads above, the sirens wound around the steep cliff. Ginger jumped off the bike and peeled the latex mask off, careful not to smudge her makeup. Then she tucked a pair of diamond earrings into the driver's shirt pocket, secured the rest of the jewels into her purse, and rushed to the jetty. The blue and green water lapped the dock as if there was all the time in the world. The police cruisers screamed in the distance, getting closer. She ripped off the top layer of her pencil skirt, revealing the short black sequin mini dress underneath. A tear in the seam would need to be sewn shut, but otherwise no worse for the wear. She fluffed her hair, dropped her gun in the water and strode up the dock.

"Right this way," the guard at the door said, before letting her through the employee entrance.

Inside, she reapplied Chanel Rouge Pirate onto her lips, and entered the black box theater from stage right, just as the curtain rose. The announcer's voice boomed: "Give a big round of applause for Ms. Ginger Price, the sparkling songbird of the cabaret."

"Thank you, what a lovely audience." Ginger blew kisses. "Compared to last night's funeral, you seem alive! No, really, you guys look great."

She couldn't feel when the ship pushed off into international waters, but Ginger felt a sigh of relief when she was on stage, a martini in hand, picturing the *polizia* shaking their fists on land. She had gotten away with it again, this time with the mother lode. Inside, among the velvet banquettes and dark bar, she could be anywhere. She'd performed in versions of this theater all over the world. Except for the porthole windows, she wouldn't know she was even on a ship.

"How many of you are rich and single?" The sparse crowd was the usual white-haired retirees who adored this cruise line for the buffet and top-notch medical staff. None of them were wealthy, but that didn't matter. The only thing worse than a poor old man was an elderly billionaire who felt entitled to buy anything he wanted. She preferred her audience docile. It was easier to get the sad sacks to fall in love with her.

"People always ask how I got into theater. It's a depressing story. My ex-husband married my ex-wife and I settled for a life of cabaret." *Ba-dum-ching.* That's when the music was supposed to start. She looked at Billy, her piano player. Instead of Billy, it was a handsome man of about forty, in a fitted tuxedo that looked made for Las Vegas. She raised her eyebrows, and he took that as his music cue. Thankfully, the stranger knew her songbook and played with an aggression that gave new life to her performance. Her schtick about looking for love and affirmation in all the wrong places worked better when she bantered with someone close in age. By the time she got to "Snuff Out the Light," she had the crowd eating out of her espadrille, and she was practically draped across this stranger's piano. The audience clapped like they were at closing night of *Dreamgirls.* Little did they realize this was Ginger Price's last show. Tomorrow morning, she'd deboard the cruise, meet a man about the jewels, and disappear into Europe as "Lea Rosen" with thirty-three million euros. Her cabaret days were over.

Ginger was sweating a bit and her blonde curls were drooping. She felt exhilarated. "Let's give a round of applause to the piano player filling in for Billy. If anyone knows his name, tell me!" The piano player smiled and winked. Then he started in on another song, the encore, without waiting for her to tell him which one.

A chill prickled the back of her neck, a performer's sixth sense. Then she understood. "Diamonds Are a Girl's Best Friend." The piano player met her gaze, and Ginger wondered if he meant to arrest her as soon as the curtain dropped. It took a lot to rattle her onstage, and this wouldn't do the trick. "Talk to me, Harry Winston!" she yelled as she sauntered through the crowd, kissing the occasional bald head.

It was there in the back, standing at the bar, she found a younger man, brown mop-top, corduroy blazer—he'd have to do. She waited until the spotlight found her. "Kiss me," she whispered into his ear. He looked startled, but then jumped in, bending her back like in an old movie. She held the microphone away and when he stood her back up, she belted out the last lyrics in her best Marilyn Monroe impression, and the crowd went wild. She dropped the microphone on the bar, grabbed the guy's hand, and pulled him towards the exit like it was all part of the act.

The piano player stopped mid-chord, but with all of the walkers and wheelchairs, he couldn't follow her out. Hand in hand, the couple ran past the bocce ball court, the pool of synchronized swimmers, the roulette table and singing croupier, and, finally, stormed through the salsa dancers shaking their replacement hips.

"Is this really happening?" the guy asked.

"It's your lucky day," Ginger said. "Now where's your room?"

***

What Ginger didn't expect was that he would have an Oceanview Suite with the highest space-to-guest ratio on the boat. "We're not going to find your wife in here somewhere, are we?" she asked with a wicked laugh.

"No," the guy stammered.

Ginger let her fingers linger on the teak furniture and marble bar. "What's your name anyway?" she asked, extending her hand.

"I'm Ben," the guy said. "Sorry, I'm a little nervous."

"Why don't you pour us some drinks?"

Ben opened the fridge, which contained only bottles of water and milk.

"We can do better than that, can't we? I'll call downstairs." She picked up the receiver on the wall phone. "How'd you find yourself on board the *DolceVita?*"

"A school auction. I'm an assistant music teacher in Pennsylvania." He looked like a teacher, with a wide, honest face and inquisitive brown eyes. "This was going to be my honeymoon," he said. His eyes flicked to the side table, where a bottle of champagne and an oversized stuffed bear held a flag that said "Congratulations."

"Oh, Champagne!" Ginger said, taking in the contents of the table and coming up with an idea. When room service picked up, she ordered a bucket of ice, a bottle of Aperol, and a sewing kit to be delivered to suite 48. "On the double!"

In front of the navy couch, instead of a television, was a sliding door that led to the balcony. The floor to ceiling glass revealed a dark sky scattered with stars and the black tar sea. No matter how many tours Ginger did, the view of the water never got old. It was an extraordinary feeling to be trapped on the ship under all this expansiveness. The undercover detective would be watching her room and her only hope was to hide out here and sneak off the ship when it docked in the morning.

"I gave her this," Ben said, joining Ginger at the window. He was holding a small velvet box.

"Why, Ben, we just met," she said. But she took the box and opened it. It was a sweet tiny thing (if she squinted). Surely a teacher could afford better than this? Then she remembered he was an *assistant* teacher.

"I loved her," he said. "She didn't think I was ambitious enough."

"You deserve better than her, and she deserves a bigger ring," Ginger said. And in a burst of inspiration, she wrenched the door open, letting in a gust of salt spray. She stepped into the sea air and flung the ring overboard. "It's time to move on," she yelled into the wind.

Ben's eyes widened and a strangled sound came from his throat. "My ring!"

"Forget about it. You need to forget her too. Isn't that why you came on the cruise?"

The wind massaged Ginger's hair and pushed her backward into Ben's toned arms.

"I don't bite," Ginger said. "Unless you want me to." There were seven hours until the ship docked. She could think of quite a few ways to pass the time.

***

Ginger woke up early the next morning in Ben's nautical suite, pinned back her curls, and reapplied her lipstick. By the time Ben rose, she had drunk two cappuccinos while waiting to reach Monte Carlo. This was where Ben would deboard and catch an overnight flight back to New York. With any luck, after breakfast, Ginger would never see him again.

"Sleep well?" Ginger said to Ben with a sly smile. "You won't have time for caffeine, but don't worry, it was cold anyway."

"Last night was . . . " Ben said with a sleepy smile, sipping from the cold cappuccino.

"Unforgettable," Ginger finished for him. "But just in case I have amnesia, I'd like something to remember you by. This bear perhaps?" She held up the stuffed bear waving the Italian "Congratulations" flag.

In response, he kissed her full on the mouth, tasting of mint and milk. She was touched that he had brushed his teeth for her. Before the kiss could go further, the cruise director's announcement interrupted them to welcome them ashore.

Ginger shouldered her purse and tucked the stuffed bear under her arm. They were going for breakfast at the most romantic café Ginger could think of. If there was anything Ginger could do, it was to make a man forget his troubles. Now if only she could forget about her own.

Ginger knew the detective wouldn't be able to monitor every exit, and she figured the "cattle" exit was her best bet. They could get lost among the crowd and slip through without being stopped. The dock was close, but it was impossible to rush, as the passengers needed time to descend the stairs, gripping the handrails like their lives depended on it. Ginger's upper lip beaded with sweat and she was trying not to panic. A man in a wheelchair ran out of steam. She grasped the handles and rolled him to the side.

"What's your rush?" a spunky lady with pink glasses scolded.

"I've got an urgent appointment with a frittata," Ginger said, wedging past the woman's walker.

They almost made it.

As luck would have it, Ginger saw the detective before he laid eyes on her. She had enough time to lean into Ben and whisper, "Café Florian," into his ear before giving him a long kiss. "I'm just going to freshen up in the little girl's room. Take my bear for me, doll. And order me breakfast." Ben nodded, pulling his suitcase, the bear dangling from his hand. He only looked back once.

"Excuse me, Ms. Price, I'll need a word." A hand with long fingers landed on her arm. Ginger smiled at the detective and the two beefy security guards behind him.

"I'm not in the mood to sing this morning," she said.

"We'll need you to come with us," the detective said, flicking his head towards the offices.

Ginger knew when to fold the cards, but she had one more trick up her sleeve, or rather, it would be at the café waiting for her.

The detective couldn't keep his hands off Ginger.

"Good grief, usually a guy buys me dinner first," she said, allowing herself to be gently pushed down the hallway, against the stream of elderly tourists stampeding towards the exit.

In the cramped security office, the detective closed the door. Ginger decided not to take a seat and stood in front of the metal desk. A porthole window revealed the bustle of Monte Carlo.

"I suspect you know what we are doing here," the man said. Italian accent. Behind the piano, he hadn't seemed so tall, or as broad-shouldered. He smelled clean shaven.

"Practicing our act?" Ginger asked.

"Will you empty your purse for me?" he asked.

"A woman's gotta have some secrets," she said, holding her purse close to her chest.

"Please," he said, leaning now against the desk.

"Well, since you asked nicely," she said, unzipping the calfskin purse and holding it out to him. "What's next? A cavity search?"

The detective rummaged through the bag, emptying onto the desk a leather wallet, lipstick, an employee card, a passport, and a sealed letter with Ginger's name on it.

The detective held up the envelope. "Any idea who this might be from?"

"A love letter?" Ginger said, only half joking.

"Do you mind if I see what it says?" The detective sliced the letter open with one finger. He scanned the page written on *DolceVita* stationary, shook his head and handed it to Ginger.

Ginger: Thank you for mending my heart. No matter how it shakes out, please know that Billy and I adore you. Love, Ben.

Billy? Her piano player was in cahoots with her lover who just walked off with a bear's belly full of diamonds. Tears sprung to Ginger's eyes as she realized what this meant. She'd be back onstage tonight.

"Rotten luck," the detective said.

The world was a cruel and senseless place, and no matter how she tried, there was no way off the *DolceVita*. Ginger sat up straighter and adjusted her hair. "On the bright side, I'm suddenly free for breakfast."

Tom McCulloch is from the Highlands of Scotland. He currently lives in Oxford with his family. He is the author of three novels: *The Stillman*, *A Private Haunting*, and *The Accidental Recluse*. Tom's short stories and poems have appeared in many magazines.

The Drop

I was once told I look like Robert Mitchum. I have been called Mitchum ever since. Even now, when only those of a certain vintage remember what he even looked like. Robert Mitchum was a bad ass. He's the only reason I still get asked to do these things. I look down at the black sports bag at my feet.

It's wet. It always rains here. It could have been doing it forever. Not that I've been here before, even though it's not that far away. Grey sky. Not a streak of white, never mind a flash of colour, just grey, grey of the oldest kind, mist rising up through the gorge to meet it. My clothes are soaked, hanging off me like there's hardly enough of me to hold them up. I am slowly dissolving.

Dan the Man.

That's why I'm here. He sat down beside me in the pub. Not a word. Waiting for me to acknowledge him.

The wooden bridge slats are dark, must have been treated with creosote—is that the stuff they use?—probably not, but coated with something a long time ago. My crisscross footprints stretch back the way I came, fading in the rain, half a print on one slat, half on another, not one full print being contained on one slat cause my feet are too big or the slat is too narrow.

"Take it to the bridge and wait for the pickup."

"Who am I waiting for?"

"You'll know."

"How will I know?"

"You'll know."

And like that my tracks are gone. There are now no clues as to how I got here. I walked to this point midway along the bridge, I know that, but no one else does. For all they know I may have been here forever. Or I could have been placed here, held by the head in the fingers of a giant hand, legs-a-twiddling, and set gently down. We all leave tracks. Tracks make it easier to understand things. Someone who leaves no trace makes people nervous. We all want to be tracked, deep down.

How long have I been here? Nobody has come and I don't expect anyone. I am on an idiot's errand, fixed as the pines on either side of the gorge. Like them, I endure. Mine too is a life lived under compulsion. I can sit in a pub, smoke a few with the paper, and drink until I'm done, answer the whim of a whisky or the need to shit. But there's no freedom in habit. I have as little choice in those matters as remaining on this fuckin' bridge. You don't want to piss off Dan the Man.

"What's inside?"

He looked at me. You could say there was a hint of a smile at the edge of his mouth but you'd be wrong.

I raise my face to avoid looking at the bag. Then I change my mind. The zipper and the little padlock gleam in the wet. I give it a quick little kick with my foot and glance around. I feel it again. A slight wobble. I felt it when I was carrying it here. A vague wobbling. Like something inside hasn't been secured and is starting to come loose. I wonder again what rolls about in a bag.

There are people emerging from the dark woods on the left side of the bridge. The east, that is; here in the great outdoors you say "east." These first people of the day in their Day-Glo waterproofs would also say "east." Mum and dad and two sprogs who undoubtedly go to Scouts or Guides, can identify animals from their shit, know what mushrooms kill you, and also say "east."

But the kids don't look too happy, heads bowed in their jackets, scuffing ahead of their parents. One of them jumps onto the safety bars and peers down into the gorge, the mum running over and pulling him back. Now they clock me. My stomach turns, wishing they weren't staring but I can't look away and here it comes, the prod, the old shame that strangers always spring.

She quickly ushers the kids past and there-they-go-a-skipping-by followed by her nervous glance and dad's thin grimace. The tracks. I saw her looking down and wondering. I'll shout after her, tell her how long I've been here, explain my lack of tracks and she'll go "aaah" and understand and we'll smile and drink coffee from their flask and exchange jokes and stories about kids, for I'll have a few of my own, one, three, no *five*, all at university but still in regular contact would you believe, home of a family Sunday for dinner and laughs and good 'ole-fashioned comfort.

They head back into the woods. The dad hangs back as the others disappear. He stops and looks back. He's going to walk slowly back along the bridge and pick up the black sports bag. But a child screeches and he's hurrying away. I remember now. There's a nature trail around here, painted signs on trees explaining the creatures that lurk in the forest but no one ever sees.

I knew today was a red-letter day, I knew it as soon as I woke up. I could have done the usual and lain in bed for hours, staring at the ceiling or clawing at the sheets till forced to masturbate, do a hundred push-ups or grab the postman's hand as he stuck the mail through. Instead, I was up like a randy jack-in-the-box because I *knew* something was happening. I was at the pub two hours earlier than usual because I *knew* that Dan the Man was going to come say hello.

"Just get there by midday and wait."

"For how long?"

"You got anything better to do?"

I hitched to the gorge. I don't know why anyone picks me up, yet they invariably do. They see something in me. Maybe Mitchum. Whatever it is, they realise a beat later they have made a terrible mistake. I am not a reassuring companion. But it's all so unexplainable in the claustrophobia of cars, and my babblings usually last to the next lay-by before I'm bundled out and maybe reversed over a few times to make sure, because why should someone who has opened his door be expected to listen to my madness? The indulgence of strangers. 'Tis a beautiful thing.

A presence.

I have a growing awareness of something I don't know is solid or spirit. I glance round and glance away. A man has appeared beside me—right *there*. How has he managed to sneak up on me? Maybe he was placed down by the same giant. I look up again and he looks down. So I look down to see that he's looking at the bag. He looks up and must have seen the tense of my shoulders because when I look up he doesn't look down again. Here's the fucker I've been waiting for.

"Morning," he says.

"_"

"Quiet here."

"_"

"I jog down here every Saturday. I've got these binoculars."

"_"

"I stop in the trees. In summer you get young couples heading for quiet spots. I watch them with my binoculars."

"Shame it's winter."

"Indeed it is my friend." And before he jogs away he tells me, "It's good to meet a man who understands."

I am filled with sudden empathy for this common or garden pervert. I want to run after him and raise the bag, shake it back and fore so he can see the wobble, the two of us crouching down to see what's inside. I have to let him into my secret because someone always has to bear witness, even this jogger with the shittiest trainers in the world, a dead giveaway to the claim he is a jogger to those in the know. There's a lope to his run, a lope that screams sex fiend, something too smooth and dirty, as if he's got an itchy arse; he's always got an itchy arse, I *know* this.

I find allies in the most unlikely of places. I lack judgement. It is why Dan the Man trusts me. Sometimes I am overwhelmed by such an intensity of goodwill towards my fellow humans that it becomes too much. I have a sudden, near uncontrollable urge to climb the barrier and fling myself off.

I wonder why the jogger talked to me, what safe reflection he saw. I can't trust my features, there's a certain quality that strangers read as familiarity. Crowded dancefloors or seething pubs, eyes lock on and over they bound to begin conversations. I'm simply a cipher for themselves. The jogger wasn't even talking to me, just talking out loud in the centre of the bridge. I was merely a lump of something unthreatening that happened to be there, fixed, like the wooden slats or the pines. It's the same in shops, the unhurried blankness of the assistant's gaze, a non-event in her day, like the blur of the pavement walking along in a daydream.

This is a popular suicide spot after all.

The gorge.

It would be like plummeting into an open mouth. I can't even see the bottom with the mist rising up.

I heard a story once. Some lunatic saying his mother flung herself off this bridge and lived, found three days later on a riverbank downstream, gibbering about fish with her clothes in tatters and clutching a pebble. Said he charted his life from that point, every thought and action being an emanation from or reaction to the image of his mother screaming about a pebble.

I see her beside me.

Maybe the jogger was watching with his binoculars as she clambered onto the rail. Maybe he thought shouting a warning would give her such a fright that she would have fallen. The last thing you want to do is fall when you're committing suicide. You want to jump. That's the whole fuckin' point. Only someone totally rational and in complete control contemplates jumping into a gorge.

Slap in the middle.

Exactly where I stood. Launching herself from anywhere else risked plummeting down through broom and gorse, bouncing and tumbling with an *ouch, ouch* like Wile E. Coyote, the whole experience unpleasant and deeply unsettling. Then again, her clothes were all tattered when she was pulled from the water by that bemused farmer. The bushes may well have broken her fall, bumping and thumping and slowing her so much she hit the water with a merry splash.

They make it a crime to kill yourself. Suicides aren't felons, those fuckers are free as a bird. It shamed me to be here. I see Dan the Man bow his head. Even a man like Dan knows truth when he sees it.

"I'll give you fifty now and a hundred when you get back."

"One fifty?"

"One fifty."

"Seems a little light."

"You think I'd only be paying you one fifty if there was two keys in that bag? Stop sweating it man."

I drop a penny to see how long it takes to hit the water. This will tell me how long it took her. It disappears into the void with a flicker of copper and I hear nothing. I need something bigger. A rock. A big, fuck-off pine branch. I might be able to hear that hit the water. But then what, what does four, six, or ten seconds actually mean? Does four seconds of falling equal instant death? It's just another guess. I would say anything over ten would mean game over, but who knows. One thing I have long learned in my cheerful swagger through this most dazed of existences is that there is always some weird variable coming trundling along the track.

"Are you alright?"

I nearly leap over the safety rail. Where do these people spring from, why must they always *creep* so?

"I mean, it's really wet and you don't have a jacket."

"_"

"We've got a blanket in the car if you want?"

"_"

"Are you cold?"

"Ten seconds plummeting equals instant death. That said, I have no proof for this conjecture."

She and the man beside her back away. I dare not speak. Look what happens, things blurt out and whether in fear or spontaneity, I do not like it. To go further, to explain my words would be to enter dubious territory of unknown destination but undeniable alarm for them and me.

She was very pretty. I saw fields of barley in her eyes. Him, I didn't like, the way he hovered behind her, behind her questions, glancing my way and looking away. He made a mess with his footprints on the slats as well, shuffling about like a jittery schoolboy. No doubt he was impatient to be gone to the forest with her. Maybe I should warn them about the man with the binoculars.

She was right about the jacket though. I don't know where that went. I had it when I was wandering along the road after the car dropped me. I had it when I took the shortcut across the field when the cow looked at me the wrong way—the way that people should—and made me feel uneasy. It was in the barn with the leaky roof. I put it over my head when I was eating that scotch egg. Steeling myself for the drop with a damp scotch egg. What would Mitchum make of that?

There are more sounds in the trees now.

Little creatures becoming a bit bolder. If I remain here long enough, I may even gain the trust of the squirrels. I can feel them running up my legs and nestling against my neck. I like the squirrels.

A raindrop quivers on the end of my nose. If I were finely balanced it would send me toppling over the barrier. I move and it is gone, falling through grey. I turn and the forest turns with me. The creatures hear but no hush falls. I have been here long enough to see what they would have seen, to see what went down, to see the woman they too saw, the bridge just as slippy, her tracks on the wood melting away as she sat on the safety barrier, staring into the unseen water.

I climb up because I have to know.

I sit there with my legs dangling over empty space. I feel the thin smirr of the rising mist on my face. I settle the bag on my lap. Still that vague wobbling of whatever is locked inside. A sudden gust of wind has me grabbing tighter to the barrier. I look behind me at the last two footprints where I was standing on the bridge, the scuffs in the wet where the bag had sat.

"The easiest money you'll make all year."

"It would appear so."

"It would indeed. You'll be back in no time and a fine evening ahead."

"I do like a fine evening."

"Nothing better than a fine evening with friends."

I see someone on the far side of the bridge. To the right, to the *west*. He's out of place, a suit for fuck's sake.

He looks alarmed and no wonder, seeing me there. I don't know if I need to worry, but he hasn't got the luxury of uncertainty. He looks like a man who has never considered uncertainty and all its beautiful enigmas. I feel a bit sorry for him. Has the poor fellow never felt like an enigma?

"I like being an enigma!"

This makes him run, the bridge bouncing a bit. He's holding out an arm even though he's too far away from me. There's a certain zombie quality that makes me laugh, more a titter. He doesn't look like a man who appreciates a good titter. He's leaving the tracks that I once left. I see them fading behind him as they faded behind me. I see him peering into the mist. He's trying to convince himself of what he just saw. I wonder what he would say to Dan the Man. I wonder what she thought as she fell. I wonder what would be grasped in my hand when they roll me over.

Journalist and author Anne Louise Bannon has been writing stories most of her life. A former television critic, she and her husband, Michael Holland, are the creators of wine education blog OddBallGrape. com. Anne is also the author of the *Freddie and Kathy* mystery series, set in the 1920s, the Old Los Angeles series, featuring winemaker and physician Maddie Wilcox and set in the 1870s, and the *Operation Quickline* series of spy novels, from which the below story has been spun off.

NICK FLAHERTY AND THE BODY IN THE LAB

With Pasadena cops swarming the lab at the small university, it was not a good time for my wife to be calling, but then she couldn't have known that. The uniformed officer about to question me looked up.

"If you want to take that, go ahead," he said. He was short and stocky with dark hair and eyes and a nameplate that read Karabedian.

Of course he wanted me to take the call. Once my phone was unlocked, he'd be able to search it. If it remained locked, he'd need a search warrant. I was about to decline, but then Karabedian got called over to just outside the lab. He hurried off with a light cough. Well, our face masks weren't going to cover up the acrid stench in the room.

"Hey, sweetheart," I said, after swiping the call on. "Can't really talk. I think I'm about to get arrested."

"Oh." Breanna sighed. "Do I need to call our lawyer?"

"It should be fine."

"Okay. I'll hold dinner."

"Thanks. I'll try to call before I leave Pasadena."

"Good luck, my darling. I'll see you when I see you."

"Can't wait, love."

I swiped off the line and sighed to myself. If Breanna didn't seem terribly concerned about my situation it was only because it was not the first time something weird like this had happened. If anything, it was the five-hundred-bazillionth time it had happened. It's kind of how my life goes. I mean, getting arrested is pretty unusual, but it's only one of many, many options on the what-the-fuck-now spectrum. I am also blessed that Breanna is exceptionally chill about it all and always has been.

I made sure my phone was locked and slid it back into my jeans pocket. Karabedian returned, pen and notepad in hand.

"All right," he growled at me, his eyes watering. "Your full name?"

I blinked my eyes. "Dr. Nicholas W. H. Flaherty, PhD."

"Doctor?" The cop looked at me.

"Yes." Okay, I was wearing my usual beat-up jeans, long-sleeved T-shirt, Giants baseball cap, and gray hoodie.

Karabedian glanced over at where the corpse was still laying. It was one ugly mess thanks to some corrosive agent, that I was pretty sure was sodium hydroxide. The light reflected off Dr. Douglas Kwan's university ID badge, which was still clipped to the remains of a blue shirt.

"Age?"

"Forty-eight."

Karabedian gave me another funny look, but I couldn't help that. Dad always says that my disreputable appearance makes me look more suspicious. He may have a point. I'm that skanky-looking white dude with the long, gray hair, scruffy beard, glasses, beat-up backpack, and skateboard you saw on the bus last week. But, hey, I don't get bothered that way and I don't get mistaken for my dad, which has been happening again since he finally let his hair go gray. Dad and I look a lot alike, or would if I shaved and cut my hair.

"You got an address?" Karabedian demanded.

"Yes." I probably should have just given it to him, but Dad and Mom always say not to tell anyone one thing more than they ask.

Karabedian shook his head. "What is it?"

I gave it to him.

"So, what are you doing here?" Karabedian asked.

"Meeting with Dr. Kwan." I sighed again and blinked at the stench and my own emotions.

"And . . . ?"

"Doug and I are friends and colleagues."

Karabedian gaped. "You're a chemist?"

"Biochemist, but yeah."

Which he might have figured out had he seen the T-shirt I was wearing. It was decorated with the words Heavy Metals in Goth typeface, along with the symbols for lead, iron, and zinc. My son had gotten it for me the previous Christmas. Then again, the odds were against Karabedian getting the joke even if he'd seen the shirt, which he couldn't because my hoodie was zipped up against the winter chill.

Shaking his head, Karabedian wandered over to the lead detective, a woman in her mid-forties with dark hair and eyes, named Lorena Salcido.

Salcido had let Adina Stenzler, the department secretary, leave about a half hour before. The detective wasn't about to let me go. Well, I had found the body and Adina had caught me going through Doug Kwan's files before calling the police. Heaven only knew what she'd told Detective Salcido, but I had the feeling it wasn't anything good.

Adina had decided years ago that I was some kind of fraud. She just couldn't get it through her head that someone who looked like me actually had a post-doc degree, was published in multiple well-respected journals, and owned a venture capital company. I was also Doug's friend, which didn't help.

Salcido walked up, while shaking her head, with two uniform cops behind her.

"Okay, Flaherty," she said. "We're taking you in."

"On what charges?" I asked.

"We'll start with burglary, and we'll see how the questioning goes."

"Hands on the wall, feet back and spread 'em," growled one of the uniforms.

"I'm carrying," I said, as I did as I was told. "Back waist holster, automatic, and I have a concealed carry permit for it."

It was the last thing I would say for a while. The cops read me my rights, then took me away. As we left the building for the cop car, my eyes swept the street and sidewalk. There was a telltale flash of movement across the street, then the cops pushed me into the back of the black and white.

I acted cool, but I sure wasn't feeling it. Having been bound and gagged a few times in my life, I hate wearing masks as it is, and even two years of a pandemic haven't made that any easier. Being masked and cuffed was one stop short of terrifying, not to mention that someone was probably tailing the cop car, and I'd just gone to meet my friend and found a stiff instead. I was not in a good place at that moment.

At the station, the officers took me straight to the questioning room. I was glad that they hadn't booked me. Funny things happen when they run my prints, and I wanted to keep my cover intact for as long as possible. I mean, I am a biochemist and I do have a post-doc degree, am published in several well-respected journals, and own a venture capital company. It's just not all that I am.

My left hand was cuffed to the table, then I was left alone, which was fine with me. I slid my mask under my nose, then shut my eyes. I was going to miss Doug Kwan. We'd been friends for almost ten years. He came over for dinner regularly. He'd come with Breanna and me to Dodger games, and both being devout Dodger fans, the two of them would gang up on me over my love of the San Francisco Giants. My two kids, Lena J and Malachi, called him Uncle Doug. He introduced Lena J to the joys of old movies, and almost beat my mom at reciting dialogue from *A Damsel in Distress*, *The Thin Man*, *Miracle on 34th Street*, and *Young Frankenstein*. Doug and I would fly to Vegas for industrial chem conferences and spend all our time gambling instead of attending seminars and meetings.

Salcido came into the room with a micro recorder in hand. "Okay, Flaherty . . . "

"You can call me Nick, and your boss can watch, but no recording," I said, pulling my mask back up.

"You can't tell me—"

"Code twenty-one, fourteen alpha, so, yeah, I can." I sighed. So much for keeping my cover.

Salcido stopped, looked at me in wonder, then swallowed. "Uh. Okay."

She left and I slid a small piece of spring steel from my belt and went to work on the cuff. A couple minutes later, I slid the cuff partway open, and Salcido returned.

"No recording?" I asked, glancing at the one-way glass.

"I had to tell the captain, but you're good." Salcido slipped into a chair across the table from me. "So tell me what's going on here."

I hesitated. "I'm an undercover federal agent."

I've been unofficially undercover, thanks to my parents being in that racket, since I was a kid. I didn't go official until 2009, when some schmuck in the CIA finally noticed my explosives certification and started sniffing around. Mom and Dad were not excited when I asked if I could join their organization, which is a shadow program under the auspices of the FBI, but they went along with it because it would keep the CIA from trying to suck me in. Those guys are real assholes.

"Undercover is what the code means." Salcido's eyebrows rose. "Somebody said that Doug Kwan was from North Korea. Is that why you're involved?"

"He was one of ours." I shrugged. "I was his handler. That's how we met."

"Really." Salcido's eyes bore into me. "So that's why you iced him."

"I didn't." I rolled my eyes. "We were meeting for lunch. When I got to the lab, there were the same signs of the struggle that you saw. I found the stiff between the lab tables, did a cursory examination, and saw the two bullet holes in his chest. I'm guessing the rest was set up to look like an accident to give the killer time to get away."

"An accident." Salcido glared. "Why don't you tell me how that was supposed to work."

I shuddered. "Well, the face and chest were burned so badly, and it smelled like sodium hydroxide."

Salcido wrinkled her nose. "What's sodium hydroxide?"

"Lye. It's a highly corrosive alkaline. It interacts with fatty acids and precipitates out glycerin, which is harmless."

"Huh?"

"It turns you into soap." I couldn't help grinning a little as Salcido covered up a gag. "My guess is that the killer splashed the NaOH on the stiff to make it look initially like he'd died as a result of an accident. Doug was using it in high concentrations as part of some of his experiments. You guys aren't going to be looking as carefully at an accident as you would a murder."

"I guess it's a good thing that his name badge was left intact," Salcido said finally, then looked at me. "Or is that how you planned it?"

She clearly was not convinced that I wasn't the killer. I thought fast. There was a side of the situation that I could not tell her, but that also gave me my out.

I sighed. "One of Doug's projects was top secret. It was for our side, but it's entirely likely that someone on the North Korean side had figured it out and came after him. I might have a few leads. The problem is, I can't share them with you because it's national security."

Salcido glared at me. "The problem is you don't have any special ID on you."

"Hello? Deep undercover?" I rolled my eyes. "I don't usually carry ID on me unless I know I'm working, and even then, I often don't. Besides, Doug and I were friends as well as colleagues, and as far as I knew today, we were just meeting for lunch."

"Oh, come on. We know you killed him. We have a witness who says you two were always arguing."

I snorted. "Did she say about what?"

Salcido folded her arms over her chest. "Why don't you tell me."

"We were arguing about baseball." I pointed to my baseball cap. "Doug is a Dodgers fan, which means he hates the Giants. I happen to love the Giants and hate the Dodgers. So of course, we gave each other shit about it. Which, obviously, Adina Stenzler did not get."

Salcido looked a little nonplussed for a moment.

I jumped on it. "How would I have known the right code for you if I weren't deep undercover? If you want, you can fingerprint me and see what comes up. I'll wait."

"Explain why you were going through his files." Salcido leaned toward me, her eyes blazing.

"I had to find whatever classified stuff he was working on and get rid of it before you showed. Only Adina showed up first and called you guys."

She grinned as if she'd caught me. "But you didn't have any files on you."

"Because his classified files were gone, and, yeah, that should worry you." I sat back. "It does me."

Breanna would say that everything worries me, and she does have a point.

Salcido frowned. "So, if I'm understanding you, you're saying that some foreign spy killed your friend, set it up as an accident, then stole his files."

"Sounds like it." Okay, I wasn't telling her everything. I couldn't. And, really, there was something else bugging me about the whole episode, but until I could figure it out, the last thing I could do was tell Salcido.

Salcido thought for a moment, then made one more attempt to catch me. "The crime scene techs said they found a skateboard in the lab. Kwan's colleagues at the school said that he doesn't skateboard."

"Yeah, but I do. Did you recover it?"

Salcido nodded and looked at me funny.

I shrugged. "It embarrasses the hell out of my kids, but it's how I like getting around."

"What?"

"I'm trying to save the planet and stay in shape. Anyway, are we done here? My wife is holding dinner and I've got a foreign spy to catch."

"But . . . " Salcido looked confused. Her phone buzzed with a text. She looked at it, then glared at me. "Looks like your lucky day. My captain says you're for real. You're free to go. I'll get the keys for the cuffs."

"Don't bother." I shook the cuff off my wrist and stood.

She gaped. "How did you get out of that?"

"You can always hide something." I shrugged. "Look, I get that you don't want your clearance numbers to go down. We'll figure something out."

Salcido sat back. Mom would have called her flabbergasted.

"Oh, and my skateboard?" I bent and picked up my backpack.

Still looking shell-shocked, Salcido got up and led me out of the questioning room. My skateboard was leaning against her desk. It doesn't look like much, but it's actually pretty righteous. I picked the board up, got my automatic back, and headed out, tucking my mask in my back pocket.

I skated past Memorial Park toward the Gold Line station when I saw that telltale sign of movement again. I was being tailed, and as I tried to figure out who was doing the tailing, it finally hit me what was wrong with the stiff. I ran onto the grass, popped the board up and waited for a moment. It was already dark and the only people visible were a couple homeless guys. I caught the flash of movement near the band shell and shook my head.

"Okay, Kwan," I called. "Get your fucking ass out here."

Doug slid out of the shadows into the dim light. He was relatively lean with a remarkably normal build. I couldn't help blinking back tears of relief as I grabbed my mask and put it on. He had his on, and I yanked him into a solid hug.

"You caught me," he said, his eyes twinkling.

"You fuck." I hit his arm. "You scared the shit out of me."

"Yeah, but you got it." Doug laughed. "How did you figure it out?"

"*The Thin Man*." I punched his arm again. "The body was carefully destroyed, but the name badge was carefully left intact."

"It was self-defense." Doug sighed. "Apparently, the folks in Pyongyang figured out that I was sending them crap and sent Lew Song after me."

"So that's who got the NaOH all over him." I winced. Lew Song was one nasty bastard. I didn't like that he was dead, but I have to admit I wasn't too upset that I no longer had to think about him. Still, I glared at Doug. "You couldn't have fucking called me?"

Doug's face scrunched in pain. "I'm pretty sure Song was

tracking me through my phone, so I had to kill it. Sorry about that." He playfully tagged my bicep.

"I'll bet." I nodded at the rail station. "Why don't you come over for dinner? We'll figure out what to do next."

Doug shrugged. "Thanks. Unless Breanna will get pissed off at a surprise guest."

"Since when?" I stopped. "I'd better call her anyway. You got our files, right?"

Doug held up a briefcase. "Right here."

I took the case. "Thanks."

"What are we going to do about Song, though?" Doug shuddered. "Once they get him ID'd, Pyongyang'll come looking for me."

"Shit. You're right." I shrugged. "We'll have to get you a new identity, anyway. What a mess. Let me call Breanna first."

As we waited for the train, I dialed my wife. She must have been more worried than she'd let on earlier because she picked up almost immediately.

"Do you need the lawyer?" she asked.

"Nah. I told you it would be fine."

"Glad to hear it. Oh. Mal is staying at my mama's for the duration, and Lena J is still at your parents' place."

Mal and Lena J are teens, and except for the first year of the pandemic when they couldn't, they mostly stay with their grandparents. It's why they still like us.

"Sounds good. You okay with Doug Kwan coming for dinner? It's been a day for both of us."

"I can't wait to hear. Call me when you get on the Expo line. I'll pick you guys up at Culver City."

"Thanks."

I swiped off the phone and emptied Doug's briefcase into my backpack, then gave the briefcase to a homeless person. Doug and I shook our heads. It's how my life goes.

W.C. Gordon is a cop, veteran, and author of the novel *The Detective Next Door*. His writing is influenced by his personal experiences in the military and in law enforcement, which he then mixes with bourbon and dark humor. He lives at his home in South Florida with his wife, son, and dog.

LIVE, LIKE A SUICIDE

Perry is in my office and we're deep in conversation about the latest innovations in law enforcement technology.

"Is it me, or have Keren's tits gotten bigger?" asks Perry.

Ok, so not exactly stimulating conversation. Well, maybe for Perry it is.

"I don't know. I don't look at them. We work together."

"Hey, you lie to girls. You don't lie to your friends. Now answer me: bigger, right?"

"Sure," I say, "much bigger," hoping this appeases him.

"I knew it! The divorce has done her good. Tightened up in a few spots. More pep in her step." Perry looks moderately aroused. I look moderately disgusted. "You've seen her tits. They're amazing right?"

"I have not seen them, thank you."

"Don't lie."

"I'm not lying. A buddy dated her in college. Not me."

"Does he have pictures?"

"Bro, that was probably the late '90s. Getting naked pics of a girl wasn't like it is today. They would've been Polaroids and they'd probably be all faded out by now anyway. Why am I explaining this? This conversation is over."

"Ok, just one more thing," Perry says with a smile. "Are they built for speed or built for comfort?"

And for the first time in a long time, probably ever, I am happy to see the boss walk into my office.

"I hope that I'm not interrupting anything important," my sergeant states authoritatively as he enters my office.

"Well, actually, Sarge . . . " Perry starts to say before I wave a hand in his direction.

"Nothing at all, Sarge. What can I do for you?" I ask, willing to take on any task to avoid continuing this ridiculous conversation. My sergeant just stands there for a moment, looking around. He has a habit of doing this. I feel like he's always assessing his surroundings. Not in an investigative way, though. He was never a detective before getting promoted to sergeant and taking over the bureau. He's assessing in more of a survivalist way. He's a former Marine and a born leader. Unfortunately, you don't so much as need a leader in the detective bureau as you do a manager who knows what he's doing. Typical police administration move to put personnel where they don't belong. A few of the detectives take advantage of this fact.

"I got a dead body for you. From what I heard on the phone, it's nothing suspicious. Probably a suicide." The sergeant and I give each other a nod and he exits my office with a near-perfect about-face that he subconsciously executes.

"Good guy. Bad detective sergeant," I say to Perry.

"Why's that?"

"You never say 'probably a suicide.' Treat them all as a homicide until you've proven otherwise. Tell that to a new guy and they go in there expecting a suicide and the whole investigation is shot to hell from the beginning."

"Yeah, well . . . it's probably a suicide," Perry says as he shrugs his shoulders.

With an exasperated breath, I ask Perry, "Wanna come?"

"God no! I hate dead bodies."

***

I print out the call notes, which give me very little information: address, name of decedent, time pronounced, and what unit is on the call. I happen to know the officer on scene so I give him a ring before I arrive. I make a quick stop before getting there and send the following text upon arrival: *here*.

Paul gets into the passenger side and I hand him his coffee. He tells me about his new Harley and picks my brain about parts. I tell him about my boat problems and he reminds me that he told me to never get a boat in the first place. After a few minutes of catching up, he gives me a quick lowdown of the scene. "Welfare check on male not responding to calls or texts and who didn't show up to work today. House was locked up when we got here. The neighbor had a spare key and we went inside. Found him hanging in the bathroom."

"Cut him down?" I ask.

"Hell no! That's your job."

"Think the neighbor had any involvement."

"Nope. Dead guy has a security camera on the front door. We checked the footage and saw him come home two days ago. Nobody enters after him. No note. Just hanging there naked," he says.

"Naked?"

"Yep."

***

That last little bit of information was probably the most useful. That could change the entire approach. I make my way into the bathroom and see the decedent for the first time.

"Who told the sergeant that this was a suicide?" I ask Paul.

"Nobody did. I talked to him on the phone and told him to send a detective out as per protocol. Told him we had a dude hanging. I never said anything about a suicide. Looks to me that this guy wasn't trying to kill himself."

As Paul says that, I nod. "Door to the bathroom closed when you got here?" I ask.

"Yep, and I bet you can guess what's attached to the back of the door." Paul closes the door when he says this, leaving just him and me in the bathroom. Well, the other guy is still hanging around too. "Looks like he wanted to cover all angles." As Paul says this, I notice an iPad propped up against the vanity mirror.

"Turn that iPad on yet?" I ask.

"And spoil all the fun for you?" Paul says with a laugh.

"Family been notified yet?"

"Nah, I didn't want to steal your thunder."

"You're so thoughtful."

Ok, time to take stock of the situation: Deceased white male. Death by hanging. Completely unclothed. One arm noted as raised overhead. What appears to be a heavy-duty eyebolt fixed into a truss in the ceiling. Rope from eyebolt to decedent, with some type of knot at the halfway point. Possibly a poorly tied slipknot? Rope is noted as padded in area around front of neck; likely to not leave ligature marks. Conjunctival petechiae present. Tongue protrusion. Rigor present and consistent with body positioning. Lividity present and consistent with body positioning. Mirrors everywhere. Ugh, the damn iPad.

"You thinking what I'm thinking?" Paul asks.

"Depends. You thinking that paying $49.99 for that Mayweather versus Paul hug-a-thon was a massive waste of money?" I ask.

"Yes, I do. So does all of America. But I wasn't thinking that."

"You're probably thinking that this guy passed away as a result of autoerotic asphyxiation."

"I'm thinking this guy died from jacking off while choking himself," Paul says bluntly.

"Yeah, well it would appear that way. Poor bastard looks like he was fumbling with releasing that knot in the rope when he went." We both look up at the rope and quietly assess the knot.

"What's your best bet on the iPad?" I ask.

"You think gay or straight?" Paul says.

I hadn't even considered that option. I was thinking more of which particular website. "A different angle than I was going. I was gonna bet BangBros or YouPorn. You added a different element to the equation."

"I don't think I did. He's still dead."

I nod as if to say, "good point."

Paul and I crouch down in front of the iPad and with my gloved hand, I press the round button at the bottom. The iPad is only in sleep mode and immediately springs to life. My eyes open wide as I hear Paul say, "Oh shit." I know that my eyes are wide because they are staring right back at me. Except my face, and Paul's, is surrounded by a little framed window that says 'live' in the bottom left corner of the screen and 'Chaturbate' in the top right. The comments below our faces are springing back to life, unlike the third party in this bathroom.

Is that guy dead?!

Did we watch that dude die?!!!

WTF?!!!

Who are those guys?!

COPS!

Seemingly at once, many screen names are logging off. I'm staring at myself, mouth agape, with Paul next to me. The rope is visible between us at the top of the screen.

"Well, I'll get out of your way," Paul says, as he leaves the room.

"Feel free to stay." My comment gets no response. I'm still staring at the iPad. IP searches. Preservation letters. Subpoenas to any witnesses. Identification of those witnesses. Who knows what countries they're in! Search warrant for a digital device. Telling the family. This investigation just got a lot more complicated. Or did it? I look at the decedent and shrug my shoulders. "It's probably a suicide," I say to nobody in particular as I leave the bathroom.

Joseph S. Pete is an award-winning journalist, the author of three local interest books, an Iraq War veteran, an Indiana University graduate, and a frequent guest on Lakeshore Public Radio. He was named the poet laureate of Chicago BaconFest, a feat that Geoffrey Chaucer chump never accomplished. His literary work and photography have appeared in more than 100 journals, including *Pulp Modern*, *Shotgun Honey*, *The Five-Two*, *The Grief Diaries*, and *Bull Men's Fiction*. The former Indianapolis resident was inspired to write this tale by a news story he covered as a reporter.

JUNKING THE EVIDENCE

The hipsters were sidled up to the bar wall-to-wall at the dive on the eastside of Indianapolis—a weathered, haunted old joint where John Dillinger allegedly once hung out after robbing a nearby bank on Mass Ave that was now an art gallery with a hulking metal vault filled with local history books just gathering dust.

They ordered Pale Ales, India Pale Ales, American Pale Ales from Midwestern craft breweries, a procession of aggressively hoppy beers until they were far enough along in the night to swill Pabst Blue Ribbon, no longer concerned with taste. They plugged the vintage jukebox with coins, playing alternative classics from The Clash, The Violent Femmes, The Pixies, The Minutemen and Sonic Youth. They came for the history and authenticity of the wood-paneled dive with the most basic banquet hall chairs, but so did the clingy ironic T-shirt and boxy spectacles crowd—en masse. The whole place ended up awash in an inescapable ambiance of pretension superimposed on the unassuming tavern of yore. They all read *My Old Kentucky Blog*; they would all head to Radio Radio and then White Rabbit as the night burned down to its ashen final butt, before heading home lonely and hopeless and ever more entranced by the evasive allure of the esoteric.

Gene nursed a Hamm's in the corner, wondering how the clientele had come to change so much in just a few years. He was steeped in a beer stupor, starting to feel it, but was stuck in a table next to a *Nuvo Newsweekly* cartoonist who was sketching and working overtime to impress a young woman who had been intrigued and came over to ask him a question about his art. Gene cringed at the opportunistic cartoonist's onslaught of charming palaver and felt a sense of relief when he finally convinced her to embark on a quest to another bar.

He drained the dregs of the cold beer can and staggered back toward the barkeep.

Gene was trying to decide between a Hamm's and a Schlitz, but couldn't hear himself think amid all the youthful commotion at the wood-paneled bar.

"So they went to go raid this Outlaws clubhouse in Knoxville or Memphis or somewhere down in Tennessee and it was just wrinkled old seniors in wrinkled leather jackets," the bespectacled loudmouth Amos proclaimed at the bar. "The SWAT team bust-ed down the door, and it was just a few senior citizens waiting around, probably for Denny's to start offering the senior dinner special after 4 P.M."

"How did that happen?" his friend Hunter asked.

The gaunt-faced Amos, who was lean and looked leaner in his fitted jeans and ragged concert T-shirt for a music festival that likely took place long before he born, took a pull from his beer.

"They had some bad intel or something," he said. "They stormed in and found a few geezers, with maybe a pocketknife and a kitch-en knife. That's all the contraband they could turn up."

"Aren't the Outlaws some big, bad biker gang?" Hunter asked.

"They are. Or they were. 'God forgives, Outlaws don't.' 'Angels Die in Outlaw States.' All that. You've heard that. Everybody's heard that," Amos said. "They're supposed to be a bunch of hard-core killers, hell-for-leather types, all that."

"They're the ones with the motorcycle logo that's a skull with pistons, right?" Hunter asked.

"Yeah, that's the one," Amos confirmed.

"That's pretty badass."

"Well, they were once formidable," Amos said. "They were like the mafia here. Indy never got as many immigrants as some of the older, more established cities back out East so there wasn't an

Italian or Irish mob. It was the bikers who stepped up or stepped in or whatever. They muscled shops and restaurants into paying protection money. They once shot people dead in the street, at red lights."

"Some serious stuff," Hunter volunteered.

"They once inspired Marlon Brando in *The Wild One*. Now, they're just a bunch of two-bit crooks stealing from corner shops and insurance companies from what I've heard," Amos said. "Now they're not so much Outlaws as hired muscle who collect like $20 in debt when the Eagles don't cover the spread."

"What happened?"

"Cops cracked down. The culture changed. People don't brook that type of old school intimidation anymore," Amos said. "There aren't even as many bikers anymore. They've been dwindling in number and declining in influence over the years. They might peddle a little pot and some crank here and there. They might do a little racketeering, some money laundering and gambling."

"None of that's above board," Hunter said.

Amos took another swig of beer, squinted at a neon Sun King sign on the wall.

"They still get their hands dirty," he said. "They might rough people up here or there. But now it's mostly low-level stuff. They're barely worthy of the Outlaws name anymore."

"Isn't Outlaw kind of a generic name for a motorcycle club?" Hunter asked. "Aren't they all supposed to be outlaws rebelling against conventional society and all that?"

"It probably is," Amos said. "But these guys were, at least at one time, the real deal, the genuine artifact."

"You mean genuine article?"

Amos shrugged.

"Yeah, of course, genuine article, sorry, a few too many beers," he said. "These dudes killed Hell's Angels. Hell's freaking Angels way back when. And they had this boss named Taco. Taco Bowman or something, he wasted five dudes on Daytona Beach with like his bare hands. He threw some dude off a hotel balcony for snitching or whatever. These were real bad hombres back in the day."

"They're thugs," his companion Sandra, who had been hunched on a barstool over the lambent glow of her phone, suddenly piped up. "Come on, a biker gang? They're troglodytes. They're throwbacks to an era that should be left in the dustbin of history."

"Now listen here," Gene blurted out, interjecting himself into the conversation he had been eavesdropping on and sounding more like a blowhard than he intended. "The Outlaws might be a little rough around the edges but they keep us safe out here on the eastside. Not everyone can afford to live in your fancy downtown lofts, not everyone is in a gilded condo tower. A lot of us are just out here working and scraping by, affording what we can."

"The Outlaws keep you safe?" Hunter said.

Gene gestured for another beer, slapped some cash down on the counter, and collected the cold can, immediately taking a swig.

"Hell yeah, they protect us," Gene said. "If anyone gets out of line, breaks into your house, robs the shop down the street, they break heads. It ain't like downtown. You can't just price out all the criminals. You've got to get a little rough."

"Aren't you talking about assault and battery?" Sandra said.

"Yeah, what about due process?" Amos said.

"What about—" Hunter chimed in.

"Not everybody is lucky enough to work at the Chase Tower," Gene said. "Not everybody gets to drive by the OneAmerica skyscraper and let out a chuckle at what cleverness that sign came up with this week. Some of us are still out here grinding. Some of us are doing the best we can, and the neighborhood today ain't what we originally bought into."

"How does that justify some bikers taking the law into their own hands and 'cracking heads'? How does that—" Sandra started.

Gene stepped in closer and started talking over her.

"Look, there are worse gangs than the Outlaws running around in my neighborhood," Gene said. "They're pushing heroin, crack, who knows what else. The Outlaws retain order. It's not like you'd ever set foot where I live. You wouldn't come to my neighborhood. You wouldn't even swing by if we had the best organic cold-pressed juice or IPA in Central Indiana."

"That's not fair. That's no way to talk to us, man," Amos said.

"What about assault and battery?" Bobby asked, mockingly. "Won't someone think of the armed robbers, the poor muggers?"

Gene looked over, gave Bobby a little knowing nod.

The enormous leather-clad biker towered over them all. The skull and pistons patch of The Outlaws bleated off his leather vest. He radiated menace and intimidation. He didn't have to say anything; his bulky frame and hostile glare spoke for themselves.

"You got something to say to me?" Bobby said.

"No sir, nothing . . . " Amos said.

"God forgives, Outlaws don't," Bobby growled.

Amos looked up at him, wide-eyed.

Bobby stared back, blank-eyed, grimacing.

Amos, Sandra, Hunter, and their friends scattered and got out of there.

After the kids disappeared, Bobby bellied up to the bar and bought Gene another beer, finally hailing the hipster bartender in the gut-hugging Courtney Barnett T-shirt.

"It's sad," Bobby said. "But they're kind of right you know. We're not what we used to be."

"Yeah?" Gene said.

"I'm one of the newer guys but even just a few years ago when I came up to the clubhouse the parking lot was packed," Bobby said. "Everywhere you went they knew you and just handed you an envelope of money. Now the club parking lot is near empty. These days no one knows you. You've got to make a scene, show a little muscle, or crack skulls to even get paid."

"Really?" Gene said. "A lot of us still see you guys as the saviors of the neighborhood. Some might grumble about the payouts, but it's a payment for a little extra security and some peace of mind. The cops don't like to come out this way. The stations out here are barely staffed. There's not a lot of other recourse. You're the only reason we can even stay, instead of selling our poor house at a big loss. Where would we even be without you guys?"

"We're not what we used to be," Bobby said. "We spend half our time draining Pabst Blue Ribbons, playing pool, and talking motorcycle repair."

"I realize it's not the heyday anywhere," Gene said. "But the neighborhood ain't what it used to be either. It's changed a lot. It's a hardscrabble place now. We need you guys here watching our backs. You keep us safe, as least as safe as can be in what's becoming a hellhole. You're like the protectors of the community, guardians in frayed denim and well-worn leather."

"That may be. And I appreciate it, brother. But trust me, it definitely ain't the old days anymore," Bobby said. "You've got no idea. You can't fathom how much we're just barely hanging on. We got guys working part-time at the UPS warehouse to make ends meet. You don't realize how small-time it's gotten."

A few beers later, Bobby hopped on his bike and rumbled off into the night. He roared out to a trucking terminal on the far eastside nearly by the ragged edge of Hancock County, arriving at the assigned time. He kept watch on the dozen semi-truck terminals, waiting for a semi-trailer to arrive so he could jack it. He kept running his finger over the safety of his Glock, eager to go to work.

All he had to do, Dustin had instructed him, was knock on the cab door, grab the driver, and yank him out of the truck. Then he would pistol-whip him, cuff him with zip ties, and leave him gagged and bound behind the dumpster. Then he could drive his bike onto the back of the semi-trailer, hop in the cab and drive off for a big payday.

Only it never came to pass. The truck terminals stayed empty for the several hours while he sat out there.

Bobby started flicking the safety on and off his handgun. He started fidgeting with the strap on his saddlebag, trying to flip it open and closed the same way.

At first, he was just trying to beat boredom. Eventually, he was trying just to stay awake.

"Damn Dustin, what the hell is this," he demanded on his cell phone. "There's no score. There's nobody here at all."

"We must have got bad intel," Dustin said.

Dustin was the boss, the head honcho, or whatever. But Bobby never took him too seriously. He hated authority and resented ever being told what to do, which is why he embraced the whole

biker lifestyle in the first place—for the pursuit of personal freedom, authenticity, the open road, and whatever the hell. Dustin
also tried to give himself the nicknames Dirty Dustin and Double
D, which he could convince exactly no one else to use.

"This was supposed to be a big score," Bobby sighed. "I needed
this. I needed this bad. I got bills to pay."

"We're working with what we're working with," Dustin said.
"Hang out there a while. See what happens. It may still transpire."

A day later, Bobby was still there. He got back on the phone.

"I've been out for twelve hours. This is a bust," he said. "I'm not
getting paid. You're not getting paid. No one's getting paid."

"Just hold on," Dustin said. "Relax. We'll see what we can do."

"What the hell can we do?" Bobby asked. "We need this money.
I need this money. How the hell am I supposed to explain this to
my old lady?"

"Don't worry kid," Dustin said. "Don't worry. We'll find another score. We'll line something else up."

"It's just nothing's going down."

"Don't worry, we'll get you taken care of. We'll get you straight."

They next day, they sent Bobby out to a Salin Bank branch with
Daryl, Dwayne, Nasty Rick, and Ole Chainmail—an Appalachian
transplant to the Fountain Square neighborhood before all the
art students arrived with their love of single origin coffee, cold-
pressed juice, and lots and lots of vino. Ole Chainmail was called
Ole Chainmail because he was always knitting chainmail back
in the clubhouse. Strangely, he never wore chainmail himself.
He claimed he just sold it all on eBay to bikers at faraway clubs.
He claimed it was popular because of cheesy action movies like
Commando, *Cyborg*, and *Mad Max*. No one believed him.

But there he was, knitting chainmail all the time, including
while they waited for the armored Brinks truck to show up.

They all had ski masks, fully automatic machine pistols, and
.45s with extended magazines as backup weapons. Ole Chainmail
just had a sawed-off double-barreled shotgun and a blackjack, not
counting the three or four knives—usually cheapo bodega switch-
blades—he always had slipped into his Doc Martens boots.

"I like to keep it low-tech," he said.

He kept breaking open the shotgun and running his finger over the shells in the breech.

"Is this going to happen?" Dwayne asked. "Is this going to go down?"

"Hell if I know," Ole Chainmail replied.

They sat in silence—dull, dragging silence.

"What I do know is if the Brinks driver is smart and prepared enough to be wearing chainmail under his uniform the only gun we've got in our whole crew with enough stopping power to put him down is this bad boy," Ole Chainmail finally said, popping his double-barrel back open and closed and running his fingers along the truncated barrel.

"Whatever," Daryl said, rolling his eyes.

After more time passed with no armored car to be seen, Ole Chainmail started knitting chainmail again. He made it halfway through the front side of a vest before Bobby called out that it was 5 P.M. and they should head over there to check if it was closed. There was no sense sticking around after it closed, he reasoned.

"It's closed," Dwayne yelled.

"Closed how?" Bobby asked.

"Closed closed," Dwayne shouted. "It says they're sorry this branch has closed because of the economy. This note is dated four months ago. We've been sitting here all day in front of a closed branch."

Bobby rang up Dustin again.

The next day, Dustin sent Bobby out to collect protection money from a Church's Chicken. He had never set foot in one before but knew them for their low prices, gizzards, and chicken livers. It smelled good, great in fact.

He strolled up to the counter and casually dropped he was an Outlaw, here for his payment.

"A what?" the greasy teen asked. "For who?"

"I'm an Outlaw. Come on kid, you surely know how this works. You didn't start working here this morning."

"Let me get my manager."

"Christ on a mother-freaking cracker," Bobby exclaimed before storming out.

He slammed the door so hard they nearly sheared off their hinges, so hard the glass nearly shattered. He pulled out his phone and called up Dustin. It went straight to voicemail: "It was just a kid. It was a kid who didn't know nothing."

The next day, five of them filed out of the motorcycle club lodge on the eastside of Indianapolis, piled into the rusty sedan, and pulled out onto a road lined with payday loan places, fried chicken shacks, and used car lots with weathered marquee signs that promised no credit checks and the cleanest interiors in town.

Many considered the eastside of Indianapolis the rough part of town even though it had neighborhoods like Woodruff Place and Irvington that once ranked among the city's finest. Now it was littered with boarded-up vacants, busted-up crack vials, and car parts shops.

They cruised past two stoplights on the pothole-ridden street until they hit a red, and—boom—got rammed from behind by a pickup truck.

Dustin got out and surveyed the damage, a scratched-up bumper that was caved in on one end.

"Goddamn it," he bellowed while striding toward the truck. "Damn it, damn it!"

He yanked the truck's door opened and roared, "Damn it, Bobby. What the hell's that? You can't ride the brakes! It's got to be convincing! We've got to convince the insurance adjuster that the damage is real, and the doctors that we've got whiplash! You've got to do it again, and don't wuss out!"

Bobby started to sputter an apology.

"Look, Bobby," Dustin said, "it's like throwing a punch. Your instinct is to pull back when you're making contact, but you've really got to punch through the impact. Punch through. Just don't kill us."

Bobby pulled the truck back a few hundred feet and scraped the curb a little, before hitting the gas so hard the tires squealed.

He slammed into the car again, sending it rocking forward this time. The bumper was crumpled.

When all else failed in these lean, diminished times, insurance fraud remained reliable. However small beans, a score was a score.

They stuck around to give statements to the cops. They figured they'd rake in at least ten grand from the insurance company.

Bobby went out to celebrate at the corner bar, where that gaunt-faced kid Amos was hanging around again. He must have put away a few beers to muster up some liquid courage. Maybe he just felt emasculated and bitter after Bobby ran him off last time. Or maybe he had the confidence of the righteous. When Bobby returned to the watering hole, Amos marched right up, confronted him, and told him what he saw. He was just out in the alley having a smoke when he saw the truck rear-end the car twice and knew everything was not on the up and up. The kid wanted his cut, just a little money to keep quiet. Bobby wouldn't get his payout for weeks but knew what to do. He told Amos he'd pay him but not here. He told him to keep calm and carry on, that they needed to be discreet. He insisted they act natural and bought him a few shots at the bar.

Then he led Amos out to the alley, ostensibly to pay him, but shoved him against a dumpster, then slammed his head into it. The kid slumped down into the dirty snow, and Bobby pulled out a pocketknife and plunged it into his back. He plunged it down again, but it got caught in the kid's ribs when he tried to pull it back out. Bobby tugged and huffed, but it was really lodged in and the blood was starting to spurt out.

Amos was still breathing faintly, but Bobby spied a cinderblock they used to prop open the back door. He handled it, assessed the heft and weight. Bobby raised it aloft. He slammed it down hard.

He slammed it down again. And again. And again.

Exhausted, he was out of breath and splattered with blood. His hands were shaky, his head a little woozy.

The gravity of the situation quickly set in.

He had a big problem, a 180-pound deadweight albatross to dispose of.

Down the alley, he saw the manhole and knew he had a solution.

He piled some trash on Amos to conceal him until he could bring back a crowbar. He thought he had one in his trunk, but he needed to run down to an Ace Hardware, which was located a few miles away in a nicer neighborhood. He was too skittish to stop to empty his bladder.

When he returned, a raccoon was licking away at the blood on the kid's face. He kicked it away and kicked it again when it hissed and swiped.

He dragged Amos, knife still protruding from his corpse, to the manhole. Blood trailed behind.

When he finally got to the edge, in a moment of rage and frustration, he again yanked at the knife. It finally came free, slicked with blood. He folded it and pocketed it.

Unceremoniously, he kicked the kid down into the sewers. It took a few sharp blows to keep him from getting lodged in the opening.

Blood was still everywhere, pointing a crimson arrow to the crime scene. Bobby figured he'd run by the car wash, get a bucket of soapy water and splash the snow-coated pavement clean.

He was thinking through the contingencies when he started to get paranoid about the body. He hoisted the manhole cover back up with back-straining exertion and saw the body just lying there inert in the filthy putrid sewage. A trickle of sewage streamed along the foul excrement-encrusted pipe, but it wasn't nearly enough to carry away the kid to some distant place where the authorities would be disinterested in forays into the fetid, slimy sewers. He had to do something about the body. He had been seen in the bar with the kid, and the manhole was right out back, so Bobby knew they'd finger him if some sanitation worker stumbled on the kid's wastewater-eroded corpse.

Bobby had to do something to eliminate the evidence but retched at the smell of the filth when he leaned closer to the open manhole. He couldn't jump down below. Then it occurred to him—sewers were filled with methane, a highly flammable substance. He hadn't realized the compressed gas could be explosive until he dropped a lit cigarette down the hole.

The first explosion seared the hairs on his knuckles. The second filled the underground tunnel, sending a fireball up to the surface and barely leaving Bobby enough time to stagger to safety. His eyebrows were singed and his face stung. The flames receded for a moment and then ignited a chain reaction of blasts that roared underneath the city. The explosions rippled through the sewer system and sent manholes flying up towards the heavens downtown. One landed on and killed an Asian tourist couple, while several more crashed through storefront windows and into vehicles. All told, five were dead.

It was a bad tragedy, but the media in Indy was less sensationalistic and more sedate than in many other cities. People in Naptown often were too cheap to subscribe to the *Star*, too homebound to grab free copies of *Nuvo*, and too invested in bad cable TV to watch the local news. The sewer explosions were a big story but it didn't make a big splash.

Bobby told Dustin what happened back at the club, and Dustin had already seen the news, which was on in the background behind the bar. He knew this was bad, potentially toxic. Bobby stared forlornly at the text scrolling underneath the grim-faced reporter on the screen.

They sat quietly, for a while. Then Dustin listened to Bobby apologize and apologize some more.

"I didn't know," Bobby said, nervously taking a swig of his longneck. "I had no idea that was possible. I thought it was . . ."

Dustin punched Bobby with a straight right into his mouth, then caught his temple with a hook.

He dragged Bobby out to the parking lot, where Dustin hit him dozens of more times before Michael ran over his head with an old Ford Taurus. They hoisted him up into the trunk after wrapping him with a tent from an Army-Navy surplus store. They dumped him on the train tracks after dusk, knowing the conductor couldn't see Bobby in enough time to stop.

Indianapolis was a city of highways, but these freight trains rumbled through regularly, rocketing through old and largely forlorn brick-clad industrial neighborhoods, carrying who knew what off to who knew where. The moon peeked through the smoggy night sky, glinting off the slightly rust-kissed tracks.

"It's got to look authentic, Bobby," Dustin whispered. "It's got to look convincing."

Meagan Lucas is the author of the award-winning novel, *Songbirds and Stray Dogs* (Main Street Rag Press, 2019). Meagan's short work has been published or is forthcoming in journals like *The Santa Fe Writers' Project*, *Still: The Journal*, *MonkeyBicycle*, *Cowboy Jamboree*, *BULL*, *Pithead Chapel*, and others. Born and raised on a small island in Northern Ontario, she now lives with her husband and children in Flat Rock, North Carolina. She teaches Creative Writing at Asheville-Buncombe Technical Community College and is the Editor-in-Chief of *Reckon Review*.

Picking the Carcass

Janelle was sweating, sprawled on the threadbare couch, ticking fan pointed at her undercarriage, when the power died; the *click-click* of the blades coming slower and slower.

"Girls!" she hollered. "Girls!" Four and eight, they were sweaty too. The little one's hair frizzed into a white blonde halo. "Make sure the windows are open, and strip down to just your shirt and panties, okay? Maddie take your socks off, baby. It's over a hundred degrees. You don't need socks."

Maddie started explaining that she didn't like the damp feel of the carpet on her feet, but Janelle couldn't hear her over Rudy barking outside. "Christ, that goddamn mutt," she whispered, picked up an old bill for something, and fanned her face with it. The ear-splitting bark seemed even louder in the new silence. She could feel each howl in the hinge of her jaw.

The cut off wasn't a surprise. She knew she didn't pay the bill. She didn't pay any of the bills. To pay bills a body needed to have actual money, not SNAP, not an IOU, not a favor. Janelle rarely had any of them, but never any cash.

"I'm hungry, Mama," the baby said.

"You two go sit out back, sun's going down, it'll be cooler out there with the breeze. I'll find something." But when she looked in the fridge, there was only ketchup. *Food would have spoiled anyway*, she thought, opening the freezer, stretching to the back, and pulling out the only thing in there: a box of old ice cream. No clean bowls, so she scooped it into three mugs with a soup spoon, and carried them to the backyard, wondering what horror she was going to have to do to get that power back on.

***

"Ice cream for dinner?" Maddie said.

"This will cool you off."

"What are the brown things?"

"Raisins."

"Why is mine crunchy?"

"It's just ice, baby. I'm sorry. I didn't buy the ice cream. Remember when Uncle Vernon came over and brought treats for you, and you watched a movie in your room?"

"When we couldn't come out?"

Janelle nodded. She hadn't remembered that part.

"Yeah," Maddie said. "He brought old man food."

Janelle didn't like rum raisin either and Vernon brought other weird snacks for the children, too: Funyuns and ginger ale. But it had been nice that he even thought of them, most didn't.

"What y'all doing back here," Jesse asked, walking around the side of the house.

"Daddy!" The girls screamed and ran to him.

"Power's out," Janelle said.

"You should pay your bills."

"You should pay *your* bills. You owe me three months."

"You owe me for summer camp."

"Bible camp? I thought it was free? I know you didn't come here for money. You know I don't got any."

"I thought you might be in the mood?" His eyes slid to the back door.

"Oh," she said and looked in the girls' mugs. She was and it was about the only thing he was any good for. She had a little time before it was fully dark. "I could be convinced." She rose, her spoon clicked against the side of her mug. "You girls stay here. I'll be right back. Don't leave the yard."

***

After, as Janelle pulled her panties up her damp legs, she said:

"Leave me a bit for later?"

"I don't have more," Jesse said buckling his belt.

"You do. You always do."

"You're getting too skinny. You don't want your teeth to look like Misty's."

"I got a long time. I'll quit before then," she said, putting her hand on his chest. "If I quit you won't be able to come over here and get this whenever you want."

"It's getting dark. You better let those girls in."

"You can tell me how to raise those girls when you start paying for them. While I'm all on my own, I do what I fucking want."

Her chances for more fun later without him were gone, but she didn't want him to know she'd forgotten about the girls or that there was all sorts of shit back there that she didn't want them getting into: bales of barbed wire, a stupid deep ditch, woods that she heard all sorts of creepy shit coming from. Plus Barry, her landlord and neighbor, had warned her not to let her girls on his land or mess with his fancy horses. The last time she'd used the girls' safety as a lever to try to wedge some money out of Jesse he'd threatened to call Child Protective Services. Jesse was halfway out the front door when he said, "Oh, before, the dog was going fucking nuts. If he gets off that chain the county is going to catch him and kill him. And they'll send you the bill, too."

"Did you go see why?"

"Not my dog. I don't know why you have it. There were some lights out in the field when I got here that's probably it, he's a dummy."

He said she got too crazy, too emotional when she was high, so she couldn't tell him that Rudy made her feel safe. It didn't make any sense. He was dangerous, a big pit mix, and she was afraid of her girls being around him. But she liked the look on bill collectors' faces when they pulled into the yard and saw him. In the night, no one could get anywhere near the house without Rudy letting her know. She didn't have anything of value, but that didn't mean someone wouldn't try to take it. A dead body was the easiest to rob, and she was near a corpse, just bones really, no meat left. She could hear Rudy barking when she called the girls back into the house, so after she got them through a cool shower and into their damp beds, she found a flashlight and went to see what his problem was.

Halfway, she stopped. His barks were frantic, goose flesh broke out on her arms. Something was wrong. *How long has he been like this?* Time always took on a liquid quality when she was getting spun out. She turned and went back to the house for the shotgun. Shining the beam of the flashlight on Rudy, he was at the end of his tether, furiously stretching towards the road where there was a dark lump. Roadkill, or trash thrown from the bed of a truck, likely. *Fucking dummy, nearly giving himself a stroke over garbage.* No strange lights, but Jesse was tweaking so he was probably seeing shit. She walked closer to the lump knowing that she was going to have to deal with it if she wanted Rudy to calm down, if she wanted to be able to get any sleep. "Please, please, please be a trash bag. Oh, or a backpack full of money."

But it was a raccoon in a puddle of something dark. She put the shotgun down on the side of the road and found two sticks. Janelle pinched the flashlight beneath her chin, and with a stick in each hand, slipped them under the thickest parts of the raccoon. She lifted gently, her hands shaking, and the animal fell off the sticks and back down into the puddle of its own goo. She felt something wet splatter against her bare legs.

She tried again.

And again.

Rudy was losing his ever-loving mind, and she couldn't hear herself think. Janelle finally grabbed the raccoon's tail, pulled it across the road, and pushed it into the ditch with her foot. As it rolled down the steep bank, the beam of her flashlight caught something shiny.

"Oh shit," she said and put her palm to her forehead trying to picture the animal she'd tried so hard not to look at. *It was a raccoon, wasn't it?* It'd been so mangled she couldn't be sure, and now that it was under some brush she couldn't really see. *What if it was someone's cat? And that glint was the tag on a collar reflecting?* She'd be devastated if Rudy disappeared. She climbed down the bank into the ditch and found the animal. No cat tag. No poor owner to call. Relief. But there was a metallic shine. *Fucking scavengers. They eat everything, it's probably a beer cap.* But still she squatted closer, curious now, and grabbed a stick and poked at the body. *It looks . . . no it can't be.* She tried to pry it out with a stick but it wouldn't budge. She stood and put her hands on her hips, chewed her lip. Then she squatted down, stuck her hand into the raccoon's remains, and wrapped her fingers around the lump. She pulled it out and looked at it under the beam of the flashlight.

A gold nugget.

What the fuck. Does gold still come in nuggets? Is that what they are called? Maybe knobs? No, nuggets, like chicken. Where do I even know about gold nuggets from? Bugs Bunny? Scrooge McDuck? Cartoons, right, this isn't real. Can't be real. Someone is fucking with me. This is some kind of joke. There is no way this raccoon was dead on the road with gold inside him. It must be something else. She looked around, swept the bushes with her flashlight looking for who was fucking with her. Looking for Jesse. But she couldn't imagine him touching a dead animal, let alone planting something in one. *If no one is fucking with me . . .* It was heavy in her palm. *Gold is heavy, right? How did you test if something was gold? Try to bite it?* She looked at it closely, black with blood and glinting in the beam of her flashlight. *I can't put it in my mouth . . .*

She rubbed it on her shirt and looked at it again. *Maybe just my teeth? Not my lips. If I can bite with just the edges of my teeth and my skin doesn't touch it.* She closed her hand around it. *Does it matter if it is gold? Yes. Bills. Food. My girls at home with no breakfast in the morning.* She bit down. It gave. *Was it supposed it give?* She couldn't remember if that meant that it was real or not. *But what if it is?*

Then she stuck her right hand back in to see if there were more.

***

She was exhausted and itchy, but Janelle felt really good walking out of the pawn shop with money in her pocket. She went to the gas station and paid her power bill, and then put fuel in her car. Then she went to Food Lion before she could make a stupid decision. She filled her cart and was checking out when the cashier pointed to the bottle of conditioner and said: "You can't use SNAP for that."

"I got cash," Janelle said and she enjoyed the scowl that wiped over that know-it-all's face. But then the money was gone. And she just had to be happy that she was picking up her girls from camp, not riding on fumes, and that she could take them home and put them in front of the window air conditioner while she cooked them dinner. It had to be enough.

"Mommy, Mommy," Maddie started as soon as they got in the car.

"Seat belts," Janelle said.

"Mommy, I want—"

"Is your seat belt on? I can't afford a ticket." When she heard two clicks she put the car in drive and pulled out of the church parking lot before anyone invited her to service.

"Mommy! Nevaeh is having a birthday party and I'm invited and I want to go. Please! Everyone is going."

"Well, I don't know baby, we don't really have anything to bring her for a present."

"It's not till the weekend and it's at the trampoline place! It's going to be so, so, so cool. And everyone is going, and I never get to go. And we don't *have* to bring a present."

Janelle rubbed her forehead with her hand. She remembered third grade. Hand-me-downs, never enough lunch, and never knowing if her mama was going to be at the bus stop when she got off. She remembered hearing about the parties. Never being asked to join. It was hard enough for the kids with no money to get invited in the first place, Maddie couldn't show up to a fancy party like that empty handed. "We'll see baby." She scratched at her arms. Just when she thought she was getting her shit together something else came to remind her that she was a bad mother.

She pulled into her driveway and turned off the car.

"No Rudy," the little one said.

"Oh shit," Janelle said. His rope stretched across the yard like a headless snake. "Go in the house," she hollered as she ran for the back fence and discovered the big hole. Barry was going to kill her. Not with his rifle, which he was known to carry, but with a big fat bill on pink paper taped to her front door. She prayed first that the dog would come home. Second that whatever damage he was inevitably causing couldn't be tied to him. *Just no evidence, baby.*

She went in the house and made the girls store brand mac and cheese for dinner. She smiled, *who'd have thought, with actual milk, not just margarine.* They watched *Dinosaur Train* and then she sent them to bed so that she could find Rudy before it was black. She grabbed the flashlight, and the shotgun, right away this time. She also licked the spoon and a little plate that she and Jesse had used the night before as a little present to herself for spending her money responsibly, but also because she was so beat she wasn't going to make it otherwise.

It didn't take long, he was a big dog, and she knew he'd go for the woods. He had found some treasure—his muzzle covered in gore—before someone found him with at least two bullets, from what she could see.

"Oh fuck. My sweet boy. Christ, I can't even take care of a dog."

She couldn't let scavengers eat him, but she couldn't carry him, so she grabbed his back legs to drag him deeper into the woods where she could hopefully pile some rocks on him. But damn it if she couldn't move him. "Fuck, Rudy. You fat beast." She yanked more but he wouldn't budge. She knelt down, emotion stealing all of her energy. "Damn it, I can't even bury my fucking dog." She petted his velvet head and rubbed his belly.

It was harder than she'd expected.

With lumps.

"What the hell?" she said, massaging his undercarriage. It definitely didn't feel right.

She remembered the raccoon. *I'm fucking high again though. That's all, I'm hallucinating.* She just needed to leave him, and call Jesse in the morning for help. He'd help her, if only because then she'd owe him. But then she'd pay him back and maybe he'd leave her a little treat. She found herself chewing on her lip and running her palms up and down her arms. But then she thought about that raccoon again, and how if there was gold in Rudy's belly, she didn't want Jesse to get any of that money. Jesse who always had gas for his car, clean clothes, and drugs, but never enough money to help feed his girls. She knew he was a regular down at Shifty's, too. She couldn't remember the last time she drank a beer in a bar. That money was hers.

She didn't have a way to cut Rudy open. She looked for a sharp rock. Nothing. She picked up the shotgun and held it against the skin of the dog's belly, whispered, "I'm so sorry, Big Guy," and pulled the trigger.

Droplets peppered her face, but she didn't care. It hadn't sounded right. It didn't sound like shooting an animal, like meat and blood. The shot sounded like metal on metal. She couldn't breathe. Back on her knees she was up to her elbows in Rudy's midsection. Her hands full of bloody golden nuggets shining in the moonlight. A flash of white light drew her attention to the trees. It bobbed between them. Someone had heard the shot. She wasn't sharing. And Barry had forbidden her from coming on his land. She'd lose her treasure and her house if he found her. She filled her pockets and grabbed her gun and flashlight but didn't turn it on as she ran for the fence.

"Sorry, Rudy," she whispered as she climbed through the tall grass, poke weed, and goldenrod, and back through the fence before she turned to see if she could still see the lights. The night was black. She pulled her hair out of her face and caught her breath. This wasn't real. No one like her found gold in their dog. If her pockets weren't so heavy, she might have thought she dreamed the whole thing.

***

As Janelle slid her handfuls of nuggets over the pawnshop counter, she noticed that one had a crust of dried blood, and she tried to pick it off with her thumbnail before the clerk noticed. She was almost finished when he asked: "Barry give these to ya?"

"What now?" she asked, trying to buy time. How could she explain?

"Barry is the only guy around here that has these, far as I know. Collects 'em. Kinda a weird thing to collect but he's nuts about them. I've been trying to get him into guns. At least guns you can use, and they hold their value. Maybe he's come to realize these are a tough investment. Maybe he's trying to get rid of 'em? Y'all are neighbors, ain'tcha? He give these to you?" His eyes were narrow and hard and didn't leave her face.

"Nah," she said, licking her lips. "I inherited them from my granddaddy. He was a miner."

"Well then. I bet Barry will want them."

"You gonna give me more than just their weight value then?"

"Nope." He piled them on a scale. "If you wanna take the risk and take them to Barry, you can. They're worth more to him than to me."

"I'd rather have the money now."

He looked at her again and she was sure that he could tell she was lying. Wasn't everyone trying to pawn something lying, though? Either to him, or to themselves? What did he care where they came from? She needed to feed her babies.

Later at home, after she'd sat next to Rudy's water bucket and cried, she paid more bills and yet again had an empty wallet. While she was microwaving some hotdogs and warming some beans, she got to thinking about Barry's weird collection, how it got in those animals' bellies, and how she could get her hands on more of it. She was pouring Tampico into the little one's sippy cup when she heard the snap.

"Goddamn vermin," she said. Maybe if she could get a little more money she could get the girls out of this place. There was a nice new fourplex on the other side of town, she wondered what the rent was. Sure would be nice to be closer to town. Nice to be in a new place where the ceilings didn't sag, the floor didn't have mushy spots, and she didn't have to pray to get the toilet to flush or the sink to drain. And then she wondered about that mouse. She hurried to dish up the beans and wieners and got the girls settled in front of *Daniel Tiger*.

She opened the door to the cabinet beneath the sink, where

she knew the mouse in the trap would be, and said a prayer it was already dead. She usually didn't check on 'em so quick, not wanting to find one in the throes, but she had to know. She held her breath as she pulled it out and set it on the counter. Its eyes were open, but it wasn't moving. It was fluffy, a brown and white field mouse that looked an awful lot like her fourth-grade class hamster. Its belly did look kinda distended though. Her heart beat faster. She prodded it with the tip of her index finger. It was too firm. Electricity ran down her arms. She opened the utensil drawer and looked for something sharp. She had a paring knife that would barely cut an apple, and a steak knife she'd stolen from a restaurant. Her stomach turned at the thought of having to saw.

She picked up the paring knife and pointed it at the animal's belly. Then she stopped and walked around the corner to check on the girls. Still TV zombies. She went back to her dissection, although it was feeling far grislier than anything she'd done in high school. She wished for the distance of that sharp formaldehyde smell, not this warm-fur pet scent. She closed her eyes, took a deep breath, and pressed the knife into the mouse until she hit the trap beneath it. She didn't feel anything hard like the nuggets, but it was difficult to tell. She spread open the cut. She still couldn't see. She couldn't imagine sticking her bare finger inside. Not here in the kitchen. Not sober. So she used the side of the blade to put pressure on the animal's abdomen and try to squeeze something out.

When it popped out it startled her. But it wasn't a nugget. Janelle realized this mouse was almost a mama. "Aw shit. Sorry," she said. "I ain't saying you're better off, but you might be. It's tough out here for us."

Janelle put the mouse and the trap in a grocery bag and took it out to the garbage can. *I'm an idiot.* She wondered why she thought she would be so lucky again. Then she looked at the new stack of bills that had arrived that afternoon, *cause I gotta,* she thought. *I gotta.*

***

Janelle had just gotten the girls to bed when there was a knock at the front door. "Please not Barry," she whispered. She turned the handle and the shitty door swung loose.

"Word around town is you've had some good luck," Jesse said, and stepped past Janelle and into the house.

"You're hearing things."

"You ain't been paying all your bills? Paying cash at Food Lion?"

She snorted. "That's gossip? Shit, this town is boring."

"You gonna share?"

"Are you?"

"You know you're my girl. I'll always take care of you. But I don't have anything right now. If you could spot me, I could get some."

"You've been hearing I'm paying my bills and you think I have anything left?"

"Shit," he said and stomped down her steps.

"Hey wait," she said running out into the grass barefoot to catch him. "You ever heard of anyone finding treasure inside an animal?"

"Inside? You mean like a prize buck? Or a bass contest or somethin'?"

"No, like actual gold, or jewels or something in an animal's belly. You know guys with a lot of money. Is that like a thing? A place to hide it maybe?"

"Shit, you're high as a kite aren't you. You used that money and got fucked up with someone else. I thought I was your guy, Janelle."

"I'm not, I swear. I'm straight. I haven't had any since you were here."

"No one fucking hides their treasure inside of an animal. How stupid would that be, if the animal ran off, your money would be gone." He pulled his hands through his hair and rubbed his face. "Speaking of gone, where's the mutt? He get loose?"

Tears started running down Janelle's face. She couldn't stop them. Before she knew it, she was on her knees in the dirt.

"You're crazy." He turned and disappeared into the night.

He's probably right, she thought.

***

Janelle lay in bed but her legs wouldn't be still. She couldn't stop thinking about Rudy. She got to thinking about how all the nugget animals were over at Barry's and how the guy at the pawn shop said that Barry collected them, and then she started thinking about the lights that she'd seen in his woods and how Jesse had claimed to see some over there the other night, too. She wondered if her story about her granddaddy wasn't that far off, if Barry was mining them. If there was gold in this ground. She imagined a little hole in the ground like a cave, maybe with a wagon that Barry pulled in and out. The she realized that all she knew about mining she'd learned from *Snow White and the Seven Dwarfs.* It might be harder than spotting a cave entrance to find Barry's mine. But all these animals were finding it, it couldn't be that hard. Finding Barry's mine and doing some of her own digging was way better than most anything else she'd had to do for money before. She didn't want to have to call Vernon or any of the others.

She slipped out of bed and put on a hoodie. She grabbed the paring knife from the kitchen, and at the back door she picked up the flashlight and shotgun. She had just slipped through the fence when she saw the lights in the distance and started heading that way. She was deep in thought about which bills she would pay first, or if she would maybe move the girls to that new apartment and wait for those bills to catch her again when she heard the scream of a coyote. She took a few more steps before she heard it again. Closer. And behind, maybe? She shivered. And then again, closer still. They were surrounding her. She racked her gun. The cries got louder and it seemed like they were everywhere, filling the darkness. She ran up to a grove of trees hoping to climb one to escape their imminent attack, and she nearly ran straight into the middle of their feeding frenzy.

A mass of moving fur was below her, writhing, the scent of

flesh, of rot, solid in the air. They'd massed on something large and dead. *A deer. Or maybe a cow?* Sometimes when it had been a while since she partied with Jesse she saw things. Detox visions. She wondered if this was real.

She turned to leave and tripped over a branch. The fall knocked the wind out of her, and when she looked up, a coyote was only a foot away, mouth open. The wet of its tongue glistening in the moonlight. She didn't think, she just pulled the trigger. The beasts scattered. She took the knife out of her pocket and cut the coyote open. She stuck her hand inside. *Bingo.* It was small, but it was there. She put the handful of hard objects in her bra.

Wiping her hand on her shirt and standing, she saw what the coyotes had been eating: a horse. A very expensive horse from the look of the parts that hadn't been savaged. She panned her flashlight over the poor beast, and saw the riding boot sticking out. "Oh fuck!" She ran to the boot and pulled it, finding it attached to a woman's leg.

"Are you okay? Hello?" she called.

"She's not," came a voice from the shadow of the trees.

Janelle pointed her flashlight at the voice: Barry.

"I really wish you weren't trespassing, that complicates things. I think I have you to thank, though, for recovering my collection. I didn't know it was out here until Billy called. I'd assumed she'd already sold it, and I'd lost it forever when I'd lost my temper."

Janelle didn't know who Billy was.

"Temper?"

"Well, you know," he said, waving at the mess. "I thought when Champ here fell on her, that was fortune shining on me. Nothing like a big horse carcass to hide a small woman while she rots. I was sad to shoot him, though, don't get me wrong."

"Billy, at the pawn shop?" she asked, trying to put the pieces together.

"Yes. Billy called and said that a woman in town, my neighbor in fact, had brought some new specimens and might I be interested in coming by to see. And, of course, I recognized them as mine and I knew the granddaddy story was hogwash, but, I also knew that you must have found them out here somewhere, that she hadn't sold them before she tried to leave, that she'd taken them with her, probably planning to fund her escape. You can imagine I didn't want to go poking around in this mess. But time, and teeth, revealed what I'd been missing. I think I have your dog to thank for that, before I took care of him, too."

Rudy, she thought, and was filled with grief and rage. Then she thought of his belly, and Janelle looked down at the horse, she looked closely at its abdomen, it was littered with bloody nuggets, gore, and shreds of leather. "In its stomach. Like the rest."

"In the saddle bag, I imagine, perhaps her purse, it's hard to tell now. I didn't see them at first, but now with all the animal activity . . . they've gotten mixed with the remains, but also brought to light."

Janelle wasn't listening to Barry. *Just like the raccoon. Just like Rudy. The coyote, too.* It made sense, they were from this land, the mouse was empty because it was not. She wondered if all the animals on this land were full of gold.

"Champ was my best worker, I suppose he can be of use a little longer and hide one more body for me," he said raising his rifle.

But she was quicker because she'd already decided what she needed to do next.

She pulled the trigger and Barry hit the ground with a thud. She climbed on top of his legs and used the paring knife to slice open his belly. She reached inside as he screamed. There were only warm handfuls of soft. Her palms were black in the moonlight. She climbed off his body and turned back to the horse. Then she lay down in the grass and put her cheek on its nose. Velvet, like Rudy. Sobs shook her shoulders. She missed him so much. She'd do Vernon every week for a year if it meant she could rub Rudy's belly again. She closed her eyes and tried to forget. Tried to trick her mind like the drugs did.

The coyotes began screaming again. "Figures," she whispered

against the horse's nose, "they're always circling. Watching. They don't even fucking wait until you're dead. Spend my whole fucking life just trying to keep them at bay."

She struggled to her feet, made a sling of her hoodie, and loaded as many nuggets as she could carry, each one a chance to put a little meat on her bones. They click-clicked against each other as she waddled across the field toward her babies, the cries of the scavengers as they descended on the bodies filling the night.

Multiple award-winning author, J.P. Seewald, has taught creative, expository and technical writing at Rutgers University as well as high school English. She also worked as both an academic librarian and an educational media specialist. Twenty of her books of fiction have been published to critical praise including books for adults, teens and children. Her most recent mystery novels are *Death Promise* and *Blood Family*. Her short stories, poems, essays, reviews and articles have appeared in hundreds of diverse publications and numerous anthologies such as: *The Writer, L.A. Times, Reader's Digest, Pedestal, Sherlock Holmes Mystery Magazine, Over My Dead Body! Gumshoe Review, Library Journal,* and *Publishers Weekly.*

WORST ENEMY

"I don't believe my brother murdered that man. I think the police are dead wrong." The woman sitting opposite Bob Harris was thin, over thirty, and pale. Her light blue eyes were teary. She tore at the tissue in her hands. Bob felt sorry for her but not sorry enough to take the case.

"Ms. Felner from what you've told me, the police have strong evidence. They wouldn't arrest your brother otherwise."

Sara Felner burst into tears. "Please Mr. Harris, just go meet Richie. Talk to him. You'll see he isn't the kind of person that has it in him to kill anyone."

A knock at the office door interrupted the intense conversation. Bob called out to the person to enter. He was relieved to see his wife Nina enter the office carrying a tray holding coffee and two cups.

"I thought you might need some refreshments," she said giving Bob a knowing look. Sometimes he thought Nina had ESP.

The Sweethearts Detective Agency, founded by Bob and Nina Harris—two NYPD detectives who opted for early retirement from the force—was strictly a small-time gumshoe operation. They'd met on the job, been attracted to each other from the first, and were married a year after their first date. When Bob, a tall, husky former marine, met Nina, a feisty, blue-eyed redhead, he started to think it was time to consider marriage.

It was Nina who initially suggested the name for the PI firm. At first Bob had groaned, but the truth was it drew a lot of female clients. Ironically, these women were generally checking up on husbands they suspected of cheating. However, Sara Felner was here on an entirely different matter.

After a short coffee break, Sara Felner again implored Bob Harris to investigate on her brother's behalf. Bob soon found himself losing patience.

"Frankly, I think you'd be wasting your money," he said. "From what you've told me, your brother is indigent. Are you so well off you can afford to shell out for an investigation? Our services don't come cheap."

Sara Felner worried her lower lip. "I understand. Can I at least pay for you to talk to his attorney? Mr. Greene is a public defender and seems to be terribly busy. I don't think he's given much thought to my brother's case."

In spite of himself, Bob felt sorry for the woman. "All right," he finally said. "You've worn me down. I'll give it a full day, talk to the lawyer and the arresting officers and give you a report."

The woman again burst into tears, this time of gratitude. "Thank you," she said in a choked voice.

"I'll be in touch. Leave me all the info."

After the client left his office, as was their routine, Bob knocked at Nina's office door. She called out for him to enter. Each morning they discussed their cases for the coming day, usually in Nina's office where they shared coffee and whole grain toast. Nina insisted on fresh fruit as well. She was committed to keeping them both in good health. A slim woman, she hardly looked her forty years. Gone were the days when Bob could wolf down a couple of donuts for breakfast. He let out a sigh of resignation.

"So what does your day look like?" Bob asked his wife.

Nina took a thoughtful nibble of her dry toast. "I'm following one Ruth Myers today. Her husband is convinced she's two-timing him."

"Lots more women cheating these days," Bob observed.

"Equal rights," Nina responded. "Who's your client? She sounded emotional. I could hear her crying right through the walls. Cheating husband?"

"No, a lot more serious than that. Her brother's been arrested for murder committed during a house break-in." Bob told his wife what he knew so far about the case. "It's a little different than what we've been doing lately."

"Doesn't sound like it'll help pay our bills for this month. But I agree that you should look into it for the client's sake." Nina gave him a smile and a kiss on the cheek.

He let out a deep sigh. "What can I say? I'm a sucker for a sob story," Bob said. "Women's tears get to me."

"That's why I love you so much," Nina responded. "To paraphrase James Cagney at the close of *The Public Enemy*, you ain't so tough."

"Yeah, but let's keep that our secret."

His wife knew he had a soft heart. Even when he voted in the elections, Bob didn't necessarily choose the law-and-order candidate. He listened and observed each individual and voted based on his gut reaction. He cared about people and wanted politicians in office who felt the same way.

***

Jeff Greene's cubicle at the PD's office was a shabby affair, but then Bob's own office was a no-frills establishment too. Greene had agreed to see Bob early the following morning before court.

They shook hands. Greene's grip was weak and slimy, like a dead fish. He was a young guy, probably fresh out of law school. His desk was stacked with files. No surprise there. Being a public defender paid badly and the office was always overwhelmed with cases.

"So what can you tell me about Richard Felner?" Bob asked.

Greene raised his eyebrows inquiringly. "I'm surprised you got involved."

Bob shrugged. "I felt sorry for the sister. She begged me to look into the matter."

Greene removed a file from the huge stack on his desk. "I think you're wasting your time and her money."

"Why's that?"

"DNA evidence. It places Felner at the scene of the crime. Frankly, I don't see how I can get this guy any kind of deal. Look over the evidence and you tell me what you think."

Bob took notes on the relevant information in the file and then decided he'd interview the detective who'd been in charge of the investigation. Detective Ralph Manning had been working homicide for many years and wasn't difficult to track down. Bob sized up Manning as a fellow veteran and figured they could relate. Unfortunately, Manning told a similar story to Greene which proved discouraging.

"Forensic DNA analysis of items from the crime scene shows hits on two men, one of them Felner. It's the most accurate tool we have as you know. We figure it was a home invasion gone wrong. The burglars didn't realize that Dave Garcia was at home when they broke in. Looks like he put up a struggle. They overpowered him, tied him up, and gagged him. Trouble was the tape covered his nose as well as his mouth and the poor guy suffocated. He was already dead when his wife came home in the late afternoon and found him. She phoned us and we went straight to the crime scene."

"You think the wife might have hired someone to bump off her husband for insurance or the like?"

The well-muscled police detective shrugged. "Doubtful. Felner was a petty criminal. He'd been convicted of breaking and entering once before. That's why we had his DNA in the system. He was an alcoholic and doper who spent most of his life homeless and on the streets. Afraid this is an ironclad case. In all the years I've been doing this, I've never seen a DNA hit proven wrong. Sorry, I can't help you."

Bob realized that the detective wasn't unsympathetic, he was just certain of Felner's guilt. But when Bob thought of Felner's sister, he wasn't quite ready to give up just yet. "Can you arrange for me to interview Felner?"

"Don't see any reason why not. When?"

"As soon as possible."

"You got it."

"Thanks, I appreciate your cooperation."

True to his word, Detective Manning made the arrangements for Bob to interview Felner at the county jail. Felner looked like a derelict. He had missing teeth, smelled bad, and was generally unkempt. The word "loser" came to mind.

"I'm here as a favor to your sister," Bob told Felner. "She doesn't believe you killed Garcia."

Felner rubbed nicotine-stained fingers over his face. "Maybe I did it. I could have. I don't remember doing it though. But I drink a whole lot and then I kind of black out."

Bob was about ready to give up on Felner. Even Felner believed he could have been responsible for Dave Garcia's death. No reputable attorney would consider putting Felner on the stand. Felner was his own worst enemy. He'd practically confessed to the crime. What more could anyone say? DNA evidence was clear proof, just as Detective Manning had observed. Yet something nagged at him.

After Bob left Felner at the jail, he went back to his office and examined the information he'd gleaned from the PD. Garcia had lived in a fancy house. When the police arrived after his wife discovered the body, they found dressers emptied, files dumped, the place ransacked for money and valuables. Mrs. Garcia's jewelry had been stolen. None of that was found on Felner. Also, latex gloves were left in the kitchen sink, wet and soapy. It appeared as if someone had tried to wash away any trace of DNA. Felner didn't strike Bob as the kind of criminal who would think to remove evidence. He just didn't have all his gray matter working. Bob found the name of the DNA analyst at the county crime lab. According to the file, she'd run dozens of tests and found an unknown DNA not consistent with Garcia or his wife on the duct tape. She ran that DNA profile through the state criminal database, but it didn't result in any hits. Felner's DNA was only found on the vic's fingernails. But could that help Felner? Maybe. Didn't it prove someone else was the brains behind the home invasion? Yet that didn't prove Felner wasn't involved. Still, the unknown assailant's DNA was on the duct tape, which contributed to the actual cause of death.

Bob paid another visit to the PD's office. He cornered Jeff Greene and shared the information he'd discovered. "If you can get Felner to tell you who his partner was, I think you can make a deal with the district attorney. It's clear Felner's too muddle-headed to have planned this. The real perp is still out there."

Greene tapped his pen against his metal desktop, thoughtfully contemplating what Bob said. "Maybe we can work a plea bargain. I'll get on it," Greene promised.

***

Bob Harris was pleased and thought Sara Felner would be as well. But things didn't turn out quite the way he expected. When she returned to his office several days after Bob's meeting with Jeff Greene, she had some surprising information to share.

"My brother told the police he didn't remember anything about the burglary or anyone else contacting him about it."

Bob was pissed off. Here he'd gone to all this trouble for the guy and the idiot wasn't willing to turn in the real perp. He was certain Felner hadn't planned the burglary himself. He told Sara Felner as much.

"I've done all I can to help your brother. If he won't help himself, there's nothing more I can do for him."

Sara Felner's eyes teared up again. "Please, Mr. Harris, please don't give up. I'm so certain my brother isn't guilty. There are things you don't know. When Richie was a child, he was hit by a car. He survived but his injuries were serious. He suffered a brain injury and his mind was never right after that. He has a poor memory and easily loses track of time. I did what I could for him after our parents passed away, but my own finances were limited. He's not a bad person or a violent one. He might be a drunk but he's not capable of deliberately harming anyone."

"I believe it could have been accidental."

Sara Felner shook her head, hair moving like a wheat field in the wind. "Please, just spend a few more days on the case. I can afford that much."

Bob finally agreed, even though he believed the woman was wasting her money. He decided to take a different tactic and do a little investigating of the victim. In that regard, Detective Manning proved helpful when Bob made another visit to the police precinct.

"We discovered that Garcia liked to hang out at a strip club. He had a relationship with one of the girls and spent a lot on her. He tossed money around and got the reputation as a big spender."

"You questioned the girlfriend?"

Manning rolled up the sleeves of his white shirt, showing his thick forearms. "Yeah, but she wasn't very cooperative."

"Mind if I give it a shot?"

"Suit yourself," Manning said.

Bob got the feeling Manning didn't expect him to do any better.

That evening, Nina watched him change his clothes and check his weapons. He holstered his Glock after loading it and attached it to the belt he wore under his jacket, then strapped a sheathed knife under his right pant leg.

"Expecting trouble tonight?"

"Just being prepared."

She gave him a hard stare. "Where are you headed?"

"A strip joint euphemistically called a gentleman's club. I'll be talking to some rough characters and no, you can't come with me."

"I'd have your back, Jack."

Bob gave her a grim smile. "It's no place for a lady, former cop or not." He kissed his wife on the lips and headed out the door.

***

Red Velvet was crowded. The bar was busy. Two almost-naked women, one on either side of the stage, were slithering down poles doing suggestive dances. Pretty much what Bob expected. He bellied up to the bar and caught the attention of one of the bartenders by putting down a twenty.

"What can I get you?" The heavily tattooed bartender asked in a gruff voice.

"Some information. I'm looking for Lana James."

"Who are you?" The bartender's eyes narrowed.

"Tell her there's some money in it for her."

That did it. The bartender picked up the twenty-dollar bill, told the other bartender to cover for him for a few minutes, and took off. Bob didn't have to wait long. The bartender returned in a few minutes, followed by a statuesque, purple-haired woman in a skimpy costume. The bartender introduced Bob to Lana James and then went back behind the bar.

"You better buy me a champagne cocktail, Mister. Our boss expects it."

Bob nodded and complied. "I want to ask you a few questions about Dave Garcia."

She threw him a hard look. "You got cop written all over you. I already talked to some detectives. I'm done." She made a move to walk away.

Bob placed his hand on her arm. "Wait. I'm a private investigator. No heat, okay? I just want to ask a few questions and we're done."

"Okay, put fifty bucks on the bar and then ask. I'll decide if I want to answer you."

He did as she demanded, knowing this was the only way he'd get any answers. She quickly scooped up the bills and clutched them tightly in her fist.

"Music's loud here. Let's find a quiet corner."

She led him to an empty spot in the rear of the establishment. "Okay, ask away."

"Word is Garcia was a free spender and was particularly taken with you. Who did you tell about that? A boyfriend maybe? Someone who had some priors for burglary?"

She let out a small gasp. Bob instinctively knew from years of experience interrogating suspects that he'd hit a nerve. Lana knew who was behind the home invasion responsible for the death of Dave Garcia.

"I don't know nothing," she said angrily.

"I don't believe you."

Her eyes narrowed into slits. "I go on in a few minutes. Get out of here while you can."

Bob watched her flounce away. But she didn't hurry backstage as he would have expected. Instead, she went and talked to a large, burly man—obviously one of the bouncers.

Bob realized it was time to leave. He'd share what he'd learned with Manning in the morning.

As he walked quickly out of Red Velvet heading down the street toward his car, he heard footsteps behind him. Just before he reached his Toyota someone grabbed him from behind.

Bob gave his attacker a hard elbow to the gut and heard a grunt; he felt some satisfaction knowing he'd made contact. As he turned, Bob got a fist to the jaw and saw stars.

It was the bouncer from the club. "Don't bother Lana again or you'll be real sorry."

The threat was followed by a quick jab to the shoulder. Bob landed a hard punch in return. The bouncer then took off, probably deciding it wasn't worth continuing with a strong opponent. The fellow might have been beefier, but Bob was over six feet tall and well muscled himself.

Nina was waiting up for him when Bob returned home. She took one look and got an ice pack from the freezer. "Told you not to go alone."

***

The following morning Bob met with Manning again and told him about the events of the previous night.

Manning shook his head. "You could have been hurt a lot worse. Rough crowd at that place. You want us to arrest the bouncer for assault?"

Bob thought about it. "Probably not. Only if he tries another time. But I doubt he will."

"We'll question Lana again. This time we'll really pressure her. We'll get Felner's partner in crime, but frankly, I don't see how that'll help him."

"You never can tell," Bob said. "I just want to get the whole story so Sara Felner can get some closure."

***

Several days passed before Bob heard from Manning. "We

made an arrest," the policeman told him. "Lana was the key. It seems she was living with one Warren McNaulty, a character who the neighbors claim is a nasty piece of work even though he has no priors. And guess what? His DNA matches the DNA left on the duct tape."

Bob was excited. "Did you question him about Felner?"

"Sorry, McNaulty wouldn't talk. Only words out of his mouth after he was Mirandized was he wanted a lawyer. Guy's no fool."

Bob felt let down. "So you don't know if there's a connection between Felner and McNaulty?"

"Nope. But the DNA implies there is."

Bob sat down hard on his wood chair. It seemed he was back to square one again. There had to be something more he could do. He realized he wasn't giving as much attention to his more lucrative paying clients, but this case bothered him. It was like a puzzle begging for a solution.

Mulling it over, he decided to discuss the case with Nina. His wife had a clever mind. She might have some helpful suggestions.

Nina listened to what he had to say, her bright eyes fixed on his. "Talk to Felner again." She licked her lips thoughtfully. "Try to pin down his movements on the day Mr. Garcia died. Somewhere there might be an alibi. Anyway, it's worth a shot."

Bob agreed and followed up with Felner at the county jail. Jeff Greene went with him, explaining that he ought to visit some of his clients who were incarcerated there as well. They sat together in an interview room. Bob led with a few questions.

"What were you doing on the evening of October 10th? Do you remember?"

Felner shook his head. He looked dazed and bewildered. Bob was certain it wasn't an act. The public defender started going through the file, examining paperwork. Greene jumped to his feet.

"Hold on. There's something." Greene turned to Felner. "It says here you were drunk and disorderly on that date. There was a medical record buried in the file," Greene said, turning to Bob. "According to this, Felner was taken by ambulance to the hospital."

"This could be important. We need to get those hospital

records," Bob said.

"I'm on it," Greene said.

Bob decided to wait for Greene to finish with his other clients and accompany him to the hospital. He hoped a court order wouldn't be necessary.

After explaining the situation, a sympathetic medical assistant proved helpful.

The records showed that Felner had been found outside a store, lying unconscious on the sidewalk. An ambulance was called by the shopkeeper. The paramedics declared Felner dangerously inebriated to near the point of death. He spent two days detoxing in the hospital covering the period Dave Garcia was killed.

"We've got a case," Jeff Greene said, his eyes lighting up with excitement.

Bob wasn't satisfied. "That still doesn't explain how Felner's DNA ended up at the murder scene."

As he saw it, there was one more thing he could do. A final visit to Detective Manning and he would be finished with Felner's case.

Manning frowned when he saw Bob. "You again. What is it this time?"

Bob explained what he and the PD had discovered in Felner's medical records. Manning conceded that it appeared Felner was innocent.

"He couldn't be in two places at the same time," Manning agreed.

Bob asked Manning to go through the medical records himself. "There could be something we missed."

Manning agreed and the two of them went through Felner's medical record for the day in question. Finally, Manning stopped reading and looked up. "I know the names of those two paramedics, the ones who picked up Felner outside the market. They're the same guys who responded to the call at Garcia's home a few hours later. They handled both patients. Must have carried the DNA from one to the other. That's what I figure. I guess maybe DNA evidence isn't perfect after all."

"Maybe someday it will be. Let's hope so."

***

After Felner's release, he accompanied his sister to Bob Harris's office. They both thanked him profusely. Felner shook Bob's hand.

"I just want you to know I promised Sara I'm going to change. This time I really mean it. You saved my life. I'm not going to be drinking anymore. I'm cleaning up my act thanks to you and her. I'm going into a rehab program."

"Glad to hear that," Bob said and meant it. "You've been given a second chance. Don't blow it."

"I won't," Felner promised.

Sara Felner was smiling for the first time since he'd met her. "Mr. Harris, would your wife mind if I gave you a hug?"

"Under the circumstances, I think she'd allow it," he said, smiling himself.

Steven James Cordin is a native of the Chicago South Suburbs. Steve has worked in banking as a repo man, foreclosure guru and fraud investigator. He writes about fraud, crime and horror fiction. His stories have appeared in *Shotgun Honey*, *Mystery Tribune* and *The Yard: Crime Blog*. Steve is currently working on a collection of crime fiction short stories.

THE DOUBLE CROSS AND THE DOUBLE CROSS

"The cops got all four of them," DiCarlo said, watching the nightly news. "Just like I said."

DiCarlo sat on the other end of the couch from Reynolds and laughed. Baxter stood by the coffee table, his eyes glued to the television. The TV showed an aerial view of the museum as four men were led handcuffed to a police van. DiCarlo couldn't make out their faces, but he knew who they were. The newscaster explained that the police arrested the robbers before they broke in. It was the lead story.

"I told you it would work," DiCarlo said, grinning at Reynolds and Baxter. He was a short, muscular young man with a blonde crewcut. He grabbed his Glock from the coffee table and stuck it in a coat pocket. "I tipped the cops off about the score, and they took Garrity's crew down. C'mon, let's go. I figure we have a few hours before the cops search their houses."

They piled into Baxter's SUV. DiCarlo rode in the back, studying his two partners. Baxter was quiet as he drove. He was a long, lanky man with thinning, dark hair. DiCarlo knew Baxter would follow his lead. They took down a bunch of scores together. He'd never worked with Reynolds before Baxter brought him in on this score. Reynolds stared out the passenger window, his reflection showed his lips set in a grim line. The grapevine said he was a solid guy to have on a job.

As they drove, Reynolds eventually turned to face DiCarlo. "You backed out of the score they were planning and dropped a dime on them. Won't they put it together you double-crossed them and ripped off their homes?"

"I've done this before." DiCarlo gave him a crooked smile. "They don't know my real name or that I know where they live. They won't get arraigned and bailed out for at least forty-eight hours since it's Memorial Day weekend. I will be long gone before Garrity and his crew get out and realize I double-crossed them."

"How do we know you won't double-cross us?"

DiCarlo's shoulders bobbed. "We will split the take tonight and go our separate ways. Baxter's worked with me before. He knows I won't screw him."

Baxter glanced over his shoulder at DiCarlo. "Yep."

Reynolds nodded and turned back to the window, his face betraying nothing of his thoughts. DiCarlo's smirk slowly faded into a frown. He sat back and looked down at his feet. DiCarlo was a professional thief, but this job was far from professional. He told Reynolds and Baxter he backed out of the museum job so they could rip off Garrity's crew. He didn't back out. Garrity threw him out of the crew. The bastard refused to work with DiCarlo and the other three went along with his decision. Garrity was a tough, up-and-coming player, expanding into girls and dope. No one wanted to cross him. *But I stuck it to that prick though, Garrity going to rot in jail and pay. They all will pay.*

Malone, one of the men arrested at the museum, had a condo twenty minutes from DiCarlo's apartment. Malone lived alone and the place was dark. DiCarlo never liked him, the dick was so full of himself. Baxter remained in the SUV, keeping a lookout for police. Reynolds picked the front door's lock in seconds. They searched each room, looking for Malone's stash from previous scores. The place was neat, almost sterile, with only a few mismatched pieces of furniture. DiCarlo wasn't surprised to find the price tags still on a few table lamps. Malone was something of a transient, never calling any one place home. Roll into a town and set up a place to sleep. Do a few jobs and then move on before anyone caught up with him. As DiCarlo searched the bedroom, it dawned on him how much they were alike.

Reynolds found Malone's loot hidden under a floorboard behind a couch: a metal box containing several stacks of cash and jewelry. DiCarlo watched him, impressed. *Reynolds is good, a shame this is his last job.*

Then they drove to Carlson's house; he was the second man arrested. The house was a small one-story bungalow at the edge of the city, an area known for hookers and drug deals. DiCarlo knew Carlson kept a key under a pot next to the backdoor. The plant inhabiting the pot had died long ago, but the key was still there. The stench of decay struck them as they entered the kitchen. The place was a mess. The sink was full of dishes beginning to look fuzzy. The kitchen table covered in partially filled takeout containers and pizza boxes.

"Christ," Reynolds murmured, shaking his head in disgust. "I hope we don't have to search his fridge."

It took longer to search Carlson's house; the rest of the place was as much of a dump as the kitchen. Carlson loved to tell stories about all the big scores he pulled over the years. DiCarlo encouraged him and pretended to eat it up like candy, all the while planning to rip him off.

"I don't know man." Reynolds stood in front of the kitchen sink, his shoulders slumping in defeat. "Maybe he didn't keep it here or maybe he doesn't have anything."

DiCarlo's eyes cut him a glare and he waved his hand in dismissal. "No. Carlson hit some big scores over the years. There gotta be some . . . "

His voice trailed off as he followed Reynolds gaze out the window above the sink.

The garage.

They found the loot hidden in a tool chest. More stacks of cash and three packets of heroin.

"You going to take that?" Reynolds asked, pointing to the heroin.

"Yep. I know someone who can move it."

"I'm not waiting on that. I'll just take my cut in cash when we are done tonight."

"Sure." *You will get your cut alright.*

"Are we going to hit Rodriguez's place next?" Baxter asked

after the others got back in the SUV. Rodriguez was the third man arrested.

"No." DiCarlo shook his head. "We will go to Garrity's cabin. Rodriguez has a wife and kids. They could be home. I don't want to mess with that. Garrity's place is out in the woods and the cops won't get around to it for a while."

"Garrity's a hard case," Reynolds warned. "He's not someone I would want to double-cross. I hear his son stays out there sometimes when Garrity isn't using the place."

DiCarlo looked up from the duffel bag he was stuffing the cash in. "Garrity is going to be away for a long time. There are three of us if the son is there. It's the perfect place for Garrity to hide his money. We're going."

I hope the son is there. DiCarlo smiled to himself. *What better way to get back at Garrity than killing his kid?*

The clock on the dashboard read four in the morning by the time they reached the cabin, a criminal's dream hideout. It was in a secluded area, miles from the nearest neighbor. The two-story building was huge and dark; the whole place was lavishly furnished and well maintained. Garrity often threw wild parties here, entertaining his drug connections and bringing girls up from his club.

Reynolds was quiet as they entered. He found the floor safe under a rug in the master bedroom in only a few minutes. DiCarlo watched him examine the safe, his hand on the Glock in his coat pocket. *Not yet, but soon.*

"It will take me a few minutes to open this," Reynolds told DiCarlo, not bothering to look up. "Why don't you look around for anything else?"

DiCarlo went back into the main room. Pale morning light streamed through the front door. DiCarlo moved toward the door, but then a large figure loomed in the doorway. DiCarlo expected Baxter to come in to help him finish off Reynolds and hide the body. DiCarlo planned to shoot Baxter afterwards and blow town with the entire score. But this was a shorter, older man with a barrel chest. He held a pistol trained at DiCarlo.

"Garrity?"

"I sent one of my guys to take my place in the heist." Garrity tossed DiCarlo's duffel bag of cash on the floor. He looked behind DiCarlo. "I took care of Baxter. We will take their bodies further into the woods and dump them."

Reynolds reached into DiCarlo's coat as he walked past and pulled out the Glock. He came to stand next to Garrity, aiming at DiCarlo's head.

"You are double-crossing *me*?" DiCarlo took a step back, ready to run.

Garrity and Reynolds exchanged glances.

"I think of it as not double-crossing my dad," Reynolds said and fired.

Ricky Sprague is a writer and cartoonist whose work has appeared in *Mystery Magazine, Ellery Queen Mystery Magazine, Mysterical-e, MAD,* and *Cracked,* and various short story book collections, including four published in 2021: *Mystery Magazine's Die Laughing* hardcover collection, *Asinine Assassins* from Smart Rhino, *Crimeucopia: As In Funny Ha-Ha or Just Peculiar* from Murderous Ink, and Moonstone's *Domino Patrick: Daughter of Domino Lady* collection. He is the author of the crime graphic novel *Gut-Shot,* inspired by his friend Ed Gorman's story "Stalker," from *Short, Scary Tales,* and the colorist for Chris Wisnia's *Doris Danger* from Fantagraphics, both forthcoming in 2022.

THE GRYFTERS

Felony 1

I handled my first carjacking with real sang-froid.

Stopped at the light at La Cienega and Wilshire, I saw a man running out of the Starbucks with what I would call a wary look on his face, casting furtive glances over his shoulder. He looked up to no good I decided judgmentally, happy that there was no reason why I should become involved in whatever that "no good" he was "up to" would turn out to be.

And yet, he seemed to do a double take when he saw my Hyundai. Well—the 2016 Accent SE *is* a practical, reliable automobile; even so, I was alarmed to see him powerwalking in my direction.

"Why is the light taking so long to change?" I wondered, directing my gaze to the radio. It wasn't on, but Mr. Up-to-no-good didn't know that. I pretended to fiddle with the dials, endlessly distracted with the task of finding something to listen to while he (hopefully) walked right past.

With a gun he tapped on the driver's side rear door window while impatiently pulling the door handle. How long could I pretend not to hear him?

"Lemme in dude!"

What was that?

"Hey! Hyundai! Open up!"

This was the longest red light in history.

"Lemme in dude I know this is Dan's car!"

Invoking my roommate's name did nothing to relieve my tension. Dan was prone to the cultivation of relationships with people that were, for lack of a better word, not entirely honest. And the Hyundai was definitely not his car. It was mine.

More to relieve the awkward tension than out of fear he might actually shoot me (surely he'd be too self-conscious to actually use his gun at a busy intersection at rush hour), I unlocked the doors and he climbed into the backseat.

He slouched, peeking out through the rear window toward La Cienega. "Stay casual. Get into the center lane and go straight through this light."

"Buh—but I need to turn left—"

"Nah. Where's Dan, by the way?"

"He—he's probably taking a nap or playing video games or something."

The light changed and I had to concentrate to keep from flooring it. I managed to maneuver the Hyundai one lane over and get stopped at the red for another long cycle.

That seemed to last.

Forever.

"He let you borrow his car?"

"This is my car. Why do you think it's his?"

"This is the one he always picks me up in," he shrugged with his voice.

That simple, casual statement filled me with a fine sense of impending doom. "When—what does—um, what d'you mean—pick you up?" I stammered. In times of stress I often trade periods for em dashes.

In the rearview mirror I saw him smile. His fingers moved furiously over the face of his cell phone. "He gives me a lift sometimes. Like you're doing now. Go right on Robertson, please."

"That's the—the *opposite* direction from where I want to—to go—"

He gave me a disappointed look into the rearview mirror. "I

just stuck my gun in my pants. Don't make me get it back out."

"You probably—um, it seems like it'd be, you know—unsafe—keeping a gun in your, um, pants like—that—"

"Keep your mind off my pants and just keep driving." Again, he looked over his shoulder.

"But I'm—I'm working—I'm on my way to—to a screening at the Globe-Ball Theatre in—in forty-five minutes—"

"Right. Dan said you work at Mountaincrest Studios. In marketing or something?"

"*International* Marketing. Who are you and—and why do you, you know—know so much about me? Nuh—no offense."

"I'm Chi-Town. This stuff back here for your screening?"

He turned his attention to the two boxes of press kits for what was certain to be another Mountaincrest Studios underperformer, *The Mountain Goat*. Each kit consisted of a presentation folder with the poster image on the outside, and pockets containing a few pages of information on the plot, characters, cast, crew, and images (which would hopefully be used by members of the Hollywood International Press in their glowing reviews and coverage) on the inside. With only seven HIPster RSVPs, we were going to have to messenger a lot of the press kits directly to their homes.

He flipped through a press kit, skimming its contents while he tapped away at the face of his cell phone. "Looks kinda dumb. But I do like Jordyn Li. She's gonna be big."

"Yeah," I said again. I turned my full attention back to the road, knuckles white on the steering wheel. "Look, I really need to—to get to my screening, you know?"

He leaned forward. In a confidential tone, his head just a few inches from my ear, he said, "Drop me off around back of the Garden of Eatin' on 3rd. Then you'll be on your way."

I felt a wave of relief wash over me, then felt resentment that I should feel relieved. This was *my* car. I was supposed to be at the screening already. Passing out press kits.

Instead, I was maneuvering into the alley behind the Garden of Eatin'. When I glanced into the rearview Chi-Town was idly twisting and folding one of the press kit folders. I decided he probably didn't respect other people's property. When the car stopped he leaned forward again, said, "Tell Dan to come here and pick me up at 12:30 tonight. Just between you and me, I actually don't need him here until one, but Dan's not the most reliable dude in the world. He runs a little late sometimes." He threw a $100 bill onto my lap. "Thanks for the unscheduled ride."

With that he got out of the car and trotted off into the building, stuffing a cell phone into his back pocket and carrying the rolled-up press kit to which he'd apparently felt entitled. I pulled forward to the end of the alley and sat waiting and waiting and waiting for a chance to turn onto 3rd. Just as I got what appeared to be a good opportunity my phone buzzed with a call from my boss, Philip. As I answered, the car in front of me stopped faster than anticipated, while the car behind moved forward, precariously closing what I'd thought was a Hyundai-sized opening in the traffic flow. Then a 2012 Prius turned into the alley, nearly hitting my car. The driver had a carelessly deranged look on his face. I slammed the brakes.

In the backseat, the press kits toppled over onto the floor. Of course. It was just that kind of day.

***

After the screening I got back to the apartment to find Dan sitting on the futon playing video games, having just awakened from a nap. I was so annoyed that I actually stalked to the TV and pressed the POWER button. For me, this was a serious rebuke.

"Hey. Didn't hear you come in."

"Um," I fulminated.

"There was something I wanted to tell you. You know how you're always saying I should make more money—"

"Don't put words in my mouth."

"I'm not trying to put anything in your mouth. But you do tell me I should contribute to rent and stuff . . . "

"That's true."

"Well, the good news is, I got a regular gig."

"That is good news."

"Actually, as I think of it, the word 'news' has a sort of negative connotation. 'Fake news' and all that—"

"Stop!" I nearly shouted. "The only reason you're telling me this now is because you know that I 'met' your friend Chi-Town tonight."

He stood and said in a placating tone, "I realize that we're all a little upset right now, but the good news is—"

"Your regular gig?"

"I was going to say the good news is that Chi-Town is very happy with how you handled yourself today in all that traffic—"

"Why did—he think he could—could just—walk up to my car in the middle of the street and get a ride?"

"He had a gun for one thing . . . "

"Guns do tend to open doors," I conceded.

"For another thing—and this relates to the good news I mentioned before . . . the regular gig? I do this sort of rideshare thing. You know, like Uber."

"Like Uber, but not actually Uber?" In my mind I was being viciously ironic. If Dan had any self-awareness or shame he would have withered under my vitriol.

"Exactly. It's not 'official,' so to speak. It doesn't even have a name yet. Some people are calling it *Crimeshare*, you know, sort of like rideshare? But that 'crime' is a little on the nose for some of us. Other people are calling it *Gryft*, you know, sort of a cross between grift and the rideshare service Lyft, with a *y*? Which one do you like best?"

I stared at him for a few stunned seconds, or minutes. Time has little meaning when you're faced with such staggeringly dumb venality. He misinterpreted the reason for my silence and added, "Grift means swindle."

"You've been using my car to—to chauffeur criminals?" I sputtered.

"I've been putting your car to good use while you slept. It would have just been parked under the building, not making any money otherwise—"

"That's why I've been burning through gas so fast lately."

"It's a win-win all around."

"How? Actually—never mind. I don't care. Stop it."

"You mean this conversation, or . . . ?"

"Stop using my car."

"Okay. After tonight I'll—"

"Stop using my car right—right *now*," I sputtered in an admittedly screechy tone. "If you're going to—to do this—this—incredibly dumb thing you're doing—then—don't—use my car—use your own car."

His face pouted. "The Monte Carlo isn't as reliable as your Hyundai."

"This isn't—just—okay—wow." I had to pause for a breath. Before Dan had a chance to fill the silence I hissed at him, "*Donoteverusemycaragainwithoutasking.*"

"That sounds pretty final," Dan conceded. He watched me a few seconds, as if waiting for me to relent. Finally he said, "Okay. I'll use Monte."

I sighed. "Chi-Town wants you to pick him up behind the Garden of Eatin' tonight at . . . midnight," I told him. "Do with that information what you want. It's your life. But if you do choose to continue doing this incredibly dumb thing, use your own car."

I went into my room, shaking with frustration. I didn't get to sleep until after Dan had left. In his own car.

***

The next morning I parked the Hyundai on the lot and carried the press kits to the Mountaincrest Studios messenger service in the Stuart Palmer Building. I filled out the paperwork to arrange for the delivery of eighty-seven *Mountain Goat* press kits to those Hollywood International Press members ("HIPsters") who hadn't bothered to attend the previous night's screening.

From there I hiked to the Gorman Building to my own International Marketing offices where I settled in with a couple of very exciting spreadsheets full of fascinating international territory gross reports, made travel arrangements for the cast of *Black Willows*, booked the Burbank Airport Hilton for a press junket, and put together a strategy memo for marketing *Postmortem 2* in the eight European and Asian territories for which Mountaincrest was handling the distribution.

Around 3:15 P.M. I got a call from Carl Cortez, a HIPster thanks in part to his status as *Bulgaria Today's* "Entertainment Reporter at Large." "I'm sorry I missed the screening last night. I heard good things about the movie—I'm sure it'll be a big hit for Mountaincrest," he said, managing to work at least three lies into two sentences.

"We missed you at the screening." See? I could lie, too.

Those polite preliminaries out of the way, he got straight to the objective of his call: "I need the passcode to unlock the cell phone."

"What do you mean?" Not to be callous, but he was an older gentleman and maybe he'd gotten me confused with his cell phone's service provider.

His response only clouded things: "Or is this something where there's a clue in the movie? I was just going to write up a review based on what Gemma told me about it, but if you tell me how to unlock the phone I'll write something positive instead."

"Um." It was part of my job to keep HIPsters happy in hopes they'd give Mountaincrest films positive reviews. But I had no idea what he was talking about. "If there was a cell phone in your press kit, I don't know anything about it."

"Oh," he said. "Well, I wonder how it got in there . . . "

"Is there anything on the home screen that shows whose it is? Picture or something?"

"No. It's asking for a nine-digit passcode. You know, my phone only needs six . . . "

"What does it look like?"

"It's a black iPhone." Just like mine, which, I noted, was safely sitting on the desk, charging on the computer.

"Hm." I was starting to get the feeling that this was going to be one of those situations I sometimes find myself in, where someone ends up dead.

"It's a good marketing idea," Carl said. "If you have a movie that's about cell phones. You could put the whole press kit on one."

"That is a good idea." A big part of my job involved humoring HIPsters.

"Say, if you do that, could you make the phones—those new Androids—what are they called . . . ?"

"I know what you're thinking of," I lied. "Hang on to it. I'm gonna ask around and I'll let you know what I find . . . "

***

I asked around and found nothing. This filled me with even more than my usual amount of consternation because even though I was certain I'd seen Chi-Town stuff a cell phone into his back pocket, I couldn't remember if it was the same cell phone I'd seen him typing on during the "Gryft." Who has two cell phones? Well, people on the grift, for instance. This gave rise to the fore-boding suspicion that one of Chi-Town's cell phones somehow made its way into a *Mountain Goat* press kit. My mind frantically played out several different scenarios. Most plausible: He'd slid it under the driver's seat and when the press kits spilled onto the floor I'd inadvertently scooped the phone into one of the folders.

Which meant I'd accidentally involved Mountaincrest and the Hollywood International Press in something that was most likely, for lack of a better word, shady as heck. And that revelation triggered my intense and nearly immobilizing sense of shame.

At that point Philip, my boss and the head of International Marketing, strode from his office and stood at my desk, towering over me with a deeply disapproving look. There was no way to pretend to be immersed in a spreadsheet. I had to acknowledge his presence as, in his thick Texas accent, he drawled menacingly, "I just got a call from Marcia Chadwell of the *Singapore Times*. Before that, Gemma Hunt of *East Europe Now*. Before that, Anatole Marquand of *Alarm France*. All of them wondering how they can finagle one of those free cell phones that Carl received."

"I'm—um—" I articulated.

"Call the messenger service and have them pick it up."

"Actually, I'm—um, I think it's—I think that I'm responsible, so—my roommate is actually responsible, so, I'm gonna have him go get it. It's his responsibility."

He gave me a skeptical look. "I have a feeling I want to be included out of this." He walked away.

Unfortunately I didn't have that luxury. When Dan answered the phone he affected a tone of wounded resentment. "Chi-Town was not at the Garden of Eatin'. I got there a little late, I admit—"

"How late?"

"12:45. Waited until almost 1:30. No-show cancellations are tough to collect on. Gryft kinda operates on an honor system which, upon reflection, is sort of a bug."

"He wasn't there at all?"

"That's what I just said. Somebody at Myth101—you know, the club upstairs from the Garden of Eatin'? No? Well, anyway, there's this club upstairs from there—okay, okay, sorry—anyway, somebody there said he was supposed to meet somebody there at eight, and he left with that person, then they went up the PCH, but that's all I could find out. Are you sure he said meet him there?"

"Yes. Look—I can't go into this stuff right now. I need you to go to Sherman Oaks and pick up Chi-Town's phone from a HIPster." I gave him an abridged overview of all the stupid things that were happening, along with my theory.

"So you want to use the Gryft, huh? How much will you give me?"

I felt astonished. "How about I just pay all the rent on the apartment this month, the way I do almost every month anyway?"

"Ouch. I really do hate to give up my parking space. I'm only two blocks down."

I conceded it was too bad to lose that space. "Still, I need you to get that phone."

He sighed, putting a nice passive aggressive twist on the end of the conversation. "All right. I guess I'll see you in a couple of hours."

Felony 2

I handled my first home invasion with real aplomb.

When I opened the apartment door I heard the sounds of

activity in the living room. My first thought was that Dan was celebrating the successful (and disconcertingly early) completion of his mission with a rousing party that would make me painfully uncomfortable.

Alas, when I went through the corridor I saw a woman with a regal, almost aloof bearing, in a long dark coat and a fitted red suit. Behind her was an enormous man, at least two hundred fifty pounds, all of it muscle.

I had no idea who they were but I had a dreadful premonition I wasn't going to like it when I found out.

She smiled the smile of a person who regarded you as less than human. Neither of them displayed any self-consciousness, despite being caught in the act of performing a sort of avant-garde deconstructionist redecorating of our apartment.

I was only able to croak out the word "What—" before she interrupted with, "You're Chris?"

"Yes. Who're—um, you? Why are you—destroying my apartment?"

"I'm Ms. Serrano. Your roommate does some subcontracting with me through my Gryft service."

"So—you, um—settled on a name?" I asked stupidly.

"Well, not officially," she conceded. "Now some people want to call it *Getaway*, sort of a play on Getaround. There was also one vote each for *Incarrigible* and *RideshareTheBlame*."

"I'd probably stick with—you know, Gryft."

She nodded and moved on: "Your Hyundai is parked under the building now?"

Without thinking I nodded. Then hastened to add, "Wh—why do you ask?"

She spoke into her Bluetooth. "It's in the garage. Oh, you're in it now? Okay."

"What—you know, what is all this?"

"Dan's been using your car working for us. I assure you I didn't know that; if I had, I wouldn't have let him. Our drivers need to use their own vehicles."

"That makes sense."

"I know that yesterday you were conscripted into giving a ride to one of my former associates, Chi-Town. Well—he was more my ex-husband's associate, actually. He stole a phone from me, turned off the remote tracking and erase, and left it in your car, intending to retrieve it later."

"This is the first I'm—um, hearing about this. Um, other than the—you know, the part about me being conscripted, as you put it. That—I was, you know—um, aware of that part." Not that I was actively counting, but this was my second lie of the day. But I wanted to make sure I actually had the phone and that Mountaincrest and the Hollywood International Press were completely separated from this entire Mystery Phone Incident before I said anything more.

She smiled. "I assumed you were an innocent bystander. But I need to find that phone. Which is why I'm going over your apartment, and why I've got people searching your car right now."

"Um—I don't have the phone."

"Naturally I believe you. But I don't trust you. Which is why my associate is also going to thoroughly frisk you."

"I wish you wouldn't do that."

"Do you know where the phone is?"

"Um, no."

"Where is Dan?"

Uh-oh. "Um—I don't know." Then, very casually, I said, "Isn't he, um—here?"

She didn't buy it. "Does he have the phone?"

"No. I mean—no."

"Give him a call. I'd like to check with him."

"Um. He doesn't—"

Her associate went through my bag, handed my cell phone to me. "That's not the phone?"

"Nuh—no. It's mine." They watched intently as I unlocked the phone and, with only slightly trembling hands, dialed.

"Speaker," she ordered.

I had to hope that Dan wouldn't answer or, if he did, that he would be subtle and not immediately launch into conversation, as he did almost every time I called him about anything.

"Still looking for Chi-Town's phone," he said immediately upon answering.

"You'reonspeaker," I hissed.

"Ol' Carl had it, but get this—"

"Hello Chris!" Carl's voice called out.

"Carl!?—why are you with—where—"

"We're on the Cahuenga Pass," Dan explained. "On the trail of the phone. Carl traded it for ganja—"

"Medical ganja," Carl clarified with elaborate dignity.

"Wait. Why am I on speaker?" Dan finally asked.

"Hello Dan. This is Ms. Serrano. I'm at your apartment with Chris. I'm so happy to hear you're looking for my phone."

"Oh snizzap," Dan said after a pause. "Hey. Hi. I didn't know the two of you knew each other. Talk about worlds colliding!"

"We, um—just met."

"I'm very anxious to retrieve that phone," Ms. Serrano said.

"Who's Ms. Serrano?" Carl asked.

"She's a crime boss," Dan said. Then: "Sorry. She's a *legitimate businesswoman.*"

"Bring me my phone," Ms. Serrano said threateningly.

"Okay. We'll have it shortly. But I'm gonna stop by and pick up Chris first."

"Why?"

"I'd just feel better if Chris was with me."

"What've you gotten me into?" Carl asked.

"Shut up. You're the one who wanted a ride into LA."

"My car won't start—"

"Fine," Ms. Serrano growled. "You can have your roommate. But I expect to get my phone back tonight."

"You will. Where's Chi-Town?"

"I don't know. I've got people looking for him," Ms. Serrano said even more threateningly.

"Hm. Well, okay, I guess . . . " Dan said vaguely.

"I'm going to give Chris my number," Ms. Serrano said.

I didn't want her number.

"We'll swing by in a few minutes, hop in the Hyundai, and get this taken care of toots sweet," Dan said optimistically.

***

Ms. Serrano's associates had been very thorough in their deconstruction of the Hyundai before getting word that the phone was definitely not in it. I'm not sure why I was so surprised that you could actually remove a Hyundai's seats and leave them on the ground outside the frame, but I was.

For this reason, the Hyundai wasn't available. So I met the Monte Carlo at the curb outside the apartment building and climbed into the backseat, which was littered with a bunch of random papers and trash.

"How'd she seem?" Dan asked.

"I—she broke into our apartment and—and tossed it. She seemed unreasonable."

"She must like you."

"Wha—huh?"

"She's ordinarily pretty ruthless with people. She killed her husband. You know that, right?"

"Why would I know that? This was the first I'd ever met her."

"She has a reputation. Anyway. It wasn't one of those genteel kind of murders where someone kills someone with an ice bullet in a locked room and then they stand behind the door so that when a crowd breaks in they just step out from behind said door and join the crowd like they just got into the room, too. This was hardcore gangster stuff. See, she cut his throat, then she reached in—"

"That's enough," I squeaked. I felt itchy all over. Then I said, to Carl: "Not that I'm not happy to see you, but why'd you tag along in this?"

"L-Train is at BowlPins. I wanted to go."

"L-Train is your dealer?"

"Of medical marijuana."

"And you traded him the phone?"

"I have back pain; don't judge me."

"I'm not judging you about that," I said in a judgmental tone.

"I'm judging you for selling the phone we accidentally messen-gered to you, even after I specifically asked you to hold onto it while I tried to figure out where it came from—" Then, realiz-ing to whom I was speaking I hastened to add: "Not that I'm, you know—actually judging you or anything—I—I just—it's obviously—um—"

"It's all cool. Just a few more minutes and we've got the phone back," Dan said, as the Monte Carlo stalled at a stoplight.

***

About a mile from BowlPins Dan called L-Train, to arrange for him to come out and hand over the phone.

"Hey, dawg. I left BowlPins a while ago. I'm at Maté's."

"That's in Santa Monica!"

"Yeah. Just come get me. I'm in the back in the Allison Wonderland Room."

After they'd hung up Dan said, "I'm gonna get on the freeway."

"Is this—the—um, Monte Carlo safe on the freeway?"

Dan shrugged. "This time of day it's all stop-and-go anyway."

The traffic in fact never went much above thirty, which was just as well, as that was the speed at which the Monte Carlo began to shake and roar violently. We only came to a complete stop seven times, and the engine only died twice.

"Now you know why I need the Hyundai," Dan told me as I returned to my seat after giving the car a push.

"I don't see how this car is even street legal," I said, coughing from the exhaust.

"Oh, it's not in California. Hence the Arizona plates."

I didn't answer, but did shake out my shirt in a vain attempt to cool myself. Of course, the air conditioning in his decrepit rattle-trap didn't work, either.

Finally we exited the 405 and made our way over surface streets to the parking structure on 3rd. Winding up over the struc-ture's ramp was a precarious endeavor; the Monte Carlo's turning mechanism required a lot of what Dan cheerfully referred to as "elbow grease." Thankfully we found parking on the third level. Dan pulled the car in, engaged the parking brake, then asked me to get out and retrieve one of the cinder blocks from the trunk and place it behind one of the back wheels.

"Can't have ol' Monte rolling away," Dan said.

The three of us went down to 3rd, then left on Santa Monica, to Maté's. There was a line of very attractive and provocatively dressed people waiting for admittance and the bouncer clearly had no intention of letting two young doofuses and one elderly doofus in. Even after we'd explained we were part of L-Train's "posse," he remained unmoved.

Carl decided to lay down his trump card: "I'm with the Hollywood International Press. Our members have readership all over the world. If you let us in I can guarantee this club will get a glowing review in *Bulgaria Today*."

That got a reaction from the bouncer. Derisive laughter.

Dan turned to the bouncer and played his own trump card, "We're here for Ms. Serrano."

He looked confused. "Ms. Serrano's not here."

I said, "Um—do you really think we should, you know—drop her name in this, you know—context?" The less association I had with her, the better, it seemed to me.

Dan ignored me. "I know that. We're here on a mission for Ms. Serrano."

"A 'mission'?" the bouncer repeated, laughing.

"Okay, an errand then," Dan said.

The bouncer called to someone inside the club who joined him to laugh at Dan's awkward yet entirely grammatically correct use of the word "mission." Dan, annoyed, turned to me and said, "Give her a call."

"I'm not calling her," I insisted. "This is ridiculous. Just call L-Train again."

"Call her and she can clear this whole thing up," Dan said.

I hissed at him, "*Idon'twantarecordofmycallingheronmyphone.*"

The bouncers looked at each other and said, "Wait. You really do know Ms. Serrano, don't you?"

"Unfortunately," I groaned. "We just have to talk to someone inside this club. We'll be in and out in five minutes."

"Otherwise," Dan said with stagey ominousness, "Ms. Serrano herself might show up."

The bouncer waved us all through. Inside, the noise that passed as music was an incoherent jumble that seemed designed to rattle and unnerve me even while the dim, confused, flashing Technicolor of the lighting made it impossible to trust my own eyes. I'd rather be riding around in Dan's car.

"I'll just wait here at the front," I shouted at Dan over the noise.

"Aw, come on back," Dan insisted. "It'll do you good—you might want to book this place for a premiere party or something."

That didn't seem possible but I also didn't necessarily want to be left alone and exposed in the front of the club, so I followed Dan and Carl back to the private Allison Wonderland Room.

L-Train was seated on the couch with a young, curvy woman in a short skirt and spiked heels. The two were avidly groping each other. Two other women stood dancing beside them. As we walked into the room, someone I took to be a customer slinked past us. My entire body seized in a massive and uncontrollable cringe. I just wanted to get the phone and get out again, go home, and crawl under my blankets and forget tonight ever happened.

Alas. L-Train greeted us with, "Glad you're here. You all can give me and Corona here a ride to Kim's Hot Take." He indicated the woman with whom he was frotting. "I'm a big fan of the Hyundai. Such an unobtrusive, practical car."

"We're in the Monte Carlo tonight," Dan said.

"It's more exciting," Carl said.

"Too bad. We still need a lift though." He put a hand on Corona's hip and kissed her mouth.

"Could you, um—you know, get an actual Gryft?"

L-Train gave me a confused look then said, "Oh, you mean Crimeshare. Why would I do that when you're already here?"

"We just, you know—we need the, um—the phone—"

"That's where we're going. To get the phone." Even with the music blaring his condescending tone was clear. "My girl Miss Z has it."

"But how—why—it's, um—it's not—"

"I owed her $200, so I gave her the phone," he explained. Corona kissed his neck. "So you'll have to buy it from her when you see her."

"Um."

"There ought'a be a finder's fee, too," Corona said, eyeing me with that dismissive "no chance" look with which I was so well acquainted. "You look pretty square. I bet you can cover it."

"What do you say— a hundred bucks?" L-Train posited.

"We're driving you," I sputtered.

"I'm considering that in the calculation of my fee. Where'd you park?"

So we all made our way to the Monte Carlo: me, Dan, Carl, L-Train, and Corona, who was definitely *not* L-Train's girlfriend— that was Miss Z, who we were on our way to meet. For some reason, it had become my job to deal with the exterior cinder block brake. As Dan turned the ignition and held it for the necessary fourteen seconds while quickly depressing the gas up and down he said, "Last time I had this many people in here, we had a tough time making it over anything with more than three percent slope."

"As long as we're not all going over the hill we'll be fine," L-Train reassured us. He kissed Corona again. They were in the backseat beside me, Corona's bottom occasionally rubbing against my hip, despite my efforts to the contrary.

Turning and twisting down the parking garage ramp resulted in a good cardio workout for Dan, two stall outs, and a lot of angry shouts and honking from the backed-up traffic. Carl noted, philosophically, that Los Angeles was a city of congestion, and to rage about it in a parking structure the height of churlishness.

With an almost majestic rattle, the Monte Carlo pulled out onto 3rd. Much as I tried to find it charming, I was beginning to feel sick with worry and stress. Why was I stuck in this jiggling flivver with four other people, on a stupid errand I still didn't fully understand? In some ways I guess it felt like a metaphor for my life, but something snapped in my brain and I couldn't think about that anymore.

I kept looking round at the traffic, self-consciously certain everyone else was watching us with brutal judgment. It was at this point I noticed the Ford Escort that had fallen into the lane behind us, keeping a fairly steady distance even as other vehicles moved in and out to the sounds of honking and shouted obscenities.

"I, um—think we're being followed."

Everyone craned their necks to look out the back window.

"Yep," Dan said. "That's the fuzz. Good eye."

"This is kind of exciting," Carl said. "We're in an incredibly low-speed chase."

"They're tailing us. But I can lose them."

I almost asked how, but decided it wasn't worth the bother. Unfortunately, Dan proceeded to answer that unasked question by suddenly pulling the wheel to the left, cutting across two lanes of traffic, then making an immediate left turn at Wilshire. He hadn't even looked before doing it; he'd simply relied on his belief that everyone else on the streets of Santa Monica actually cared about their cars, and would stop or swerve. Which they all did. He then made a right on a side street and pulled up to the curb. It felt like it had all happened with jarring rapidity. But in fact I knew we'd never topped thirty, as the Monte Carlo never rattled or stalled out.

"We'll let them pass," Dan said.

"Shouldn't you—actually shut the car off?" For some reason, I was whispering.

"It's too much hassle to start it again."

"Too late. The po-po found us," Corona said.

The Escort pulled up beside the Monte Carlo and I tried to position myself behind Corona and L-Train while awaiting the mocking laughter I was sure was to come. And the arrest. The driver turned his smiling face toward us and said, "You know how hard it is to tail a clunker like that?"

"*Classic*, not clunker," Dan corrected.

"You were driving pretty erratically back there," the driver pointed out. "In your *classic*."

"Sorry about that. Traffic patterns are a little different here than they are in Arizona."

"Are you two the police?" Carl asked.

The driver nodded. "I'm Officer Rudolfo Alvarez, and this is Officer Andrea Goldstein. We're with the Transit Division—"

"Shouldn't you be staking out the bus stops?" Corona asked derisively.

As the two officers glared at her, I felt my entire body go painfully tense. The driver said, "We heard that one of you invoked the name of Ms. Serrano back at Maté's. We're very curious about her."

"Must've been someone else," Dan said in a confused tone. He looked around at his passengers who all, with one notable exception, shrugged and made questioning sounds. "We've never heard of this . . . Miss Cyrano, did you say?"

"She allegedly provides a service—sort of a casual criminal rideshare thing. Sometimes called the Gryft, with a *y*, like Lyft, or *Car-Treband*, or—"

"*Car-Treband?*" Dan asked exasperated. Then he turned toward the backseat and said softly, "That's one I never heard before."

"I don't like it," L-Train said.

"It's pretty strained," I agreed.

Carl said, "Officers, I don't know if this matters, but I'm Carl Cortez, an accredited journalist and a voting member of the Hollywood International Press. Each year we award the Platinum Orbs. These people are working with me on an important work of entertainment journalism. So we need to get on our way. If you're not going to charge us—"

Everyone else in the Monte Carlo either gasped or groaned.

"Charge you? Why would we do that?" Officer Alvarez asked, eyebrows raised. "Have you done something you should be *charged* for? Aside from all the traffic violations committed while driving your classic, I mean."

"No, it's not that," Carl said, fumblingly. "It's just—you pulled us over—"

"We didn't pull you over. For some reason you stopped your jalopy—with the engine still running—here at the curb. We just stopped to find out what you were up to."

"Well, I've told you. I hope that my important work of

entertainment journalism doesn't have to morph into a scathing indictment of police harassment."

"None of you know who Ms. Serrano is?"

"Honestly, we don't."

Officers Alvarez and Goldstein consulted with each other for what felt like hours. Finally, Officer Alvarez turned back toward us and said, "Have a good night." The Escort drove away.

"That was easy enough," Dan said.

"Too easy," L-Train said. "Something's up."

"Maybe you should, um—get an actual Gryft, rather than—"

"You're not trying to get rid of me are you?" L-Train smiled menacingly.

"Nuh—no!"

"I'll stick with you to Kim's," L-Train said. He returned his attention to Corona and Dan pulled away from the curb, at which point the Monte Carlo's engine died and we drifted to the curb on the other side of the street.

I got out and pushed while Dan restarted the Monte Carlo.

A lot of the trip turned out to be downhill which was a time saving bonus. Two of the engine stall outs occurred at points where gravity went a long way to keeping us in motion.

***

Dan parked in the $20 lot about a block away from Kim's. Carefully and painfully I climbed out of the backseat (barbarically the Monte Carlo had only two doors) and stood on the sidewalk, stomping my legs to get the circulation going again. I heard a bloodcurdling squeal and raised my head in time to see the young woman I correctly guessed to be Miss Z rushing toward us in a very short skirt and impossibly high heels, brandishing her purse in one hand and a Cosmo in the other hand.

"I know you didn't bring *Corona* here!"

I was standing between Miss Z and Corona. Before I could step out of the way, L-Train held me in place and said, "Corona came with my boy Timmy."

I really hate the name Timmy. Before I realized what I was doing I blurted, "My name's not Timmy."

Everyone looked at me, either expectantly, annoyed, or both.

Corona embraced me with sweaty arms, pressing her pleasingly voluptuous body against mine. "Baby's name is T-Roy. You know that L-Train."

Miss Z looked skeptical. "You two—?" was all she felt she needed to say to express her incredulity. As if Corona couldn't land someone like me.

"Oh, yeah," Corona said, slobbering on my cheek. "T-Roy's my main squeeze."

I grimaced; an entirely involuntary reaction. The slobber she was now smearing on my face and lips was at least partly L-Train's and, well, who knew who else?

"You two look real close," Miss Z snarked.

"Girl, I thought you and Corona were okay?" L-Train asked innocently.

"*We're* fine," Miss Z pointed out. "But you, me and *her*"—here she gestured angrily at Corona—"are *not*."

I didn't understand the subtle nuances of their relationship and I was starting to resent having to deal with it at all, so I blurted, "Are you—do you have the phone?"

L-Train prevented her answering by taking her by the shoulders and leading her off to the side, where he started cooing at her, presumably in a very romantic way. Corona stood beside me, arms crossed, watching them. After a few seconds she glanced at me and said, "Way to sell it, dummy."

"It's not you, it's him," Dan said. Then he stage-whispered "Germ-phobe."

"You seem—um, very lovely," I said placatingly.

She smiled. She was an attractive woman. She leaned into me, arm draped over my shoulder. "For an uptight guy you're kinda cute, T-Roy."

"What's with these nicknames? Is this a criminal thing? No offense. But. L-Train, Miss Z, T-Roy, Chi-Town . . . "

"You know Chi-Town?" Corona asked.

"Yeah. Well, kinda. I mean, he carjacked me."

"That's Chi-Town," she smiled knowingly.

"You know where he is?"

She shook her head.

"It's his phone we're trying to find."

"Hm," she said. Then she let out a squeal and rushed for Miss Z and L-Train, who had apparently smoothed things over enough to begin making out against the wall of the building. She called out, "I have *got to* get inside and use the bathroom!" grabbing Miss Z by the arm.

"Let's all go in awhile," Carl said. Unbeknownst to any of us, he'd struck up a conversation with a man who appeared to be perhaps half his age, with close-cropped hair and a leather jacket.

I started to suggest that we just get the phone and go, but everyone was on their way into the club. So, of course I followed. I hoped the bouncers would turn us away but there was no resisting Corona and Miss Z.

Inside the club was dark, with flashing lights of various colors, pulsing at odd seizure-inducing intervals. The music was so loud you could feel it inside your skull, rattling around like an unwelcome "legitimate" businesswoman tossing your apartment.

Miss Z and Corona disappeared off to the bathroom leaving me, Dan, L-Train, Carl, and Carl's brand-new friend Brett, to make inaudible small talk. The one bit of conversation that was clear to me occurred when L-Train leaned toward my ear and said, "I hate to bring this up, but, you owe me three hundred bucks."

"Um. I thought it was two hundred."

He nodded. "Right. I forgot. And by the way—don't get any ideas about Corona."

Startled I said, "Um—of course not. Do you—know Chi-Town?"

"Sure. Good ol' Chi-Town. Everybody knows him. Kind of a character I guess you'd call him. Why?"

"Well, he's the guy who carjacked me."

L-Train laughed. "Like I said—a real character!"

At that point the women returned. Miss Z rushed to me with such alacrity that I flinched. "You're the one who wants the phone, right?"

"Yes!" I felt a wave of relief wash over me. Finally this horrifying night was over. The entire episode was finished and I could crawl back into bed and sleep for, well . . . for about three hours before I had to get back up and go to work again.

"I gave it to Copper."

"The police?"

"No!" She laughed. "I gave it to Copper! P-Dog!"

"Of course," I said, deflated. "You gave it to someone with two nicknames."

"What?" she cried over the music.

"Where is Copper?" I shouted.

"He's down the PCH!" She started moving her body to the music. To Corona she said, "Dance with your T-Roy!"

Corona grabbed my hands and put them on her hips while she moved against me. The fabric of her dress was shockingly thin. This created in me a mixture of feelings I'd rather not discuss here.

"Not that I don't—you know, appreciate this—um—diversion—but I need to—you know, um, get to—down the PCH!—and get the phone from—Copper!"

Corona pouted at me. "You've got to loosen up, T-Roy!"

"Um," I said.

Carl added, "Yeah, I'm in no rush!" He was leaning forward talking to Brett in a very friendly way. Naively I hoped this meant he wouldn't be joining us on what I hoped would be the last leg of our journey.

But of course, he did. And Brett wanted to come, too. So now the Monte Carlo had me, Dan, Corona, Miss Z, L-Train, Carl, and Brett. As Dan went through what I had come to think of as the Ignition Ritual, he smiled sheepishly and said, "I don't see any way we'll get very far with this much weight!"

Instead of inspiring an open and honest conversation on the need to have so many people come along, Dan's carelessly tossed off warning elicited carefree whoops of joy from the others.

The Monte Carlo began its rumbling journey. Carl had Brett on his lap in the front seat, while Miss Z was on L-Train's lap and Corona was practically on my lap beside them. She ran her fingers through my hair, kissing me lightly on the cheek. "If the car doesn't make it," she whispered, "will you give us a nice hard push?"

"Um," I said. Unfortunately this was the most exciting relationship I'd had in a year.

The sound of a ringtone came from Miss Z's purse. She laughed, opened her bag, and removed a cell phone. Started punching the screen. I looked over Corona's shoulder and saw that Miss Z's bag contained another phone—a black iPhone.

She tossed her phone back in her purse and returned her attention to L-Train. The purse hung open. There was the phone. Possibly. Why would Corona and Miss Z lie about giving it to Copper?

My breath was shallow and my heart beat madly. I said, "Corona, I—um, I find you quite—fetching . . . "

"What? You do?"

"Yeh—yes. I think that sitting this close to you is—um, it is very exciting—"

She leaned in closer to me, her arms around my neck. She kissed my nose. "You're so adorable I swear . . . "

I leaned in, put my arms around her, and reached for Miss Z's purse. With sweaty and trembling hands I deftly extracted the phone while Corona kissed my neck. I ignored the sensations (arousal mingled with revulsion) her actions produced, scrolling through to wake up the phone.

The Monte Carlo's pace slowed to a crawl, with horns honking and angry shouts all around as other vehicles with fewer engine problems and less weight easily passed us.

"I really love your rounded shoulders," Corona cooed to me. "It's so nice that you don't have much of a chin . . . "

Ordinarily I'd go for her dirty talk in a big way. But I was too worried that we were being led into a trap for some reason. As the car traveled down the grimy, dark streets of Malibu's industrial district I felt my skin crawling with fear. Also arousal.

"It's up at this turn here, isn't it?" Dan asked.

"Yeah," Corona said, turning her head from me.

The phone's home screen was blank save for the prompt for a nine-digit passcode. During the carjacking I thought I'd seen

Chi-Town sending a text. But what if he'd been changing the passcode? He'd specifically mentioned liking Jordyn Li—the character she played in *Mountain Goat* was called Billie-Lou. Without the dash that was nine characters.

Those nine characters unlocked the phone.

So, Miss Z hadn't given Chi-Town's phone to Copper—she wanted us to deliver it . . . Actually, it occurred to me at that moment that as soon as I'd mentioned it was Chi-Town's phone we were after, Corona had insisted on going to the bathroom with Miss Z.

"Turn up here," Miss Z said.

Clutching the phone in my sweaty palm I pulled away from Corona and said, nonchalantly, "I—um, I'm getting a, you know—a text, um—"

She regarded me wryly. "You'd rather check your phone than me?"

"Just—um, you know—this has been a—um, it might be, um, work—"

"T-Roy takes work very seriously," Carl said gravely, nuzzling Brett's neck.

Surreptitiously I palmed the phone in such a way that—I hoped—made it appear I was removing it from my back pocket. Being in such cramped, uncomfortable quarters helped sell the illusion. I held the phone so the face was tilted away from Corona and scrolled through.

"Turn up here," Corona said to Dan.

It didn't take long to find out why Ms. Serrano was so interested in retrieving the phone.

"Ooh, honey," Corona said, pulling me close. "Your heart's going a mile a minute."

"You're, um—you're doing something, um, to me—"

"It's the next right," Miss Z said.

With great effort Dan made the turn onto a cul-de-sac. At the end of the road stood the most dilapidated beach house in Malibu. It was still probably a ten-million-dollar home set just below street level and overlooking the beach. A particularly unscenic part of the beach, but still Malibu. The Monte Carlo suddenly felt like a death car, if such a thing exists.

Wait—what had Dan said about Chi-Town missing his ride the previous night and going up the PCH with someone? I had a bleak feeling of apprehension that finally overcame my sense of shame as I squeaked, "Dan, I think we should turn around—*turn around* Dan, um *floor it* and *turn around* go back go back *floor it Dan*—"

Dan floored it.

The Monte Carlo rattled to a stop at the end of the cul-de-sac, directly in front of the dilapidated home's driveway.

Felony 3

I handled my first hostage situation with genuine dignity.

Inside the Monte Carlo was heavy silence that lasted several seconds before Corona reached past me and opened the door, then pushed me out. I stumbled into the street. She got out behind me and made a call.

Copper, sometimes known as P-Dog, was an intimidating man with lean muscles and a hard look in his eyes. Also, he had a gun handle sticking out of the top of his pants. Why do people stuff guns down their pants? I'm no expert on the matter, but it seems potentially quite dangerous—

Anyway. Emerging from the front door he smiled and said, "Welcome to Malibu!"

By now Dan was out of the car and standing beside me. L-Train and Miss Z were standing beside the car. Carl and Brett reluctantly stepped out of the car.

"Everybody, come on in," Copper said. His eyes were wide and his nostrils flared with the labor of breathing. He had, for lack of a better word, a very bad look about him.

"We're actually just here to pick up a cell phone," Dan said with admirable calm. "We'll get it and be on our way."

Copper removed the gun from his pants. "Nah," he said. "Let's stay awhile, anyway."

None of us seemed particularly interested in contesting that suggestion. All of us filed into the house. The furniture, which was arrayed in such a way as to suggest a hasty clearing of space, had a grieving, dollar-store chic to it. There were papers and trash on the floor. And of course there was what appeared to be a new bloodstain in the middle of the room. That stain was smeared, suggesting to my naïve mind that a bleeding person had been dragged down the hallway toward the back of the house.

The whole place smelled like grimy, squalid death.

Miss Z, perhaps for the first time realizing the potential danger of the situation, said, "Copper—I've got the phone right—" Then her voice broke off as she searched her bag. It was one of those tiny bags with space only for a cell phone and small wallet and maybe a couple of keys. So it shouldn't have taken her nearly as long to search as it did. Partly she was incredulous that the phone was gone, and partly she was intoxicated. "I did have it—"

"Where's the phone?" Copper demanded.

"I don't know," Miss Z said.

Corona turned to me with an expression of incredulous realization. "You made out with me to—to distract me—"

"What's going on?" L-Train asked, waking up.

"T-Roy's got your phone," Corona said viciously, gesturing toward me.

I really didn't want to give him the phone. "That's not—I mean, I don't—where's Chi-Town?"

"I don't know where Chi-Town is."

"Give him his phone," Corona said.

Part of me felt wounded, somehow. "You're a—a femme fatale," I squeaked.

She smiled. "I guess so. Give him the phone."

"I don't—it doesn't—um—" I stammered.

Copper pointed the gun at me. "Stop messing around. I want that phone."

That got everyone to back away.

"Just give it over," he said.

With trembling hands I gave the phone to Corona, and she hip-swayed to Copper. She handed it to him and they kissed. Again, irrationally, Corona's actions hurt me. Imagine how I would have felt if I'd known her more than three hours.

"Finally," Copper said. He examined it, nonplussed. Then, "What's the code?"

"He knows it," Corona said. "I saw him scrolling through it."

Copper's eyes widened and his nostrils flared. "Tell me the passcode," he hissed.

"I—um, I—I don't—it's—" At that point a couple of things happened. First, I noticed Brett making a movement that I interpreted in a very reassuring way. Second, the Monte Carlo crashed through the garage door with a thunderous noise that rocked the house like an earthquake.

Copper, startled, fired in the direction of the crashing noise. The sound was shocking and painful, far worse than any of the throbbing nightclub music I'd heard earlier. Dan lunged for him, wrestling the gun away, in the process knocking me over while striking Copper on the back of the head with butt of the gun. I rolled out from underneath Copper, then deftly rose from the floor to avoid touching the bloodstain.

Then I noticed that one of the papers on the floor was a rolled page from the interior of the *Mountain Goat* press kit.

Brett moved toward Dan and said, "I'm Officer Fontana with the LAPD Transit Division. You'd better let me have the gun."

"Thanks for the help," Dan said ironically.

"You moved a split second before I did," Brett said defensively.

Carl whined, "You were a bus cop all along?"

Taking the gun from Dan, Brett said, "Alvarez and Goldstein sent me to Kim's to 'meet you,' to find out what exactly you were up to. Something about this cell phone?" He leaned down and picked up from the floor—from the very spot where I'd fallen—a black iPhone.

An eerie quiet fell over the room. After a few seconds, Copper moaned.

"We should—um, probably call an ambulance. Also—I think Chi-Town is—um, back there—" I pointed toward the back of the house.

Officers Alvarez and Goldstein appeared at the door, guns drawn, but with what appeared to me to be inappropriately casual expressions. Officer Alvarez said, "You need to have your brakes looked at. Your classic just started rolling down the driveway."

"Monte's a real lifesaver," Dan said.

Brett returned from the back of the house. "There's a body back there. I assume it's Chi-Town."

In the distance, sirens blared.

Within minutes the house was swarming with police and emergency medical people. It was a frantic mess that took several hours to unwind. After a few attempts at unlocking the phone, Officer Alvarez gave up and said, "We've got software for this." Appropriately, he was standing on the page from the press kit at the time.

Felony 4

I handled my second home invasion with style. It was old hat.

Corona, Miss Z, and L-Train all remained with the police. They had outstanding legal issues to address. Carl decided he'd had enough of the Monte Carlo and employed the use of a legitimate rideshare service to take him back home.

Crashing into the garage had done only minor damage to the Monte Carlo. It was, in fact, difficult to see any difference. Certainly not in its performance.

When we arrived back at the apartment, Ms. Serrano was waiting for us, along with two of her large associates.

"You had an exciting night," she said.

I handed her the phone. "Too—um, you know—exciting for me—"

"Thank you for not turning it over to the bus stop cops."

Dan looked at us, agog. He said, to me, "You gave them *your* phone? Are you, like, a criminal mastermind now?"

"Nuh—no!" I blurted.

Ms. Serrano gave us both a sinister look. "I hold grudges. I also don't forget when someone has done me a good turn. You are both owed a favor from me." She'd meant that last sentence to be reassuring but that certainly wasn't how I took it.

When she left Dan asked me what was on the phone and why I'd given it back to her while giving the "bus stop cops" my own phone in its place.

"You remember how you told me there were rumors that Ms. Serrano made herself a widow? Well—that cell phone was her, um, ex-husband's. There were texts on it that suggest that, um, she might have had a good reason for . . . what she did."

Dan whistled. "Stuff that you didn't want the police to know?"

"It—um, it involves her daughter."

"Wow. What are they going to do when they find out you gave them your phone?"

"Well, you know, in all the confusion I didn't know which phone was which," I said. "Besides, I always use a very complex passcode—they might never crack it. But just in case, I'm going to remote erase it and get a new one."

"Look, Chris, I feel kind of responsible for everything that happened," Dan said magnanimously. "Tell you what—I'll let you drive Monte to work today, so you don't have to ride the bus or anything."

"Thanks," I said in a viciously ironic tone. "And while I'm at work I expect you to put my Hyundai back together."

"What?"

I smiled. "Make sure it's done before I get home. Or I'll have to talk to my friend Ms. Serrano."

ACKNOWLEDGEMENTS

Thank you to Gary Anderson for your work and confidence, as well as our moniker, *Jacked*.

Thank you to Aaron Jacobs and Daniel Sparshott for your input, dedication, and support on this project and others.

More thanks to Garth Jackson (our fabulous cover photographer) and Gretchen Jankowski (our fabulous cover designer) for making everyone look so good.

Also, thank you to our Assistant Editor, Krysta Winsheimer, the unsung hero of this anthology, for challenging every last dangling participle. On behalf of everyone involved, we bow at the altar of your Chicago style.

Lastly, thank you to our authors, all twenty-one of them, for entrusting us with your most excellent works.

Lightning Source UK Ltd.
Milton Keynes UK
UKHW040653190722
406066UK00002B/459

9 781733 352697